A Wedding

SONG

IN LEXINGTON, KENTUCKY

A Wedding
SONG

IN LEXINGTON, KENTUCKY

JENNIFER JOHNSON

BARBOUR
PUBLISHING

Scripture taken from the HOLY BIBLE, NEW INTERNATIONAL VERSION®. NIV®. Copyright © 1973, 1978, 1984, 2011 by Biblica, Inc.™ Used by permission. All rights reserved worldwide.

This book is a work of fiction. Names, characters, places, and incidents are either products of the author's imagination or used fictitiously. Any similarity to actual people, organizations, and/or events is purely coincidental.

Cover design: Faceout Studio, www.faceoutstudio.com

Published by Barbour Publishing, Inc., P.O. Box 719, Uhrichsville, Ohio 44683, www.barbourbooks.com

Our mission is to publish and distribute inspirational products offering exceptional value and biblical encouragement to the masses.

ecpa Member of the
Evangelical Christian
Publishers Association

Printed in the United States of America.

Dedication

This book is dedicated to my husband, Albert. I will always remember the first time I saw him. I was a sophomore (cheerleader). He was a senior (quarterback). He was sitting on the football bench, his head ducked down—he'd just been hit in the back and was catching his breath. I'd never seen him before, but I knew he was The One. (From that moment, the poor boy didn't have a choice but to like me back. It's true—I'm quite persistent.)

I love you, Al!

Chapter 1

The floorboard creaked. Megan McKinney leaped from the office chair, her stapler clattering to the ground. Ignoring it, she twirled away from the copier and toward the front door of the law office. At the sight of a client, she placed her hand against her chest to still her racing heartbeat. She forced a smile. "Sorry 'bout that. I didn't hear the door."

The red-haired woman rolled her eyes then stared at long, manicured fingernails. "Obviously."

Megan sat and straightened in the chair. Dumb machine jammed up papers more than it copied them. Clients often scared the life out of her, coming in when she was elbow-deep in yanking out documents.

She forced a smile as she took in the woman's lime-green, spring sweater, the shape enhanced by modern medicine, and the white capris that exposed the lace outline of some very skimpy undergarments. No doubt about it, the redhead was here for Justin.

Megan raised her eyebrows. She had to give the woman credit: the silver rhinestone sandals were the most adorable she'd ever laid eyes on.

Lifting her chin, Megan prepared herself for the woman's tirade if she wasn't the younger Frasure's scheduled appointment. She had endured more than her share of self-centered fashion plates since coming to work for the law offices of Frasure, Frasure, and Combs six months ago.

"You gonna tell Justin I'm here?" The woman offered a quick glance of contempt and placed her hand against her chest. Megan noted the gargantuan marquise diamond on her left ring finger. Engagement ring. No wedding band.

Megan bit back the urge to ask the woman if her fiancé would also be available for the appointment. She shook her head. None of her business. "Let me check. What is your name?"

"Never mind, darlin'."

At the syrupy-sweet shift in tone, Megan followed the woman's gaze and saw that her divorce-turned-adoption-attorney boss, Justin Frasure, had opened his office door.

Megan gritted her teeth and forced a smile. Justin furrowed dark, thick eyebrows above chocolate-drop eyes. His stunning and impossibly delicious looks never failed to send a shiver down her spine and then a wrinkle of disgust to her nose. She couldn't stand men like him.

He motioned for the redhead to enter his office. Megan looked away until she heard the door shut behind him.

Sucking in her gag reflex, she twirled her chair toward the computer screen. She highlighted Justin Frasure's latest appointment as an indication that the client had shown up. *Something tells me that woman isn't here for adoption advice.*

She clicked a few buttons on her keyboard and switched to the university home page. With a huff, she typed in her username and password. Still no posted grade from her spring class. She logged off, and Justin's appointment book flashed on the screen.

Her stomach turned. *Justin Frasure must have run out of the hot divorcees in the city. Added engagees to his list instead.* She wrinkled her nose. *Is there such a word as* engagees?

The last secretary had warned Megan he would hit on any pretty woman who crossed his path and that Megan, as quite the "adorable cutie," would be a prime target.

But he hadn't hit on Megan. Hadn't even flirted with her. Not that Megan cared. She didn't want the man's attention. Not in the slightest. After dating Clint Morgan in high school, she and God had enough issues to work through when it came to trusting men.

Besides, what did she care about who came into the law office? Scooping up the nonurgent messages she'd taken throughout the day for the three lawyers, she made her way to the office mailboxes outside their doors. She'd cringed when she'd placed Justin's messages in his box, remembering how one woman with a strong southern accent had whined incessantly because she couldn't speak with that "handsome, young lawyer" directly.

Megan bit back the growl that threatened almost every day she worked. Nothing upset her more than a man who played women. The Holy Spirit nudged her heart. She shouldn't judge him. The Bible told her to pray for those who got on her nerves. Maybe, not in so many words, but she knew her flustered feelings wouldn't change the guy's behavior. She blew out a long breath. *Forgive me, God. Bless Justin.* She gulped. *And the redhead.*

Okay, so maybe her heart didn't feel the silent prayer she'd sent upward, but it was the best she could do for now. She made her way back to the desk and flopped into the seat. The heart could be deceitful. Obedience was the key. God had proven that time and again.

Shaking away the thought, she focused on the letter the elder Frasure had given her to type. She glanced at the clock. Only two more hours to work, and then she'd be off for a three-day weekend.

She finished the letter, e-mailed it to Mr. Frasure for final approval, then checked the college website again to see if the grade for her education class had been posted. She sighed when the space remained blank. "Well, my professor has to post by Monday," she whispered as she scooped a pile of folders in her arms and headed to the filing cabinet.

The door to Justin Frasure's office opened, and the redhead walked out, shutting the door hard. Frustration, or more like fury, seemed to etch her brow and purse her lips as she nodded toward Megan and headed for the front door. Megan placed the last file in its appropriate place. She stood to her full height and flattened the wrinkles from her blue checkered skirt.

She rarely talked with Justin. It was Mr. Combs and Justin's father who seemed to need her assistance the most. But Mr. Combs was on a cruise with his wife, and the elder Frasure was with a client—a very attractive client who would probably be with him awhile. It had only taken a week for Megan to realize the acorn didn't fall far from the Frasure tree.

She exhaled a long breath. She had no choice but to remind Justin she wouldn't be in the office the next day. Glancing toward the door, Megan hoped his mood didn't mirror the client's.

Forcing herself to lift her chin in confidence, she knocked on the doorjamb, cleared her throat, then opened the door. The younger Frasure's head snapped up from whatever he was studying at his desk. His eyes flashed, ready for confrontation. She sucked in a breath, realizing she hadn't waited for him to invite her in.

Then his expression softened, and his entire body seemed to exhale. Megan swallowed and balled her fists at her sides, willing her legs to stay strong beneath her. The man was sinfully attractive. It wasn't fair.

She cleared her throat again. "Mr. Frasure?"

"I've told you to call me Justin." His voice, though deep as Mammoth Cave was long, whispered to her like a butterfly kiss on her cheek.

"I know." She nodded as she reminded her brain to continue to send the message to her legs to stay upright. "But you're my boss, and I feel it's appropriate. . ."

His lips curved up ever so slightly on the left side, as if he found her determination for propriety, or possibly her discomfort at being in his office, somewhat humorous. "All right, Ms. McKinney. How can I help you?"

"I just wanted to remind you I will not be at work tomorrow."

A shadow fell across his face, and he looked down at his desk. "I'd forgotten." He picked up his iPhone from the desk and punched something into it. He looked at her again. "I remember now. You asked for a personal day. Do you mind my being nosy about it?"

Megan shook her head. "Not at all. I'm going on a canoeing field trip with my sister's sixth-grade class. I went with her last year. It's a lot of fun. The water is calm, practically unmoving, or so it seems, and only waist high in most areas. We all have to wear life jackets the entire time, so it's very safe for the students. It has to be. Her school takes eighty students each day with only eight or nine chaperones. But, it's. . ." She clasped her hands in front of her waist as she realized she'd become quite animated in her description of the trip. She cleared her throat. "It's a lot of fun."

A full smile curved his lips. "Sounds like it." He leaned back in his chair. "I haven't been in a canoe in years."

"It's nice." She took a step back from his door then lifted her hand in a hesitant wave. She had no idea why the man made her so nervous. "I'll—I'll see you Monday."

"Okay."

Unclenching her fists, she rubbed her clammy hands together.

"Hey, Megan."

She turned at Justin's voice, realizing that may have been the first time she'd heard him say her given name. If only his voice wasn't as enticing as his looks. The man had been entirely too well formed in his mother's womb. "Yes?"

"Your blue outfit really accentuates your eyes."

He looked away from her and focused on his computer screen. For a moment, Megan felt glued to the carpet. She stared at Justin, her jaw dropping slightly. Blinking twice, she found her voice. "Thank you."

Once again having to force messages from her brain to her legs and feet, she turned on her heels and headed toward her desk. *Did he just hit on me? Was that flirting?*

She gnawed the inside of her cheek. He acted as if he'd merely stated facts, no emotions, no ulterior motives. She shut down her computer and grabbed her purse out of its cubby. *I'll believe it was simply an observation, a kind observation. Nothing more.*

Megan awakened early, made some coffee, then walked onto the back deck with her java, devotional, and Bible to enjoy the sunrise. She was a natural early riser, and God never ceased to amaze her with the beauty of His creation each new day. Having been raised on a small farm in southeastern Kentucky, she missed the smell of cattle, freshly cut grass, and honeysuckle blooming in spring. She missed watching the sunrise over trees and through hills.

And yet she and her sister Marianna had managed to find an apartment in the midst of Lexington that overlooked a well-groomed, nature-filled park. The sun rose just as spectacularly here. Megan sat in the black patio chair and took a sip of her cream-filled coffee. The warmth covered the slight nip of the early spring air, and she couldn't help but grin.

The back door opened, and Marianna stepped onto the deck. Her sister's long blond mane reminded Megan of the bird's nest they found every year in the dogwood tree in front of their parents' house. Though alike in so many other ways, Marianna had never learned to appreciate the glory of a sunrise in the morning. Megan met God in the morning. Marianna preferred the night.

Megan waved to her sister, younger by three short minutes. "You're up early."

Marianna groaned as she flopped into the chair beside Megan. She folded her legs up onto the seat, wrapped her arms around her calves, and dropped her chin on her knees.

Megan laughed. "Happy birthday, sis."

Marianna wrinkled her nose and grinned. "Happy birthday to you, too. What a great way to spend our twenty-fourth birthday—in a canoe with a bunch of sixth graders."

"Are you kidding?" Megan nudged her twin sister's arm. "This trip is a blast."

Marianna grabbed Megan's coffee cup off the patio table and took a sip.

"Hey!" Megan grabbed it back from her. "I don't want your cooties in my coffee. I'm telling the teacher."

Marianna rolled her eyes. "I am one of the teachers. We'll have a lot of fussing and tattling today. They're eleven- and twelve-year-olds, you know."

"Oh I know." Megan nodded. "And you love every minute of it."

Marianna started to grin, but a yawn took over, and she swiped her eye with the back of her hand. "You're going to love teaching, too. Did you get your grade back yet?"

"Not yet." Megan stared out over the park, so peaceful and still. Only an occasional bird chirped. A squirrel raced from one tree to the next. She knew God wanted her to use the musical talent he'd given her. She'd always assumed it would be through contemporary Christian music, but when she'd had the opportunity to work with her twin in the school system over the last year, Megan realized she wanted to teach children as well.

Marianna dropped her legs out of the chair then wrapped her hands around her bare arms. "It is absolutely freezing out here. I'm going in." She hopped up, stepped through the door, and looked back at Megan. "First dibs on the shower."

Megan shook her head and waved her hand through the air.

"You always take a shower first, and you always use all the hot water, too."

"You know what they say: the early bird gets the worm."

"I got up a full hour before you."

"But you sit out here on the deck, enjoying the nippy fifty-degree weather."

Megan laughed. "Go get your shower, and save me some water."

Marianna shut the door, and Megan turned back toward the park. She picked up her Bible and turned to the scripture she'd read every birthday since she was sixteen. Her Sunday school teacher had insisted the teens memorize it. She opened to Jeremiah, *"'For I know the plans I have for you,'" declares the Lord, "'plans to prosper you and not to harm you, plans to give you hope and a future.'"*

She shut her Bible and sucked in a long breath. That year had changed her life. Having gone to church every Sunday with one of her neighborhood friends, she'd accepted Jesus into her heart when she was fourteen, and He was her Savior, her Redeemer from sin. Accepting Him was the best choice she'd ever made.

But sixteen? Sixteen was a year she'd never forget. It changed how she looked at things. What she thought. What she felt. God was still working on her heart and mind, getting her through the hurt and confusion.

She closed her eyes and whispered into the breeze. "You've brought me so far, precious Jesus. Keep loving me. Keep molding me. I am your clay."

The phone rang inside the apartment. Megan opened her eyes and spied one of the elderly neighbors as he puttered down the sidewalk, his small poodle on a leash in front of him. The phone rang again. Megan gripped the arms of the chair.

JENNIFER JOHNSON

Marianna was in the shower and wouldn't be able to answer it. Megan knew who it was. She knew she should answer it. God would want her to answer it.

Pushing herself away from the chair, she walked toward the rings. Even if everyone she knew would agree with her right to ignore the call, Megan would obey the Spirit.

She'd obey, and maybe one day her heart would follow her actions. She walked through the door and glanced at the caller ID. Just who she'd expected. Sucking in a breath, she grabbed the phone off the receiver. "Hello, Mom."

Chapter 2

No one ever choked to death swallowing his pride.
HARVEY MACKAY

Gripping the sides of the canoe, Colt Baker jerked his head around at the sound of a blood-curdling scream. What in the world would be causing such a ruckus?

In an obvious attempt to get the canoe turned around, his niece paddled her oar feverishly on the right side. "Colt, come on. Something's gotta be wrong. Looks like Miss Megan, and she's got Stephanie with her."

In just a few strong strokes of his paddle, Colt maneuvered them around, and he and Hadley headed back toward the still squealing teacher. This couldn't be good. Stephanie was impulsive and often too physical. She showed little affection and frustrated easily. But Hadley had a soft spot for the autistic child, and she was often able to settle the girl down.

As they drew closer, Colt spied the young, blond-haired teacher in the back of the canoe holding Stephanie tightly against her chest. To his surprise, Stephanie wasn't fighting the teacher, but both of their paddles had fallen into the creek. Several canoes filled with students floated around them, but no one tried to hand the paddles to the twosome.

"What's going on?" Hadley yelled before Colt had the chance.

"A snake's in their canoe," one of the boys said. Colt remembered the kid had been one of the "tough" guys in Hadley's class, always bragging, sometimes bullying. He sure looked scared out of his mind over a snake—which Colt had to admit was a good thing. It could be a cottonmouth that found its way into the canoe, and if it struck one of them, they'd have a hard time getting the victim to a hospital quick enough.

Colt looked back at the teacher and Stephanie, realizing it wasn't the teacher howling; it was his niece's young friend. He guided their canoe closer to the boys. "Hadley, I want you to hop in their canoe. I'll go get the snake."

The smaller boy reached out to take Hadley's hand. His eyes were as big as his fists, and the poor guy was drenched from head to toe, probably having "accidentally" fallen into the water as many of the students had.

"No, Uncle Colt." Hadley shook her head and pushed the boy's hand away. "Stephanie's about to lose it. You need me over there to calm her down."

"Her teacher can calm her down."

"That's not our teacher. That's Ms. McKinney's sister. Stephanie probably don't know her at all."

Colt looked at the woman who seemed to be gripping Stephanie so tightly the child was likely losing oxygen. He could see the woman was saying something in Stephanie's ear, probably trying to calm the girl. But fear wrapped Stephanie's expression, and her hands trembled. At any moment, the girl could snap and try to jump out of the canoe, possibly making the snake strike her or the woman. "Okay, but you will stay as far away from the snake as possible, you hear?"

Hadley nodded. " 'Kay."

"I'm in front." Colt grabbed ahold of the boys' canoe and pushed his way toward the front while Hadley weeded her way around him. With as few strokes as possible, they paddled toward the canoe. Colt knew he couldn't call out to the woman that they were there to help. Stephanie might panic. Instead, he sat up as tall as he could to see inside the canoe. Relief washed through him when he saw the reptile.

"Not poisonous," he whispered to Hadley. He could almost feel his niece's sigh of relief behind him. "Big black snake. Must've got in before we started."

"Thank the Lord."

Colt grinned at the sound of true thanksgiving in Hadley's voice. "Once we get just a tad closer, on my three, you grab the side of their canoe, and I'll grab the snake and hop out."

Silently they drifted a few feet closer. He turned and nodded to Hadley. He lifted one finger. Two fingers. "And three!"

In one swift motion, he jumped up, grabbed the black snake with his hand around the head, his pointer finger pressed against its bottom jaw and his thumb firm against its top, and then jumped into the water with it. The every-bit-as-healthy-as-he-expected snake's body fought to take flight along the water, but Colt tightened his hold. If he released the critter, the kiddos would freak, and he'd have a string of flipped canoes and screaming twelve-year-olds to deal with.

He trudged through the waist-high water to the muddy bank. Glad he'd worn his work boots, he dug the strong heels into the mixture of mud and rocks until he'd made his way out of the water. After walking several yards away from the students, he released the snake into a grassy area, watching as it slithered through the field.

He wiped his brow with the back of a saturated sleeve. "Poor feller probably hadn't expected so much activity today. All he'd done was take a nap in an unused canoe."

He turned around and saw that Stephanie had climbed into the canoe behind Hadley. She held tight around Hadley's waist, her face, even her glasses, pressed against his niece's back. "Uncle Colt," she hollered. "I'm going to take Stephanie back to the starting spot. You come back with Miss Megan."

Colt looked at the woman sitting alone in the canoe. Her already pale complexion had drained of all color. Shocking blue eyes peered at him with intense emotion. He walked back to the bank and into the water. Without a word, he pulled the canoe over to the side and got in behind the frightened woman.

He wanted to pat her shoulder to assure her everything was all right but didn't want to startle her with his soaking wet hands. She was as spooked as a wild buck, but she was also as pretty as a field full of daisies. His insecurities flared like he was in the sixth grade all over again.

"It'll be all right." He managed to speak the four words as he paddled back toward the starting point. The woman Hadley had called Megan didn't say anything the entire ride. He couldn't help but wonder why Stephanie had been in the canoe with her to begin with. Stephanie often had a resource teacher with her on field trips. In his thinking, the canoe trip would warrant a teacher coming specifically for Stephanie. It seemed odd the science teacher's sister would be the one taking care of an autistic child.

Not that this Megan had done anything wrong. By all appearances, she seemed to have kept Stephanie as calm as could be expected. The more he thought about it, the more surprised he was that Stephanie had gotten into the canoe with Megan at all. Usually she would only venture with someone she knew well.

He paddled up the concrete bank, and Hadley's science teacher, Ms. McKinney, helped her sister out of the canoe. Their resemblance was striking.

Ms. McKinney wrapped her arms around her sister. "Oh Megan, I can't believe that happened."

"How's Stephanie?"

Colt looked at Megan. The concern in her tone was evident.

"She's fine. Are you okay?"

"I'm fine. I knew it wasn't poisonous. I just couldn't get Stephanie to settle down."

The frustration in her voice made him want to defend her. "Normally a special needs assistant or a chaperone goes with Stephanie." He glared at Hadley's teacher, even though his words were intended for Megan. "Don't be upset with yourself. You shouldn't have been in that situation. She should have gone with someone she knows."

"I was her chaperone."

Colt looked at the woman who hadn't uttered a peep the full thirty minutes he'd paddled upstream. She crossed her arms in front of her chest and glared at him. "I thank you for helping me. I needed it. But I do know Stephanie. Her mother asked me to be her chaperone today. Please do not insinuate my sister is not doing her job."

Before Colt could respond, the woman stomped toward the restroom facility. He looked at Hadley's science teacher. Embarrassment swelled in his gut and tightened his throat.

She clasped her hands in front of her. "I can assure you, Mr. Baker, I would never do anything to put a child in danger. My sister has been Stephanie's music teacher this entire school year. They are actually very close. The snake was more than Stephanie is used to handling, and—"

Colt raised his hand. "When a man's in the wrong, he should swallow his pride and 'fess up. I assumed something without knowing the facts. I'm sorry."

Ms. McKinney's cheeks tinted pink, and she nodded. "Thank you." She pointed toward the picnic area. "Hadley and Stephanie are already eating lunch if you'd like to join them."

"I think I will." Though he'd already eaten his fill of humble pie, Colt sauntered toward his truck, took his lunch cooler out of the back, then made his way to Hadley. It wasn't his fault he'd thought Stephanie didn't know the teacher's sister. Hadley hadn't known. It was an honest mistake, and he took pride in being a guardian who cared about the well-being of his niece and her friends.

He sighed. That didn't make him feel better. He pulled the wet T-shirt away from his chest, but once released, it clung to his frame again. Being wet didn't help either. But at least the sun shined bright and warm. It wouldn't be long before he dried.

He sat beside Hadley and opened his lunch. "How are you doing?"

Hadley smiled at Stephanie, exposing deep dimples in both cheeks. "Much better now."

"Hi, Colt," Stephanie said as she dipped her chin so she could peer at him above the rim of her glasses.

Colt lifted his fist, and Stephanie knuckle-bumped it with her own. She giggled then wrapped both hands around her sandwich.

"How are you doing, Stephanie? You having fun?"

"There was a snake, Colt." Stephanie's thick, dark eyebrows rose, the right higher than the left.

"Hadley put her hand on Stephanie's shoulder. "Yep, but it's gone now. Right?"

"Right!" Stephanie waved her right arm in an exaggerated motion. "All gone."

Pride swelled in his heart for his niece. The sandy-haired, green-eyed cutie was hardly bigger than a fencepost, but her heart was as big as a barn. And she had spunk and fight in her. The girl handled a horse better than most men. And yet her heart was as tender as a mare's for her foal. He loved the girl with every breath in him.

Colt took a bite of his sandwich. Out of the corner of his eye, he saw Ms. McKinney's sister exit the restroom. He could tell by the damp strands of hair around her face and neck that she'd washed up. He wanted to talk to her, to apologize for accusing her sister. Instead, he watched as she sat at a far table with Ms. McKinney and several teachers.

She and her sister sat side by side on a bench that faced him. He could tell they were identical twins—both with light skin, blue eyes, and long blond hair, but Megan had a deeper dimple in her left cheek when she smiled, and her eyebrows seemed to be a shade darker.

"Ms. Megan's awesome." Stephanie's words interrupted Colt's thoughts.

"She's a good piano teacher?" Hadley asked.

"Miss Megan's the best. She's awesome."

"I'd like to learn piano someday," Hadley said. "Maybe you could show me."

Stephanie moved her fingers through the air like she was playing the instrument. "You go like this."

Colt smiled as Hadley laughed and mimicked Stephanie's motions. Maybe it wouldn't be such a bad idea for Hadley to start taking piano lessons. His niece loved to sing, and it was often too quiet in their big family farmhouse with only the two of them.

He gathered up his, Hadley's, and Stephanie's garbage and headed toward the trash can. It would give him an excuse to talk to Megan and apologize to her. As he made his way toward the picnic table, one of the teachers stood up and motioned for the students' attention.

"When you can hear my voice clap once."

A clap sounded from the teachers and many of the students.

"Clap twice," she added.

This time almost all the students clapped twice and faced her. In a matter of seconds, the entire picnic area grew silent with all sixth-grade faces staring at their teacher.

The woman raised her hands in the air. "Today is a very special day. It's Ms. McKinney and her sister, Megan's, birthday. Let's sing happy birthday to them."

The students cheered and then began the birthday chorus. The sisters were petite enough that a couple of the girls walked toward their science teacher and her sister and wrapped an arm around their shoulders with ease.

Once the song ended, the students and teachers made their way out to the open area for a few games. Megan stayed at the picnic table, cleaning up the mess. Colt walked to her and grabbed some items off the table.

"I'm sorry for my assumption."

Megan jumped and placed her hand on her chest.

Heat warmed Colt's cheeks. "Sorry. I guess I should have let you know I was here."

Megan smiled, exposing the deep dimple on the left side. "I think I'm still a little jumpy about the snake." She pitched several wrappers into the trash. "It's okay. I was a bit shaken for Stephanie." She turned and peered into his eyes. "I really am grateful you helped us. I don't know how I would have gotten her to calm down."

"It was nothing." His stomach knotted up talking to her. It had been a long time since he'd felt anxious talking to a woman. He cleared his throat. "Well, Stephanie's been bragging about you being a terrific piano teacher."

Megan smiled again. This time he noted the beautiful white teeth and a twinkle in her eyes. "She teaches me more than I teach her, and that's the truth. Music is her gift."

Colt rubbed his hands against his pants then clasped them together. "I was wondering if you'd be interested in giving lessons to my niece Hadley. She's the one who got Stephanie out of the canoe."

"I know who Hadley is. I help with my sister's class every chance I get. I'd love to give her lessons." Megan reached into a side pocket on her lunch bag and pulled out a card.

Colt raised his eyebrows. "You keep business cards on you? Even when canoeing?"

She shrugged and grinned. "You never know when you'll need them."

Colt laughed out loud as he flicked the card. "I suppose you're right." He put the card in the front pocket of his jeans. "I'll give you a call this week."

"I'll look forward to it."

He watched as she walked toward the open area to join the students and teachers in their game. He was the one who could hardly wait.

Chapter 3

No battle plan survives contact with the enemy.
Colin Powell

A horn blew from outside the apartment. The front door swung open. "You're being kidnapped!"

Megan jumped up from the couch and smacked her hand against her chest. "Amber! You scared the life out of me. What are you talking about?"

Marianna ran down the hall and into the living room. "What's going on?"

Another friend, Julie, pushed past the petite brunette. She wore an orange and red party hat on top of her short dark curls. She blew a whistle that hung from her neck. "Amber already told you what's going on. You're being kidnapped. Get your shoes."

Amber raced to her and looped her arm around Megan's. Julie rushed to Marianna and grabbed her hand. "Let's go."

Still in a daze, Megan slipped on her flip-flops and allowed herself to be pulled out of the apartment. She gazed back at Marianna. "Grab a key."

With her sister's eyebrows still raised and her jaw dropped open, Marianna nodded and reached for her purse despite Julie's nudging to get out of the house.

Once shoved into the backseat of Amber's car, Megan looked at Marianna as she clicked her seat belt across her waist. "Did you know about this?"

Marianna shook her head. Amber and Julie slid into the driver's and passenger's seats and began a chorus of an off-key rendition of "Happy Birthday to You." As understanding dawned, Megan and Marianna laughed. Megan smacked the seat. "Of course."

"Should have known they'd do this," said Marianna.

Amber winked into the rearview mirror, and the twins joined the singing. When the chorus ended, Marianna chimed in with a new chorus about smelling like a monkey.

Megan shook her finger in front of Marianna's face. "I don't think so, little sister."

Marianna stopped and dipped her chin, zeroing in on Megan with a deadpan expression. "Really? You're still trying to call me 'little sister'?" She lifted up three fingers. "Three minutes is nothing."

"It's something on the birth certificate." She pointed to her chest. "Makes me the oldest. The more mature."

"Whatever. You sound really mature right now."

Julie twisted in the passenger's seat and flicked both of them in the knee.

"Ow!" they squealed in unison.

"I can't believe you two still fight over three minutes. Every year it's the same thing."

Megan shrugged. "She just can't stand that I'm older."

"Babies have more fun."

28

Amber interjected, "Well, we're all going to have fun tonight."

Megan grinned at her sister as she trailed her fingertips along her pinned up hair. She glanced down at her clothes, thankful she'd chosen a matching shirt and pair of shorts after returning home from the canoe trip and taking a shower. "Julie, Amber, you two are crazy."

Marianna added, "You definitely surprised us."

Megan looked at her sister who still hadn't taken a shower. A giggle welled up inside of Megan and spilled out. She pinched her nose. "What was that you said again? Something about *me* smelling like a monkey? I was worried about not having on any makeup, but at least I don't stink."

Marianna wrinkled her nose and shoved Megan with her elbow. Megan pushed her back then shifted away from her sister, rolled down the window, and stuck her head out.

Amber looked at them from the rearview mirror. "Now, now, birthday girls. Do I need to call your mother?"

Megan bit her lip as she rolled the window back up. The one conversation with Mom had been enough.

Julie turned in the passenger seat. "We couldn't let your birthdays pass without some kind of celebration."

"I hope we're not going anywhere where people will have to smell me," Marianna huffed. She glared at Megan with obviously feigned offense.

"No worries. We can sit outside." Amber pulled into the parking lot of Megan's favorite frozen yogurt shop.

Megan rubbed her stomach. "Orange Leaf! I hope they have fresh blackberry topping tonight."

"Since it's our birthday, I'm getting confetti cake yogurt."

Marianna pinched her thumb and finger. "Maybe a smidgen of red velvet, too."

"Not me." Megan shook her head. "I'm getting my usual—coconut, pineapple, and pomegranate."

Marianna jumped out of the car. "I love this place. I don't care if I do stink. . . ."

Amber grabbed Marianna's arm. "Hold on, flash. Julie and I are buying you all's dessert."

Julie added, "Yeah. We know you're going on your annual birthday shopping spree with each other tomorrow, but we wanted to do something for you today."

Megan hugged Julie then Amber. "You two are the best. What a great way to end our birthday."

Marianna opened her arms. "Will you risk a hug from me, too?"

The friends laughed and shared a group hug. Megan had spent a good deal of the afternoon flustered over the incident with Stephanie and the snake. She was thankful for friends who knew just how to make her smile.

"Surprise!"

Megan opened one eye and glanced at the alarm clock on her nightstand. Seven was way too early to rise on a Saturday morning. Surely Amber and Julie hadn't come for a second birthday kidnapping.

She rolled over in bed and stretched her arms. She could hear someone talking to Marianna in the other room. She grimaced. Didn't sound like their friends.

"Wake up, Megan."

Her mother stood inside the door. The voice had sounded happy coming from her sister's room. Not so much now.

Megan blew out a sigh. "Hey, Mom."

Her mom forced a smile. Really, it was ridiculous. If the woman didn't want to spend time with her, it wouldn't break Megan's heart.

"I want to take you girls to breakfast. Maybe a little shopping."

Marianna wrapped arms around their mother from behind. Their mom's face lit up, and she laughed as she turned to give Marianna a hug.

"I love surprise visits," said Marianna.

Their mom patted her arm. "Me, too. Go get dressed."

Marianna ran off, and Megan heard the bathroom door shut. That was great. She'd have to wait half of forever for her sister to get out.

Her mom clapped her hands. The smile was gone from her face. "Let's go, Megan."

Megan pushed herself to a sitting position. She loved the morning. Maybe not this early on a Saturday. Especially after they'd spent a good deal of the night watching romantic comedies on the DVD player. Still, normally she liked an early morning wake-up call.

But not when it was her mother glaring at her from the bed-room door.

"I'm coming. Give me a second."

Her mom left the doorway. Within moments, she heard the coffeemaker brewing. She loved her mother. At least she tried to. But it was pretty obvious she didn't want to spend time with Megan as she did with Marianna.

That was fine. Don't feel obligated. Megan wasn't overly thrilled with the idea of spending her birthday fussing with her mom either.

Once Marianna finished, Megan took her turn in the bathroom. Within half an hour, they were ready and heading to breakfast. Marianna selected her favorite restaurant. It wasn't Megan's choice, but she hadn't expected her mom to ask. It didn't matter anyway.

Megan seated herself at the table across from Marianna and her mother. They busied themselves discussing wedding plans. Discontent niggled at Megan's heart. She wished her relationship with her mother wasn't strained. It hadn't always been this way.

Eight years ago everything changed, and though Megan knew in her mind she should forgive her mother. Her heart felt otherwise.

Her mother hadn't forgiven her either. Hah. What a laugh! Megan had done nothing to warrant her mother's anger. Well, she did date the guy her mother didn't like. Truth be told, her mom had said she wasn't allowed to date Clint. But really, was that such an offense that would warrant eight years of a strained relationship? Talk about holding grudges.

"So, how are things going for you, Megan?"

Her mother's voice sounded tight, and she stuck her nose in the air. The pompous attitude may have worked in her office before she retired, but it didn't intimidate Megan.

"You know she finished her last class," said Marianna. "All she has left is student teaching."

Megan grinned at her sister. Ever the peacemaker between her and their parents. "She's right. I can even student teach on the job if I'm hired."

"Really?" Her mother fluffed her short, red curls then adjusted the collar of her short-sleeved blouse.

"Yep. Maybe she'll get a job at my school." Marianna dipped her head. "Wouldn't that be great, Megan?"

It would be wonderful. She hoped she could work in the same building as her sister. She preferred the elementary students, but she wouldn't turn down a job at the middle school.

Her mother pursed her lips then focused again on Marianna. Though Megan enjoyed discussing wedding preparations with her sister, she had no inclination to make small talk with her mother. When she was younger, she'd tried to win her parents' affections again. After high school, she'd determined to seek God's approval.

If her parents wanted to reconcile, she'd be willing, but she wouldn't alter who she was to bow down to them.

Are you really willing to reconcile?

She shifted in her seat at the niggling of her spirit. God wanted her to forgive them, even without their request. And she tried. At least she wanted to try. But forgiveness didn't happen easily. Especially when it wasn't requested.

Megan twisted in her seat as she scanned the restaurant. Where was their waitress? They'd been here—she looked at her watch—a full ten minutes. She was ready to get this day done.

"In a hurry, Megan?" Her mother's sarcastic tone grated on her nerves.

As a matter of fact, this is not how I planned to spend my day. She bit the inside of her mouth, thankful she hadn't said the words aloud. "No. Just hungry."

Her mother studied her, and Megan determined not to look away from her scrutiny. A piece of her hoped to see a sliver of reconciliation, some sort of desire to make amends in her mother's gaze. As usual, it wasn't there.

Their waitress arrived, and Megan let out a long breath. She did wish things were different between them.

Megan pushed through the front door of the law office. After a mostly wonderful weekend, Monday had arrived faster than she'd hoped. The morning with her mother had been tiresome, but she and Marianna had shopped to exhaustion once she left. She'd purchased a couple of adorable outfits to start a school year—if she landed a position.

Sunday had also been filled to the brim with activities: Sunday school and church service, choir practice, and children's church in the evening. Going to work would provide her a bit of rest after such an eventful weekend.

"What in the world?" Her gaze took in the oversized arrangement of white daisies and pale pink roses. Her heartbeat sped up as she gently touched the satin bow wrapped around the neck of the clear vase. The last time she could remember receiving flowers was when she'd gone to her senior prom. *And as I recall, I picked those up myself since my date was just a friend.*

She bit her bottom lip as she pulled the card off the prong. Who would have sent her flowers? Her mind raced with the possibilities. There was that new guy at church who had paid a lot of attention to her, but he also got her and Marianna mixed up often enough that she felt pretty sure he wouldn't have been investigative enough to find out where she worked. She grinned. He'd have probably put the wrong name on the front as well.

She read the single word written in black ink on the marbled white card. It was definitely her name written on the front.

It could have been her sister. She scrunched her nose. She doubted it would have been Marianna. Rent was due in less than a week, and her wedding was only a couple months away.

A face popped into her mind. The guy from the canoe trip. What was his name? Colby? Cody? Colt.

That was it. Megan could tell the guy felt bad about accusing her sister of being incompetent as a teacher. He'd asked her about giving his niece piano lessons, and then on the trip back to the school, he seemed to search for things to say to her or Marianna. He probably sent flowers to her sister as well.

It was silly to keep guessing. She pulled back the envelope flap.

"Good morning, Megan." The senior Frasure's deep voice boomed through the room.

Megan sucked in her breath and placed the card against her chest. Either she'd become jumpy the last few days or people around her had grown bent to scare the life right out of her. "Good morning, Mr. Frasure."

He motioned toward the flowers. "Lovely arrangement. Must be from some young fellow who has his sights set on you."

Megan's cheeks warmed. Very few men had sought her out in a romantic way. She figured she was pretty enough. Marianna received her share of attention until her engagement with Kirk. But Megan wasn't interested in dates or boyfriends. And she must have put off some kind of antiman vibe, because she hadn't gotten any offers in a long time.

"So, who're they from?"

"I don't—"

Mr. Frasure opened his hand to stop her. "Sorry, Megan. That's none of my business." He pointed toward his office door. "I need you to get your notepad. I have a couple of letters that need to go out first thing this morning."

Megan bit back a sigh as she put the card on her desk and scooped up her notebook. The senior Mr. Frasure had to be the only businessman in the United States who still wanted his secretary to shorthand a letter before it was typed. Mr. Combs and the younger Frasure communicated with her almost solely through e-mail messages, an occasional phone call, or even dictation.

She grabbed a pen from the tray and started to follow him to his office.

He stopped midstep and turned toward her. She bumped into him, gasped, and jumped a few steps back. "I'm so sorry, Mr. Frasure. I didn't expect you to stop."

He waved away her apology. "Not a problem. While I get settled, run into the conference room and get me a cup of coffee."

Megan nodded, placed her pad and pen on a seat, and walked to the room the lawyers used for talking to clients and other attorneys. She measured the coffee, filled the filter, and poured two bottles of water into the pot.

While it brewed, she straightened the eight cushioned, brown, leather chairs sitting around a long, rectangular mahogany table. Various fake plants sat in small and large pots around the perimeter of the plain room. The only other furniture in the room was an oversized, ornate bookshelf that held more legal manuals and books than seemed necessary to exist. Her bosses seemed to have every legal reference book written, except a Holy Bible—the most important reference of all.

Not that it surprised her. The senior Mr. Frasure only dated women who were twenty years or more his junior, and he never dated the same woman longer than six months. At least that's what the previous secretary told her, and so far Megan had seen two young women come and go from his life. Mr. Combs was married and seemed to be happy enough, but he spent every opportunity given to him on the golf course. And the junior Frasure—Justin's reputation preceded him, as well as the steady flow of beauties who continually sought his expertise.

Megan huffed as she picked up the coffeepot and poured the hot brew into an oversized ceramic mug. She needed to be a godly witness to the men she worked for. She scrunched her nose. Even if they were the kind of men who turned her stomach.

She headed back toward Mr. Frasure's office. She tripped on the plush carpet when she spied her younger boss inspecting the paperweight on her desk. Breathing a sigh of relief that the coffee hadn't spilled; she straightened her shoulders and lifted her chin before Justin realized she was in the room.

She cleared her throat. "Hello, Mr. Frasure."

He gazed at her and smiled. He looked amazing in a pinstriped charcoal suit and deep red satin tie. His eyes, so dark and mysterious, beguiled her like the spider drew the fly. Once caught in the web, the fly could never escape, and more than once since she'd started working here, Megan feared falling for the handsome lawyer.

He pointed to the paperweight she'd received the first week she and Marianna visited the church a year ago. "Do you go to church here?"

She nodded.

"Do you like it?"

She nodded again. Her throat seemed to have filled with cotton, and her mind shifted to blank. She couldn't seem to get words of any kind to form.

His eyes danced with humor, and she would have sworn he bit the inside of his cheek to keep from laughing at her. "Do they have Bible studies?"

He lifted his hand before she could nod again. "Wait. That's another yes or no question. I'm a lawyer. I should know how to interrogate people better."

He cleared his throat as he straightened his shoulders. "Ms. McKinney, on which night of the week does this church"—he pointed at the paperweight again—"have a Bible study that I could attend?"

He winked, and Megan felt her legs turn to rubber, as they seemed to have a habit of doing in his presence. Swallowing, she forced her mind and mouth to work together at the same time. "I go to Bible study on Thursdays."

"Is it a Bible study I could attend?"

She shrugged. "There are about fifteen of us. It's a singles' class."

"Perfect. What time does it start?"

Megan furrowed her brow. She wanted to be a witness to her bosses, but she really didn't want any of them joining her Bible study. She allowed herself to be vulnerable with her group. They were close, and each of them was seeking God's will with their whole heart, not looking for their next date.

Conviction welled in her spirit. How could she be so arrogant? So pompous? It wasn't *her* group. It's was God's group. *Forgive me, Lord. Justin wants to learn more about You, and I'm being selfish. About a Bible study group!*

She looked into his eyes. He seemed genuinely interested to

know more. Warmth filled her, and she felt a smile lift her lips. "We meet at seven. It would be wonderful if you could go."

"Great. I believe I will." He placed the paperweight back on her desk then started toward his office. He turned toward her again. "Your flowers are pretty. Who are they from?"

"I still haven't had a chance to read the card."

"Well, read it." He opened his office door, stepped inside, then shut it behind him.

Megan glanced at the senior Frasure's office door. Any minute he'd be stomping down the hall looking for her. *This will only take a second.*

Plucking the card once again off the prong, Megan smiled as excitement welled within her. She opened the envelope flap and pulled out the card. Her jaw dropped. Only three words were written on the card. "Happy Birthday."

She swallowed the knot in her throat and the fear that clenched her heart. Why would this man send her flowers? What were his intentions? His motives? His. . . She blinked at the questions swirling through her mind. She gazed at her youngest boss's office door as she spoke the last word on the card. "Justin."

Chapter 4

Temptation is like a knife that may either cut the meat or the throat of a man; it may be his food or his poison, his exercise or his destruction.

John Owen

Justin walked into the small fitness center and looked up at the clock above the mirror-covered wall. He had thirty minutes before his buddy, Kirk, arrived to lift weights. Plenty of time to run three miles on the treadmill.

He nodded to the dark-haired desk attendant as he shoved his iPhone and keys into a wooden cubby. The large gym he'd used since college had metal lockers with combination locks. He looked around the small open facility. There was no need for locks here. He could see the cubbies from anyplace in the building.

He stepped onto a treadmill, put in his earphones, then plugged them in so he could watch the Reds' game on the TV in front of him while he ran. Releasing a sigh, he realized he'd miss the familiarity of his old gym, but he wanted to help Kirk get back into a workout routine, and his friend felt uncomfortable in the larger facility. Justin selected a challenging course of speed and inclines, and soon lost himself in the rhythm of the workout.

The changes he'd made in his life proved more difficult than he'd expected. But God knew that, and Kirk had told him his faith wouldn't be without challenges.

His mind drifted to his meeting with Sophia the week before. She was a temptation to him. And she knew it.

Memories of dates they'd spent together poured into his mind, and he pushed the button to speed up his run. He'd pushed himself at the gym a lot since he'd given his life to Christ two months ago. God wanted to be first in his life, but women were his weakness.

And two months was a long time.

He yanked the earplugs out and pumped his fists harder in sync with the run. Staring up at the ceiling, he asked God for the strength to think of something else. Anything else.

Work. He was busy at work. Two couples were coming into the office the next day to sign adoption papers. One of the couples had been foster parents to their son for three years. Tomorrow they would finally become his legal parents. He and Megan had spent hours combing through the documents to ensure the signing would take place without a hitch.

The three miles complete, he slowed his pace to a fast walk. He wiped the sweat off his forehead with the back of his hand. Thinking of Megan was dangerous territory, too.

There was something about her. She was pretty but not gorgeous like most of the women he noticed. Still, she invaded his thoughts at the oddest moments. She was easy to be around with her sense of propriety and efficiency at work. She didn't bat her eyes or flip her hair over her shoulder like most of the women he knew. She intrigued him. Her faith was apparent in more than just the paperweight on her desk.

He turned off the treadmill and stepped down. He took a long swig of water and tossed the empty bottle in a nearby trash can. He didn't need to think about Megan either.

"I don't believe we've met."

A soft hand touched his elbow, and Justin flinched. He looked at the woman and inwardly sighed. Tight black and pink fitness getup. Legs as long as his. Silky dark hair pulled in a ponytail. Emerald green eyes. *God, is this some kind of test?*

He forced a smile and extended his hand. "Justin. I just joined."

Her nails tickled his wrist before she shook his hand. "Brandy." She pointed to the logo on her too-tight shirt. "If you ever need anything, you just let me know. I work Tuesdays and Thursdays."

Justin nodded, trying to act uninterested. The woman smelled delicious, nothing like a person who worked at a fitness club.

She lingered, apparently waiting for his response. He wished he still stood close to the treadmill. He could have stepped back on as if starting the second half of his workout.

The front door swung open, and Kirk walked inside. He waved to Justin, blew out an exaggerated breath, and shoved his keys in a cubby. "Sorry I'm late, man. Traffic was a killer."

Justin sent up a silent prayer of thanks, nodded to Brandy, then headed toward his friend. "Perfect timing."

Kirk squinted his eyes. "What's going on?"

Justin tilted his head to motion behind him. Kirk looked past him, and Justin punched him in the arm. "Don't look."

Kirk gaped back at him. "Brandy hit on you?" He shook his head. "Man, she is so hot."

"What would your fiancée say if she heard you say that?"

"She'd say, 'Man, she *is* hot.'"

Justin growled as he made his way to an open weight bench. Kirk followed behind him. "Seriously, I want to trade temptations."

Justin added weight to the bar then lay back on the bench. "How can you even begin to compare your addiction to mine? Video games don't waltz up to you after a workout and start up a conversation."

"Are you kidding? Every time I walk past the electronics section of a store or even turn on my computer, a little voice in my head says, 'Come on, just one game.'" He shrugged, tapped his temples with his fingertips, and lifted his eyebrows. "It's evil."

Justin laughed at Kirk's dramatics. "Nowhere near the same as a live person."

"I don't know about that. Mine's even in my house."

Justin let out a long breath. "I suppose you're right. Temptation is temptation, and yours is no less than mine."

Kirk sobered. "But I do have a big support system. God. Marianna. My family. My Bible study group."

"I have you and God."

"You could join my study."

Justin wrinkled his nose and shook his head. He'd tried to visit Kirk's church once, but something just seemed off to him. Maybe it was the fact he'd dated the preacher's wife in high school. Sure, it had been thirteen years, but it still felt weird.

"Yesterday you mentioned a Bible study you planned to try out."

"They meet tonight."

"You going?"

"I think so. My secretary goes there, and. . ." Justin laughed when Kirk ducked his chin and peered at him. He lifted his hands in surrender. "I promise it's on the up and up."

"What church is it?"

Justin told him the name, and Kirk nodded. "That's where Marianna used to go. She switched to my church when we got engaged. Her sister still attends, and she loves their Bible study."

"That's great." Justin patted the top of the bar. "But if we don't start working, I'm not going to make it."

Kirk growled. It had only been a few months since Justin reconnected with his high school sweetheart. But Justin knew as soon as Kirk muttered, "I do," his friend would give up the gym membership.

"Marianna had better appreciate all I'm doing for her."

Justin switched places with Kirk and stood behind the bar to spot while Kirk completed his reps. "When am I going to get to meet this girl?"

"Soon. She's been nuts teaching middle school and planning the wedding. But she's anxious to meet you."

"I'll try not to steal her away."

"Not funny, man."

Justin laughed as Kirk lay back against the bench and frowned. "You used to love to work out in high school. Remember baseball conditioning?"

Kirk grimaced as he pushed the bar up until his arms were straight. He dropped it onto the bar. "That was before I discovered how delicious pastries and sodas are. I've changed quite a bit since high school."

Justin nodded. His friend was not the same guy he'd known during his teen years, and Justin was thankful he'd run into the metamorphosed version.

Justin rubbed his hands together to ensure his palms weren't as damp as he feared. Normally he was a man of stoic confidence, one people sought out for assistance and assurance. But he was out of his natural element.

Standing outside the megachurch's front door, he realized he had no idea where the Bible study would be located in such a massive building. He'd visited here once before, years ago, with a woman who'd needed his assistance through a nasty divorce. He flinched at the overpowering memory of his motive for attending church with her. She was yet another woman he needed to seek out to ask forgiveness.

Sophia had taken his apology just as he'd anticipated she would. The gorgeous redhead walked into his office assuming he wanted to start up their relationship again, but when she'd learned he only wanted to apologize, she'd flown into a rage.

Her nostrils flared as she pierced her cool blue eyes into him. "You called me over here for what?"

He'd tried to explain again he'd accepted Jesus into his heart, and though he didn't deserve her forgiveness, he wanted to apologize for the way he'd treated her.

She'd jumped to her feet. "Don't flatter yourself, Justin." The anger that lit her eyes shifted to one of seduction as she placed her hands on his desk and leaned toward him. "I make my own choices." She leaned closer to him and raked one hand through his hair.

Shivers raced through him at the light scratch of her fingernails, and he forced himself to stare only into her eyes. She was a temptation to him, and she knew it.

He'd cleared his throat and forced his gaze away from hers. "I just wanted to apologize. I won't bother you anymore."

She'd stood there for what was probably only a few seconds more but seemed like an eternity. He didn't want what he'd had with Sophia, and too many other women. He wanted God's peace and contentment in his life, not just momentary satisfaction.

Snapping back to reality, he reached for the church's door handle then hesitated. *You've changed me, God, and yet I still feel as if I'm not good enough to walk into Your house.*

"You're not, but I am."

He pulled open the door and walked inside, remembering his dad's words that the church walls would fall in if he stepped inside one. Justin shared the sentiment until he'd reconnected with Kirk. His friend led him to the Lord and assured him the walls should fall in on everyone.

A welcome desk sat to his right, but no one was in the lobby. Heavy oak doors he remembered led to the sanctuary were closed in front of him. Long halls extended on his right and left as well as more entrances to the worship area and stairs that led to the balcony.

He looked around for some kind of poster or map. But he didn't even know where the class met. His thumb rubbed the hard new leather of his Bible. He gritted his teeth. He could have planned this better. Asked Megan how to get to the class or if she'd meet him in the lobby. Aggravation swelled in his chest, and he turned and headed for the door.

Megan opened it and gasped when they made eye contact. "You came?"

Embarrassment warmed his neck and cheeks. What was wrong with him? He hadn't acted this way since he was in middle school. He cleared his throat and nodded. "I did."

He watched as she bit her bottom lip. He couldn't read her expression. Was she simply surprised? A little apprehensive? Or upset? An ache twisted his stomach at the idea she wouldn't have wanted him to join her class. He knew she was a Christian. Her faith was evident, and he'd hoped her Bible study would teach him more about his faith.

Her lips curved into a genuine smile, and the heaviness in his gut lightened. She motioned to him. "Come on. We'll go together."

He fell into step beside her. His gaze took in the various children's paintings of crosses and flowers covering the walls. The sign on the first door was labeled nursery, then toddlers, then twos, all going up chronologically. A bulletin board was covered with pictures of children hunting Easter eggs in the back of the church's property.

One particular picture caught his eye. It was of Megan sitting on the ground with her legs stretched in front of her. She had a basket filled with candy between her legs. Two boys and a girl sat around her, pillaging through the goods. But Megan was looking up, smiling at the camera with her right cheek twice its normal size, obviously stuffed with candy. She looked so happy and carefree and innocent. It yanked at his heart.

"I'm glad you came."

Justin snapped from his reverie. Megan's voice was softer than usual, and for a moment, he wondered if she felt obligated to say it. Then she looked up at him, and his heartbeat sped at the fullness of her smile.

He gripped the Bible tighter in his hand. "I've been looking forward to it." He opened his arms wide. "This is all so new to me, but I know I need to find a church."

Megan shifted her weight and studied him. Under her intense scrutiny, he had to resist the urge to adjust his polo's collar. Finally, she nodded. "I think you'll like our group. We have a lot of fun together."

She opened the door, and Justin followed her inside. The room was bigger than he'd expected. According to the sign on the door, it normally housed eight-year-olds. He assumed the sign was accurate by the children's materials lining the walls. Metal chairs were set up in a circle.

Justin looked around at the women in the room. One slightly plump, a shorter lady with flaming red hair and bright pink glasses. Another woman, average-length blond hair, crooked teeth, possibly blue eyes, just kind of plain. There was another woman with highlighted brown hair. She was already seated, but if Justin guessed right, and he usually did, he'd say she was probably a little taller than average, five feet seven or five feet eight.

Megan interrupted his analysis. "Justin, this is Kat. She's our discussion leader this week."

Justin took in the dark-haired woman. Deep brown eyes. Small button nose. And lips that would make Angelina Jolie envious.

Kat extended her hand. "We're glad to have you."

Before Justin could respond, voices sounded from the doorway. Justin looked as a tall brunette and a strawberry blond walked in and took seats beside each other.

He swallowed the knot in his throat as he glanced around the seven women in the room. *God, is this some kind of joke?*

He cleared his throat and addressed Megan. "Is this a girls' Bible study?"

Megan narrowed her eyelids. "Are you looking for a girls' only Bible study?"

The insinuation behind the question stung, but he knew his reputation preceded him. It was one of the reasons he'd determined to apologize to the women he'd treated as little more than momentary amusement. The truth of the reputation was why he needed to drown himself in God's Word. He stared into her eyes, hoping she'd see the truth. "No. I'm not."

Kat said, "I'm sorry about this, Justin. The guys had a make-up baseball game tonight. Their Tuesday night game was rained out."

Justin cocked his head. "Baseball?"

Kat nodded. "Yep. Started two weeks ago. They could use a few players."

Justin opened his mouth to offer to play. It had been four years since his last college game. He missed it something fierce.

"Maybe Justin will play. He's really good. Played in college."

Megan's comment stunned him. It was the first time he'd heard her call him by his given name, and he couldn't imagine how she knew he'd played in college.

Kat's expression brightened. "You did?"

He nodded but looked back at Megan. "How did you know that?"

"Your picture's on your dad's wall."

He pursed his lips. He'd forgotten. For some reason he kind of hoped she'd known because she wanted to know, not because the picture was right in front of her face. He shook his head. He didn't need to be thinking like that. He was avoiding his temptation.

Kat smiled. "Terrific. I know they'd love to have you." She clapped. "But for tonight. It'll just be you and us girls."

Justin glanced around the room once again. Just what he needed to encourage his faith. A Bible study filled with a bunch of women.

Chapter 5

Nobody, who has not been in the interior of a family can
say what the difficulties of any individual of that family may be.
JANE AUSTEN

Megan twisted the wire around the tulle pew bow. She stuck her hand through each loop and twisted the material into a shape Marianna wanted. Once satisfied, she handed it to Marianna to attach the silk yellow Asiatic lilies, orange Gerberas, baby's breath, and deep red ribbon. Her sister's wedding color choices were bolder than Megan would have selected, but she had no doubt her sister would pull off one of the most beautiful celebrations she'd ever seen.

Megan clenched and unclenched her fists then wiggled her fingers to relieve the stiffness. "How many more?"

Marianna pointed to each as she counted. She wrinkled her nose as her lips spread into a sheepish grin. "Only thirty-five."

Megan huffed as she let her head fall against the back of the chair. "There is no way we'll finish all these today."

"I know, but I thought maybe we'd get half of them done."

"Ten more?"

Marianna pushed the tulle closer to Megan. "Yep. That's all." She twisted the wire, connected two of the flowers to a red bow. "It's not too bad. Especially since you aren't taking any classes right now."

Megan folded the tulle, making uniform loops. She'd finally gotten her grade for her spring semester class. An A, just as she'd expected. The only thing left was student teaching, and if a music position opened over the summer and she landed the job, she was eligible to complete her student teaching on the job.

Megan peered at her sister. "I do have other things to do today."

"Like what?"

"I'm going to Hadley's house. Her uncle asked me to give her piano lessons."

"I forgot. The day of the canoe trip, right?"

Megan nodded as she twisted wire around another bow.

Marianna clipped most of the stems off two of the orange flowers and attached them to a large yellow lily. "He's really protective of Hadley."

Megan snorted. "I could tell."

Marianna set down the flower arrangement. She brushed a stray hair away from her eyes. "What I mean is you must have made a great impression for him to ask you to teach Hadley. I've never had a parent, especially a man who isn't even the girl's biological dad, be so involved in what we're teaching and how we're teaching it."

Megan growled. "Great. So, he's going to be a pain in the neck?"

Marianna shook her head. "No. He isn't rude or intrusive, but he is involved. And he's a Christian. And he's good-looking."

"Where are her parents?"

Marianna shrugged. "I don't know the details, and even if I did, you know I couldn't tell you. Confidentiality." Marianna shuffled her eyes as she reached across the table and pushed Megan's arm. "I do know he's rich."

Megan's cheeks warmed. "Marianna, I can't believe you would say such a thing."

Marianna laughed, and she rubbed her hands together as if she'd just found the fictional pot of gold at the end of the rainbow. "Well, he is."

"You know I'm not interested in dating."

Marianna sobered, and Megan shifted in her seat. She knew what was coming. Part of her wanted just to get up and go to the restroom or go get a drink from the kitchen. She didn't want to hear any lectures. Though Marianna stood beside her during the worst time of her life, her sister had no idea how bad it was to live it.

Marianna's voice softened. "It's been eight years, Megan. Maybe it's time."

All that time had passed, and yet when Megan closed her eyes and allowed her mind to travel back, she could still recall every detail. Even the smell of Cajun leftovers. She hadn't touched spicy food since.

Megan shook her head. "No. I don't think so."

She stared at the mass of flowers, tulle, wire, and clippers sprawled on top of the table. She knew Marianna studied her, her expression a mixture of frustration and pity. Megan noticed the calendar hanging on the refrigerator. She looked back up at Marianna. "When are we supposed to have the fittings for the bridesmaid dresses?"

The diversion worked. Marianna jumped out of her seat and walked to the refrigerator. She moved her hands across the dates on the calendar. The thing was covered with appointments and sale dates of various wedding items.

Marianna tapped the calendar. "Here it is. Next Monday, five o'clock." She looked back at Megan. "Once you get a little bit of sun, I know you'll love the color."

Megan bit the inside of her mouth to keep from responding. She still couldn't believe her sister was forcing her to wear a strapless yellow dress. Megan was pale as a ghost. Yellow was the last color she would ever choose to wear. And her shoulders were covered with freckles. Which was why she enjoyed keeping them covered.

Of course, Marianna's two bridesmaids were both tall brunettes with killer long legs and willowy shapes. They'd look gorgeous in the light color. Megan would look like a short yellow cupcake.

The only redeeming facet of the dress was the thick red sash around the waist. She just wished the whole dress could be that color. But Megan would be a good sister. She wouldn't mention that her sister had condemned her to a lifetime of embarrassing photos and memories. It was Marianna's day, and Megan wouldn't fuss about what she had to wear.

"You know Mom's coming for the fittings."

Marianna's voice interrupted Megan's thoughts. Megan knew she would. They'd seen a lot more of their mother since Marianna's engagement, which was to be expected. Megan knew her emotional estrangement from her mom and stepdad were not what God wanted, but she couldn't forgive them.

Marianna continued, "Bill wants to come with her."

Megan sighed. "I'm not surprised."

"You need to make amends."

Megan frowned at her sister. "They don't mind that our relationship is superficial. They don't care that—"

"But you're the Christian."

Megan smacked her hand on the table. "I get tired of being the one who has to forgive and forget. They've never once apologized to me, and you know they were wrong."

Marianna averted her gaze and picked at one of her fingernails. Megan knew her sister. She was trying to figure the right words to say to make Megan change her mind. Well, this was too big. God should understand why she couldn't just forgive and forget.

Marianna opened her arms. "You're right. They owe you an apology. But you may never get it."

Megan squeezed her eyes closed. Why did God ask her to forgive people who didn't deserve it, didn't even want it? A fresh wave of realization of Jesus' covering of her sin washed over her. She hadn't deserved forgiveness, and yet God granted it to her.

But God was bigger than her. He was God, after all. The Maker of heaven and earth and all of creation. He had a lot more power within Himself to draw from. And yet He still wanted her to forgive. She knew scripture said it. Knew God commanded it. But she didn't feel it. And she didn't want to.

Wind whipped through Megan's hair as she drove the old country roads that led to the small town of Midway. She tapped the top of the steering wheel. Her fingers still ached from making pew bows with Marianna earlier in the day. And they were only half through with the pew decorations. She cringed at the thought of starting up on them again.

Megan turned a curve and slowed to a near crawl behind an

oversized tractor. She allowed her gaze to sweep the countryside. She'd missed the beauty of her mountains and hills in eastern Kentucky, but the rolling pastures of Midway were just as breathtaking.

She passed a farm with several horses grazing. An ornate white barn with a gray roof and black-trimmed doors and windows sat a thousand feet or more away from the road. She lifted her brows. "Haven't seen many houses nicer than that barn."

She glanced at the GPS suctioned to her windshield. If the gadget was right, she'd stay on this road for two more miles. She lifted her pointer finger in the air and spoke in a monotone voice. "Then I'll arrive at my destination, on right."

She laughed at herself as she continued at a speed that would challenge a turtle. Two cars had slowed behind her, but with so little traffic on the road, she didn't expect the farmer would pull over and allow them to pass.

Passing another horse farm, she drank in the whitewashed brick walls on each side of the entrance. Portfolio antique verde lights hung on the brick walls on each side. Though the decorative wrought iron gate was closed, Megan still spied the house that looked as if it had been copied off the pages of *Gone with the Wind* and planted in the small town of Midway. She whipped her hair over her shoulder, threw back her chin, and proclaimed, "After all. . .tomorrow is another day."

The GPS jabbered at her, and she looked at the entrance to her destination. Though not as gaudy, the brownstone and wrought iron entrance opened up to a two-story white vinyl farmhouse with a charcoal roof and deep red shutters, an oak front door, and a wrap-around porch.

She shifted into park, scooped the piano books and her purse off the passenger's seat, then reached around to the outside of the car to open the door. She sucked in a deep breath as she shoved the door closed with her hip. "Marianna was right. Definitely rich."

She had taken just a couple of steps toward the house when Old Yeller raced across the yard barking at her. Megan bit back a squeal as she booked it to the front porch. She loved dogs, and golden labs had been one of her favorites since reading about this one's twin as a girl. She clenched her jaw when the massive creature leaped onto the porch and bared his teeth at her.

"Old Yeller!" A male voice sounded from behind the house. Colt walked around to the front and patted his thigh. "Get over here, boy."

Megan blew out a breath and offered a weak smile when the animal nestled against Colt's leg then sat beside him. "Your dog?"

Colt nodded. "Yep."

Megan loosened her grip on the piano books. The canine winked, an involuntary motion she was sure, but adorable just the same. The dog panted heavily but remained obediently beside his master. He looked up at Colt. "His name's Old Yeller?"

"Don't you think he looks like him?"

"Definitely." Megan lowered her hand palm up and started to bend down. "He won't hurt me, will he?"

"I'd reckon not. Old Yeller's about the sweetest dog I've ever owned."

Colt patted the dog's side, and Old Yeller walked to Megan and sniffed her hand. Once Megan had received a slobbery lick, she petted the animal's head and neck. Old Yeller moved closer, and Megan fought the urge to wrap her arms around the dog's thick neck.

Megan stood and wiped her hand on the side of her denim capris. "Is Hadley ready?"

Colt looked at his watch. "She should be back any minute. She's been practicing her barrel racing."

Megan lifted her eyebrows.

Colt cocked his head. "It's a rodeo sport where the competitor rides around three barrels in a cloverleaf pattern as fast as she can without knocking them down."

Megan shifted her weight. "I know what it is. I just didn't know girls did it, especially girls as young as Hadley."

Colt scoffed. "Well sure. Hadley's one of the best in the nation." His lips parted into a smile that would outshine John Wayne. "You should go with us to a rodeo sometime."

Heat crept up Megan's neck as she realized how accurate her sister had been in describing Colt as quite a hottie. She knew he was just bragging about his niece. He wasn't asking her on a date. Besides, it was Hadley's barrel-racing, sweat-flying, steed-stomping rodeo he was talking about, not some moonlit ride on a pair of tame horses. "Well, I—"

"That was some ride."

Megan turned and saw Hadley stomping toward the porch, patting her hands against her jeans. Old Yeller bounded down the steps and ran around the girl until she bent down and petted the canine.

"You were supposed to be back half an hour ago to allow time to clean up." Colt frowned and crossed his arms in front of his chest.

Hadley looped her fingers through the waist of her jeans. "I know, Uncle Colt, but Fairybelle was riding like a champion, and I had to let her keep practicing at that pace."

Megan watched as Colt's expression softened. She had a feeling the preteen had her uncle wrapped snuggly around her pinkie finger.

He pointed toward the house. "Get on in there and clean up quick. I'll show Miss Megan the piano."

Hadley grinned as she rose up on tiptoes and kissed her uncle's cheek. She waved to Megan. "Be right back."

Megan's heartbeat sped at being left alone with Colt again. She wished Hadley had listened to her uncle and been ready when she arrived. She also wished Marianna hadn't cursed her into noticing Colt's good looks.

Colt didn't make a move to guide her inside. He just sort of stared at her. Which made no sense. What did he want her to say? Surely he couldn't tell she thought he was quite the cutie. She inwardly growled. She had news for him. There would be no baring of the soul, no admission of his good looks.

He waved toward the house. "Come on in."

Megan rolled her eyes at her own dramatics as she followed the man into his home. Listening to her sister go on about Colt Baker had her mind all in a tizzy. The man wasn't that good-looking. Just because he had dirty-blond hair, blue eyes, and the swagger of a true homegrown cowboy didn't mean he was any more than the average Joe she passed each day on the street.

She rolled her eyes at her wayward thoughts as she followed Colt through the living room and down a hall. The house didn't look like a bachelor pad. Though a bit dated, the décor was one of the more feminine Americana styles she'd seen.

He guided her into a room, and Megan gasped. The walls were covered with books and Victorian figurines. Dusty rose-colored drapes and an elegant swag cascaded from the top of the window.

Beside a tall lamp sat an ivory satin-covered wingback chair. But it was the Victorian baby grand that stole her breath.

She gestured toward the instrument. "Does it work?"

"Tuned and ready."

She placed a hand on her chest and nodded toward it. "May I?"

"Yeah. Give her a whirl. Let's see how she sounds."

Megan sat down on the bench. She caressed a few keys before placing her hands in position. But what to play? Something Victorian would be best. She searched her mind. She knew little from that era by heart, but there was surely something she could play a few chords of.

She remembered a song she'd learned in high school. Her fingers danced across the keys, and she threw herself into "The Dying Poet" by Gottschalk. She didn't think with her brain, just allowed her fingers to remember the notes. The soothing melody filled her and reminded her of a time of happiness and innocence.

When she finished, she stared at the black music holder. She'd learned the piece just before she'd started the tenth grade. Things were easier then. Good and bad was absolute. Life wasn't tainted.

"Am I gonna learn to play like that?"

Hadley's question broke Megan's reverie, and she twisted in the seat. She rubbed her hands together and smiled at the girl. "Absolutely."

She glanced across the room at Colt. He was leaning against a bookshelf, his arms folded across his chest. Surprised pleasure etched his features, and she looked away from him. He really shouldn't look at her like that.

Chapter 6

Generosity is giving more than you can,
and pride is taking less than you need.
KHALIL GIBRAN

Colt blinked and shook his head as he pushed away from the bookshelf. He didn't know enough about Megan to be swept away into some kind of strange ooshy-gooshy land just because she played a few chords. She reminded him of his mom. For a moment, he was the proverbial fly stuck to the wall, entranced by Cozette Baker who sat at the piano playing an elaborate tune. Her husband, Wade, leaned against the doorjamb, mesmerized into a deep calm after a laborious day on the farm. Colt knew his mother's playing soothed his dad's soul. He hadn't realized how much it comforted his own. He missed her. His mom. And his dad.

With a wave of emotion threatening to rise out of his chest, Colt retreated from the room and headed to the front door.

"That was so pretty, Megan. Play another."

Hadley's awe-filled voice filled the foyer, and Colt wasn't able to make it to the door fast enough. Another rhythm pealed from the piano. He recognized the old hymn "When the Saints Go Marching In."

A low growl slipped through his mouth. That was the *perfect* song to uplift his spirits. One about when God's children left this world to meet Him in the heavens. He sucked in a deep breath then stepped out into the warm spring air and lifted his gaze to the cloud-dotted sky. "God, I miss Mom and Dad."

Growing up, life had been perfect. Better than anything shown on old television sitcoms. His dad, the hardworking farmer, and his mom, the doting wife and mother, raised his brother and him in God's majestic Kentucky countryside. They'd attended their small country church each time the doors were opened.

Then things changed. His brother befriended Tina. They started drinking and doing drugs. She got pregnant. Then came Hadley. Then Mom and Dad's car accident.

He pushed the spiraling gyro of hard recollections from his mind. No reason to dwell on them. He had a farm to tend. Horses and Hadley to raise. And God and his church stood beside him. Past was past. And he wasn't going to allow a few tunes on a piano to set him off to wallowing in sadness about things that couldn't be altered.

His big yellow dog meandered up the stairs and nudged his leg, begging for attention. "Hey, Old Yeller." Colt bent down and petted his buddy, who'd been around nearly as long as Hadley. A constant companion through the ups and downs of the last decade. "Let's say we go check on the horses."

Old Yeller barked and took off toward the stables. Colt had finished his chores early and had planned to stay in the house for Hadley's first piano lesson. He wouldn't go far. Wouldn't stay out too long. But he'd get away for just a bit. Get his thoughts and feelings back in check. Next time Megan came for a lesson, he'd be better prepared to hear the old piano come to life.

He thought of the young woman sitting on the piano bench. Though most of it was pulled back in a ponytail, blond wisps framed her face. Complete serenity etched her expression when she closed her eyes and dug into that first song. She felt the music with every fiber of her body, and it stirred something primitive within him.

He smiled. She was a good woman. Not like Tina. He could trust Megan with Hadley. She loved God. He could just tell it. Only a relationship with Jesus could cause such a peace in a person. He picked up his pace toward the stable. She was someone he could be proud of. Call home about. Even if there was no one but him and Hadley left to answer.

More than an hour passed. He pushed the saddle back on the rack. He'd gotten so wrapped up in oiling the thing he'd forgotten to check his watch. Megan may have gone ahead and left. He hoped not. She hadn't been paid. And he hoped she'd let him know Hadley was alone before hitting the road.

He took long strides toward the house. But she may have had somewhere she needed to go, and he couldn't fault her if she'd gone. People who were late grated on his nerves. He glanced down at his watch again and gritted his teeth. Fifteen minutes was a long time to wait when a person had somewhere to go.

Reaching the back door, he barreled in without stamping the dirt off his feet. He pulled off his ball cap, walked through the mudroom, coming to a halt at the kitchen door. Hadley and Megan stood over the island countertop. Hadley wore his mother's pink-and-white polka-dotted BEST GRANDMA apron. She shaped a chunk of prepackaged cookie dough into a ball. Megan placed a ball of dough on the cookie sheet.

A knot formed in his throat, and he swallowed it down. It had been a long time since he'd seen a woman in the kitchen—outside of Hadley, and he most certainly couldn't call her a woman. He cleared his throat. "Sorry I'm late. Got caught up with stuff in the barn."

Hadley and Megan looked at him. A blush swept across Megan's cheeks, and Hadley stuck out her bottom lip into a dramatic pout. "Uncle Colt!" She jabbed her hands onto her hips. "If you'd have waited ten more minutes, we'd be done with our surprise."

He raised his eyebrows and made eye contact with Megan.

She placed a ball of dough onto the cookie sheet then wiped her hands on a paper towel. "Hadley wanted to bake you some cookies. She said they're your favorite."

Colt's heart raced. Her shy gestures and deep blue eyes cantered on his senses like a horse in competition. "That was awful sweet."

Hadley smacked her hand against her thigh, causing him to shift his attention back to his niece. She wrinkled her nose and wiggled her shoulders and head from side to side. "Yeah, but you had to go and ruin it and come back too quick." She stuck out her lower lip. "You never let me surprise you."

Colt bit the inside of his lip. The older Hadley got, the more dramatic she became. Some days the young'un would set off to stomping through the house and crying for no reason he could figure at all. It was as if turning twelve had caused some kind of weird metamorphosis in the girl about which no one had given him fair warning.

Having been raised with just himself and his brother, Colt didn't know what to expect as a girl got older. He knew there were things young ladies dealt with that boys didn't, and he figured he probably needed to look into finding out more about those things, but Hadley was only twelve. Not even a teenager yet. Surely he had a few more years before he needed to start initiating uncomfortable talks with his niece.

A wave of nausea swirled in his throat at the thought. Raising the girl on his own was more than he'd bargained for. Not that he regretted or begrudged it. He loved her more than just about anything in the world. In fact, he couldn't think of a thing he loved more. Still, he hadn't the faintest clue what to do with these emotional outbursts.

She shouldn't be mad at him for showing up too soon when he was a full fifteen minutes late coming in from the barn. Hadley picked up the cookie sheet and shoved it into the oven with a bit more force than necessary. The kid made no sense.

Actually the whole thing was quite comical. He pulled out a stool from underneath the island and lowered himself down onto it. "Well, Hadley, I'm sorry for showing up too soon, even though I'm fifteen minutes late."

She glared at him. "Don't make fun of me, Uncle Colt. I was wanting to do something nice for you."

Megan placed a hand on Hadley's forearm. "Why don't you play the tune I taught you? He'd probably like to hear it."

Warmth swelled up in Colt's chest as he drank in the ease with which Megan handled his niece. Her voice was calm. Her expression sincere.

Hadley tumbled right into Megan's charms. Her expression

softened, and her eyes lit up when she looked back at Colt. "You wanna hear?"

Colt stood and motioned toward the piano room. "Absolutely."

Hadley pushed away from the counter and raced away. Colt noticed Megan set the timer on the oven before following his niece. Hadley's impulsive behavior and mood shifts didn't seem to faze the piano teacher. She took his niece in stride, and he wished he'd made himself stay and watch the lesson. See them interact. Spend a little time with Megan.

He knew Megan was a Christian. And from what little he'd seen, she seemed to be a good influence on his niece. The girl needed a woman's influence. A woman who loved the Lord and lived for Him. Megan may be the answer to his petition to God for help with Hadley.

She may be more than that.

The idea wrapped itself around his brain. He hadn't been looking for a woman in his life. He'd been filled up with farmwork and Hadley. But now he'd met Megan and seen her in action with his niece. Thoughts and feelings were coming to him that he couldn't recall the last time he'd pondered. To his surprise, the notions set kinda good with him.

He followed Megan to the piano room. She surely wasn't hard to look at. Small frame with curves in all the right places. Blond hair, shiny and as soft looking as fully-ripened wheat. Eyes so blue they shamed the sky for color.

Megan turned to him. He stopped short and felt heat rising in his neck. It was a good thing she couldn't read his mind.

"She already knows the keys and where to place her hands. Teaching her will be a snap."

Colt nodded. He wished he knew something clever to say. He'd never known exactly how to act in front of a woman. Hadn't been overly worried about it anyway. He reached into his back pocket and pulled out the check he'd written to her. "Here. Before I forget."

Megan accepted the money. "Thank you."

A broken tune sounded from the piano, and Colt focused his attention on his niece. Though she stopped and started over several times, he recognized the tune. The same one Megan had been playing when he'd walked out. Only Hadley didn't add the extra melody to "When the Saints Go Marching In." She played the tune simply.

After several moments of starting and restarting, pausing and moving her fingers to correct notes, Hadley finished the song, looked over at Colt, and smiled. "Whaddaya think?"

Now she wasn't mad at him. Now she was smiling, eyebrows lifted, expression in anticipation of his approval. The kid never failed to confuse him. He walked to his niece and patted her shoulder. "Sounds great. I can't believe you got through the whole chorus after only one lesson."

Hadley's smile lit up the room. It surprised him how such simple praise from him meant so much to her. The older she got the more he tried to remember to tell her when she did a good job. She seemed to need the reminding.

But it wasn't in his nature to always be spouting off one compliment after another. To his thinking, less meant more. He tended to enjoy seeing the results of his hard work. He didn't need to talk about it. Didn't need a pat on the back. But Hadley sure did. The girl wore him out with her neediness lately. Still, he wanted to encourage her. And she was a good kid—when she wasn't being moody.

Colt turned to Megan. "She's doing great."

"Like I said, she already knows a lot. Hadley may be the easiest student I'll ever have."

Hadley jumped off the piano stool and raced to Megan. She wrapped her arms around her. "I'm glad Uncle Colt asked you to come. Stephanie says you're the best, and I know it's true."

Colt took in the affection Hadley already felt for Megan. She'd always been a loving child, quick to give hugs, but he could see she really liked Megan. He sent a silent prayer of thanks that God had brought her into their lives. Hadley needed a female influence.

"Do I have to wait until next Saturday?" Hadley looked from Megan to Colt. "Couldn't I have two lessons a week? Maybe she could come on Tuesdays, too?"

Colt glared at his niece. "Hadley! I'm sure Megan has other things to do than come over and—"

"Actually," Megan interrupted him, "I wouldn't mind at all giving you two lessons a week. On one condition."

Hadley clasped her hands and bounced on her heels. "What?"

Megan looked from Hadley to Colt. A slight blush colored her cheeks and she bit her bottom lip. The mixture of mischief and hesitation in her expression drew him. He couldn't wait to hear the condition.

"What?" Colt and Hadley asked together.

She blew out a breath. "I used to ride horses when I was a girl living in eastern Kentucky. Could we maybe work out a trade, the extra hour lesson for an hour of riding?"

Colt's jaw dropped. That was what she wanted—to ride horses? The woman couldn't be more perfect for Hadley. Or him. "Are you serious?"

She wrinkled her nose and shifted her weight from one foot to the other. "Yeah."

Hadley snorted. "Well sure. We can do that." She motioned outside. "We can go out there right now. I'm always open to a horse ride. I didn't know you rode horses."

Megan chuckled. "It's been awhile. I may be a bit rusty, but hopefully it's like riding a bike. It'll come back to me."

Colt motioned to the door. "You wanna go now?"

"I would love to." Megan shook her head. "But I can't. My sister's getting married in July. We've been working on some decorations, and we still have a ton to do."

She picked up her purse from the settee and gave Hadley another hug. Colt wished she'd offer one to him, but he wasn't going to hold his breath. Maybe another day.

He followed her to the door. "So, we'll see you Tuesday?"

"Sounds great. What time?"

"You can come for dinner if you'd like," Hadley answered.

Megan shook her head. "That's awfully sweet of you, but I'm having a dinner with a friend. Would six be too early?"

"Sounds good to me," said Hadley.

Megan looked at Colt, and he nodded. He wished she would come to dinner as Hadley had suggested. He hoped her plans weren't with a date. Here he'd been having all these thoughts of her being a perfect mate for him, and he didn't even know if the woman had a boyfriend. He hoped she didn't.

"Okay. I'll see you then." Megan waved and walked down the sidewalk.

Hadley looked up at Colt. "I really like her."

"I can tell."

"She'd be good for you, too."

Colt didn't respond. He ruffled her hair then walked away from the door. The oven beeper sounded, and Hadley ran to the kitchen. Saved by the bell. He didn't want his niece to see he thought she was right.

Chapter 7

Character is doing the right thing when nobody's looking.
There are too many people who think that the only thing that's
right is to get by and the only thing that's wrong is to get caught.

J. C. WATTS

Justin looked at his reflection one last time in the full-length mirror. He appeared comfortable in his newly pressed khakis and bright melon polo. A fresh shave and a recent haircut completed the look. The last time he'd felt so nervous was when they'd gone to trial for the Jones's divorce proceedings. He'd had to squelch more than one bloodbath with those two arguing over their five million dollars in family assets.

At the time, he'd dug into the case, anxious to make Mrs. Jones the victor and him a benefactor of the win. Now it hurt to think he'd been so excited and consumed in helping the desolation of a thirty-five-year union. Some moments he still wondered if Mrs. Jones would have been willing to try counseling if he had suggested it.

But past was past. He couldn't change it. And God had forgiven him. He picked up the brown leather study Bible he'd been making good use of and headed downstairs. He hadn't told Megan of his plan to visit her church. She probably assumed as much since he'd gone to Bible study on Thursday, but he'd been busy on Friday, and they hadn't really talked about Sunday morning services.

He hadn't wanted to discuss it with her anyway. This was something he needed to do on his own. Free of women. His stomach churned when he thought of the possibility of running into Amy. He hadn't seen her in years, but she had once attended the church, and she might still be there.

Memories of his relationship, if he could call it that, with the woman flooded his mind. She was beautiful. Her husband had an affair. She didn't want the divorce, but her husband did. She'd talked about her faith and cried for God to help her. She'd been vulnerable but determined. Then succumbed.

And Justin had congratulated himself for it.

Justin clamped his eyes shut and pressed the Bible against his chest. "God, I can't do it. The walls will fall in if I walk through those doors on a Sunday morning."

A scripture from 2 Corinthians washed through his mind, *"Therefore, if anyone is in Christ, the new creation has come: The old has gone, the new is here!"* He couldn't fathom why God would save him. Why He would choose him. His sin was so ugly. So arrogant. So self-serving. When he thought of the way he'd treated people, especially women, it sickened him to his core.

Learn to fellowship with believers. He'd read Paul's books over more times than he could remember. Paul claimed to be the worst of sinners, seeking out the destruction of Christians, encouraging the stoning of Stephen. And yet when Paul gave his life to Jesus, he changed. Radically. Completely. And without hesitation.

Opening his eyes, Justin grabbed his keys off the foyer table. He had to go to church. Had to hear God's Word. He didn't deserve the right to walk through those church doors, but God had given the grace, and he could not deny his Lord.

Justin made his way out of the house and to the car. Christian music pealed from the speakers as he drove the short distance. He just had to make it through today. Sit in the back. Talk to as few people as possible. Just take the first step. Going alone felt so different than going the one time with Kirk. His nerves surprised him.

He pulled into the parking lot and watched as people walked into the church. A family with a little boy and infant. A teenage girl and a woman who was probably her mother. An elderly couple. A middle-aged man.

He waited as the flow of members and visitors became more sporadic. Glancing at his watch, he knew the service started in less than five minutes. But he wanted to wait until the very end. Normally he ate up attention from people. Looked for a pat on the back or a word of praise for showing up. Today he just wanted to slip in. Be invisible.

See if Amy was there.

If she was, he would need to apologize to her. If not today, soon. She may smack his face or laugh at him. Spit on him maybe. He would deserve all of it. She had been a conquest. And he had won. His gut churned anew at the memory.

Pushing the thought away, he opened the car door and stepped out. The church doors had shut. Hopefully the men who were standing there welcoming people inside had already gone to their seats.

He walked up the stairs and opened the large wooden door. An older woman with graying light brown hair stood beside the door that opened to the sanctuary. Her dark red lips parted into a welcoming smile as she handed a bulletin to him. "We're happy to have you."

He accepted the paper and nodded. "Thank you."

She pointed to the left side. "There are some open seats in the back."

He went inside. To his relief, the congregation was standing and singing a song he didn't recognize. It had a contemporary beat, but he hadn't heard it on the radio. He assumed there were many songs he wouldn't recognize. "Amazing Grace" maybe, but that might be it.

The words to the song were displayed in large letters on a screen in the center of the wall. A tall red-haired man stood behind the pulpit singing with a fervor Justin had witnessed from a television worship leader when he'd been a boy shuffling through stations. The man waved his right hand back and forth to the beat of the music. As a kid, Justin thought the guy on TV looked goofy. But this man obviously sang with his whole heart.

Justin slipped into an empty pew in the very back of the room. His plan to go relatively unnoticed was working until the music stopped and the worship leader invited everyone to "reach around and shake someone's hand."

He cringed but plastered a smile on his face as one person after another made his or her way to him to greet him and shake his hand. He hadn't seen Megan. Or Amy. In truth, he didn't want to run into either of them.

They finally sat down, and Justin went ahead and opened his

Bible to the passages listed in the bulletin. Music started again, and he looked back to the front.

Megan was there. Alone. She held a microphone. She was going to sing?

"I'm not going to play today." Her voice reverberated through the room.

A grunt of disapproval washed over the congregation, and Justin looked around. People could act like that in church? Someone could speak from the pulpit and the congregation could respond, and with a negative sound? He thought old men stood behind the pulpit and preached the truth about hell, and the congregation listened. Maybe a few of the older men said, "Amen" or something, but there wasn't any actual interaction.

Megan continued, "But I'm still going to sing."

Laughter and applause sounded from the people, and Justin looked around again. This church was nothing like he expected. Completely different from Kirk's. He settled back in the pew and studied his firm's administrative assistant. He'd never heard Megan sing. He knew she played piano. Figured she must be pretty good, because she had a degree in it. He probably should have assumed she sang, but he'd never put much thought into it. She wasn't the kind of girl he went after.

She was pretty enough. Not gorgeous but pretty. She wasn't flashy like the girls he dated. Didn't have a husband or a boyfriend whom he needed to best and steal her away from. He inwardly growled. How he hated the man he was. He thought it might take the rest of his life to restore his reputation. And he wouldn't be able to do it. God would have to.

The background music continued, and then Megan joined in.

Her voice little more than a whisper, she sang of forgiveness. The music flowed softly, like water trickling across a creek bed, and Megan's voice, gentle yet sure, added the message to the flow.

As the song progressed, the music crescendoed, and Megan's volume rose as she sang of God's triumph over our mistakes and the strength of His restoration. Her voice mastered confidence and beauty and conviction. He felt the words, the sound, the truth to the depth of his being.

As the song ended, Justin watched her. Megan transformed when she sang. Her face, her voice, her body language. All of it spoke of a woman completely overwhelmed with adoration for God. How had he never really noticed her?

He had no intention of *really* noticing her now. He was focused on the Lord and building a relationship with Him. He needed to spend time making God the true Lord of his life.

Still, Megan stirred something in him. It was different than he'd felt with other women. It was pure. Holy. He didn't want from her. He wanted to give to her. It was a different feeling than he'd ever known. Even though he didn't know what to make of it.

For now, Justin didn't need to dwell on it. The song had given him the confidence he needed to sit in the church. He was a sinner, but he was forgiven. He could start anew.

The preacher walked to the pulpit. The man was younger than Justin had anticipated. He wore a white button-down shirt and green striped tie and brown pants. His sandy-colored hair was cut short, but he wore a mustache and wide goatee. He looked more like a dressed-up Harley Davidson rider than a preacher.

Then the man spoke, leading the congregation in prayer. Justin knew he was a man following God. Humble. Sincere. Honest.

Immediately Justin wanted to hear the message this man would deliver.

With his eyes still closed, he felt someone slip into the pew on the far side away from him. To his surprise, his heart raced at the thought of Megan sneaking in from the back and choosing a seat close to him.

When the prayer ended, he glanced to the end of the pew. The couple looked at him and nodded. Then recognition dawned. It was Amy. And the husband Justin helped her divorce.

The sermon was agonizing. Justin didn't hear a word the preacher said. Instead, he battled over whether he should talk to Amy. Was she married to the man again? Did he know about her and Justin?

She was on his list of women to whom he planned to apologize— but at church with her ex-husband, boyfriend, husband, whatever the guy was? Justin wasn't sure this was the most appropriate venue.

The service finally ended. *God, what do I do?* He glanced at Amy. The guy had already stood and made his way to Justin. With his pointer finger, he poked Justin's shoulder. "What are you doing here?"

Justin's old nature, which hadn't had much time to change, erupted, and he grabbed the man's finger and pushed it away. "Attending a church service."

"I know what you did." Fury laced the man's eyes and etched his jaw. He balled his hands into fists. "Did you come here to see my wife?"

Justin cocked his head. He owed Amy an apology, but if this guy thought Justin would sit by and allow himself to be pummeled, he'd learn real quick that white-collar workers could fight as well. Especially when provoked. "Ex-wife?"

"She's my wife again. No thanks to you."

Justin's brow puckered. "If I remember correctly, she came to see me because of you."

The man pulled back a fist, and Justin readied himself to lay the guy flat on his back.

"Timmy, please." Amy grabbed the man's arm.

Justin simmered when he looked at Amy's face, etched with embarrassment. His mistreatment of her haunted him more than any other. He wished he could change it. She was a Christian woman going through a very hard time. And he'd taken advantage of her.

Justin looked at her, hoping she could see how much he meant the words. "Amy, I'm sorry."

Timmy bristled up again. "Do not talk to my wife."

"What's going on?"

Justin turned and saw Megan standing behind him. She held a Bible and some other materials against her chest.

"Nothing. We're leaving." Timmy grabbed Amy by the arm and, before another word could be spoken, ushered her out of the church.

Justin let out a long breath. He'd been nervous about attending church, but he hadn't expected to make a scene. He glanced back at Megan, expecting her to inundate him with questions. Instead, she studied him. He felt uncomfortable, which didn't sit well. Normally he was the epitome of confidence. He shrugged. "Sorry 'bout that."

"Didn't look like you caused it."

"Oh, I did."

Megan cocked her head, and Justin grew more ill at ease at her scrutiny. He wanted to explain himself to her. He needed to be honest with her. For her to know the truth—the whole truth—

and still accept him.

"So Megan, who's your friend?"

Justin looked at the owner of the masculine voice. Up close, the pastor looked even younger than he had at the pulpit. He might even be in his twenties.

Megan pointed to Justin. "This is one of my bosses, Justin Frasure."

Justin accepted the pastor's extended hand. She motioned to the minister. "Justin, this is Pastor Wes."

"It's good to meet you."

"You, too. We're glad to have you here this morning. In fact, we've got some church baseball practice later this afternoon. Could use a few more members. You interested?"

"I'm actually already planning to be there. Kat told me about it at Bible study Thursday night."

Pastor Wes smiled. "Terrific." A young woman grabbed his arm, grinned at Megan and Justin, then pulled the pastor away.

Megan chuckled. "That's his wife. She probably needs help with their twins."

Justin looked at her. He needed someone to talk to. To tell him the church wouldn't spontaneously combust because he'd attended a service. "Would you be willing to have lunch with me?"

Megan's eyebrows rose, and she took a step back. "Well, I. . ."

"I could really use someone to talk to." He clasped his hands. "If you're not busy."

Megan adjusted the Bible and other materials in her arms. She didn't answer right away, and Justin wished he could take back the invitation. She looked down then nodded just a bit. "Okay."

He held up his keys. "I can drive and then bring you back to the church."

Megan shook her head. "No. I'll drive myself. Where would you like to go?"

They decided on a restaurant, and Justin followed her to the parking lot. He had no idea why he'd invited her to lunch. She was probably the last person he needed to talk to. He didn't spill his guts on a regular basis. Until recently he didn't have guts to spill. He'd spent his life not caring about people or how they felt.

Now he'd invited Megan, his secretary, to have lunch with him so he could talk with her. She'd just shown up too soon after the confrontation with Amy's husband. He didn't need to share anything with Megan. He'd just take her to lunch, and he'd see her the following day at work. One lunch. No problem.

Chapter 8

Stolen kisses are always sweetest.
LEIGH HUNT

Megan squirted a dollop of hand sanitizer into her palm, rubbed her hands together, then dropped the bottle back into her purse. She placed her purse on the booth close to the window. She glanced to the front of the restaurant where Justin had taken their flashing pager. He placed it in the basket then collected the two trays containing their individual size pizzas and chopped salads.

They'd chosen to eat at one of her favorite places. Not only did she love the "smashed" tomato sauce on their pizzas and the homemade vinaigrette dressing on their salads, but she also adored the atmosphere of the place. On one side, a brick wall was painted green and trimmed in red. Videos of Italy scrolled across a large-screen television. Large windows covered two walls, allowing for natural light. The kitchen area was open, and she could watch as the cooks placed pizzas in the oven set over 800 degrees. They served real Italian pizza, and she loved it.

Justin arrived at the booth and placed the trays on the table. He smiled as he slid into the seat across from her. Man, the guy was entirely too good-looking. And that melon polo looked amazing against his naturally dark skin. She felt like the ugly duckling sitting across from him. But having already reached adulthood, she felt fairly confident she wouldn't be changing into a swan anytime soon.

He extended his arms across the table and opened his hands. "May I pray?"

Nervous about touching her boss, just the two of them, at lunch, in which he insisted on paying, she rubbed her thumbs against her fingertips beneath the table. Her nerves were ridiculous. She lifted her hands and placed them in his. "Of course."

She bowed her head and listened to his petition to God. His heartfelt words and humble offerings to her Savior melted away any uncertainty she had about lunch with him. She knew what happened between him and Amy. The whole church knew.

Timmy had confessed all his sins in a couples' Bible study he'd agreed to attend with Amy. The only problem was he'd confessed all hers as well. She didn't know Amy well, but she knew enough about her to know she was a private woman with a very sensitive spirit. Megan couldn't imagine she'd have wanted her failures to be publicized. Megan sure didn't.

When he finished the prayer, Megan opened her eyes and looked at Justin. He was a changed man. A lot different than he had been when she first started working in his office. For a moment, she wondered if Clint would have been different if he'd accepted the Lord.

The thought sickened her, and she wrinkled her nose and swallowed back the bad taste in her mouth. That guy was vile. Treacherous. Deceitful. Manipulative. The pressure of his knee against her leg washed over her anew. She touched the spot as her body trembled, and she forced the memory from her mind.

"You okay?"

Megan straightened in the seat and lifted her chin. "Mm-hmm." She pierced her fork through the salad then shoved a bite into her mouth. She nodded, hoping he'd erase the concerned expression from his face. She swallowed and pointed her fork at the dish. "My favorite salad in the world."

Justin took the bait. "I like it, too."

She wiped her mouth with the napkin. "So, what did you want to talk about?"

Justin pushed his fork through the salad. He seemed hesitant, uncertain. She'd never witnessed those qualities in him before. She hoped he didn't want to talk about Amy. It wasn't any of her business, and it wasn't as if he needed to clear the air between them so they could build a relationship together. She had no inclinations for a relationship, and most especially with a man who'd studied as many women as he had law books. Even if he had changed.

He looked up at her, and her stomach fluttered at the intensity of his gaze. "You have a beautiful voice, Megan."

She hadn't expected him to say that. She cleared her throat. "Thank you."

He leaned back in the booth. "That song was like a wave of peace, like a. . ." He crinkled the napkin in his hand. "I'm not good with pretty language. More of a law guy, you know."

He winked at her, and her heart dropped to her ankles. Inwardly she picked it up, shoved the organ back in place, and hammered some boards around it. There was no way she'd allow this man's words to get to her.

He continued, "It was what I needed to hear. God's forgiven me. Just like the song says. I'm restored, and I need to move on from this place. Forgive myself and move on."

Megan didn't know what to say. She watched as he looked down at his plate. He picked up the knife and cut off a piece of his pizza. She noticed his hand trembled. Not much. No one would notice unless the person was studying him.

But Justin Frasure did not tremble. He was strength and certainty. He was the spider who seduced the fly.

He glanced back up at her. "I'm not the same person I once was. Do you believe that?"

Megan swallowed. It was almost as if he asked for her forgiveness. But he'd done nothing to her. He didn't need her approval, and she couldn't give it. It wasn't her place. Her heart was untouched by him, and it would stay that way.

His dark brown eyes searched hers. They reminded her of a puppy begging his owner for a pat on the head or a rub on the belly. She couldn't simply not answer him. Sucking in a deep breath, she determined to state the facts of what she'd seen in him. Facts only. No feelings. The heart had a way of being deceitful, and she wouldn't be tricked by it again. She nodded. "I have seen a change in you."

Relief washed his features. "I'm so glad. I've worked so hard."

Megan lifted her hand and shook her head. "Justin, it's not about your work. You can work as hard as you want. God does the changing."

Her words pricked her spirit. Her sister's comment about it being time to move on from the hurt eight years before flooded her mind. Megan had worked hard to build the walls, layers of them, around her heart. She loved her sister, her friends, and the kids she worked with in church. Once she became a teacher, she knew she'd adore those children just as much. But her parents, her old boyfriend—even though he was dead—and any man who'd dared to look at her since, she'd pushed away, placing an invisible barrier between herself and them.

She was safe that way. She'd put in a lot of work building her safe haven. She hadn't allowed God any changing.

Emotions warred within her. She couldn't stay here with Justin. Couldn't sit here and give him advice she'd only just realized she wasn't heeding. But she couldn't forgive. Surely God wouldn't require it of her. Some things were too sacred, too pure.

Clint didn't deserve it. He didn't even need it. He was dead. Her parents didn't want it. They didn't care. Didn't even know they needed to be forgiven. They still blamed her.

She thought of her Christ, who was punched and mocked and placed on a cross for the world to see. And He'd done nothing wrong. He'd loved. He'd served. He'd come to save. And they had killed Him.

And He forgave.

But why did He do it? They were unworthy. He'd hung on that cross because of her sins as well. She was unworthy. She didn't deserve salvation, but Jesus had given it to her.

And she was to be like Him. God commanded it. But how? She loved the Lord, read her Bible, served in His church. She'd forgiven the guy who'd rear-ended the car she'd driven off the lot only one day before. She'd forgiven Marianna more times than she could count for taking long showers and leaving her with cold water. She'd forgiven the woman who'd neglected to pay her for her son's piano lessons before they moved to another state. She'd forgiven many people for various reasons over the years since she'd become a Christian.

But Clint and her parents. It was too hard, and they weren't sorry.

Visions of a movie she'd watched about Jesus's crucifixion streamed through her mind. Soldiers wagering for Christ's clothes. Mocking Him with looks, laughs, and even blows. And Jesus forgave them.

Open her heart to everyone. That's what God wanted her to do. To be a vessel He could use. To be willing to be hurt. To love unconditionally.

She smacked her napkin atop the table. *Fine, Lord. You win. I forgive everyone, and I'm moving on with my life.*

She stood and walked over to Justin. Without a word, she leaned over, grabbed his cheeks in both her hands, and pressed her lips against his.

Shaven, his cheeks were soft against her fingertips, but not as soft as his lips. His mouth was perfect. Inviting. Delicious. An arrow of pleasure shot through her, and she deepened the kiss.

Realization of her actions punched her gut, and she opened her eyes. His were closed, and he seemed to enjoy her touch as much as she did his. Her brain jolted, and she jumped away from him as if he were the 800-degree oven at the other end of the restaurant. She pressed her hands against her lips. Heat washed over her, and she shook her head. He was a man. He was a womanizer. He was her boss. "Mr. Frasure."

"Megan." Though surprise still filled his expression, he didn't seem upset she'd flung herself at him. He reached for her hand.

She brushed him away. "Mr. Frasure, I am so sorry."

Before he could respond, she raced out of the restaurant. Shoving her hand in the bottom of her purse, she rummaged for her keys. "How hard can they possibly be to find? I have a big pink monogrammed key chain attached to them, for crying out loud."

She yanked out the key chain as she reached the car. Her hands trembled when she tried to stick the key in the lock.

"Miss Megan."

Megan jumped and squealed at the sound of her name. She placed her hand on her chest and looked at Stephanie and her mom. She forced a smile to her lips. Lips that still felt the pressure of Justin's against them. "Hi, Stephanie. How are you?"

Her voice was too high. Even to her own ears.

Stephanie tapped the side of her face with her palm. Something she did when she felt nervous or unsure of a situation. "Are you okay, Miss Megan?"

Megan let out a breath and forced her nerves to calm. "I'm fine, Stephanie. May I have a hug?"

Stephanie smiled, and she wrapped her arms around Megan. Hugs always worked with the autistic child. For her, they affirmed everything was okay. Megan waved as Stephanie and her mother walked to the department store beside the Italian restaurant.

She turned back to her car. Justin stood in front of it. Heat rose up her neck and cheeks again. She hadn't even seen him leave the restaurant. He stepped closer to her. "Megan."

She looked to the heavens as she opened the car door. "Please, Mr. Frasure."

"Do not call me Mr. Frasure."

She looked at him, noting the hurt in his eyes that she addressed him formally. She dipped her head. "Justin."

"We can talk about this."

Her strength returned as she shook her head and looked back up at him. "No. I promise there is nothing to talk about. I have no idea why I did it. I don't just go up to men and kiss them. I don't even date."

He drew his eyebrows together. "What do you mean you don't date?"

"Just what I said. I don't date. Period. Ever. I haven't in eight years. I don't plan to ever again. I apologize for my actions. That was not like me."

He placed his hand against his chest. "I'm not offended, Megan. You don't owe me an apology."

"I don't want to date you."

"Did I ask you to date me?"

Megan shook her head. "No. Of course not. I'm the one who— I shouldn't have. I don't know why I did it. I don't. . ."

He lifted his hands in surrender. "Okay. I get it."

"I don't want to give you the wrong impression."

"'Kay." He smacked his hand against his thigh. "You don't like me. I get it."

"I'm sorry, Mr. . ."

He glared at her, and she cleared her throat. "Justin." His name slid through her teeth with a mixture of frustration and pleasure.

He nodded. "Okay. I'll see you tomorrow at work."

She slid into the car and turned the ignition. She felt his eyes on her even as she pulled out of the parking lot. *God, what in the world possessed me to do that? You're talking to me about forgiving people, and I jump up and kiss Justin?*

She drove toward the apartment. She was one mixed-up, crazy

woman—that's what she was. The memory of his lips against hers still niggled at her mouth. It was the first kiss in eight years, and she couldn't believe how delicious it had been. So different than the one years ago.

The one before it had been insulting and suffocating and too-often haunting. She hadn't realized until moments before a kiss didn't have to be that way.

She didn't want to think about it. She couldn't think about it. Not only was she not going to get involved with a man, but she most certainly would not get involved with a man who'd dated more women in Lexington than lived in her small hometown. Okay, maybe that was an exaggeration, but the truth was Justin Frasure was an experienced man.

Even if he had changed.

Megan pulled into her driveway. She had other things to think about. Like getting the children's church lessons ready for the evening service. She still needed to run by the grocery and pick up snacks and drinks for the kids.

She also needed to look at her closet. She needed to find the least attractive thing she owned and press it to wear to work tomorrow. She wasn't glamorous and gorgeous like the women who'd strolled through the law office doors many times before. Still, she had no intention of leading the youngest lawyer at the firm to believe she was dolling up for him. Justin Frasure was the last thing she wanted.

Chapter 9

We can decide to let our trials crush us,
or we can convert them to new forces of good.

HELEN KELLER

Megan tied the oversized red bow around the back of the waist of the bridesmaid dress. She dropped her hands to her sides and twisted left to right in front of the full-length mirror to drink in her reflection.

The design was adorable. The strapless sweetheart cut enhanced her chest and cinched in her waist. The slight flair of the skirt stopped just above her knees, a length that accentuated her muscular calves. If only the dress weren't yellow and she didn't have a smattering of freckles covering her shoulders.

Marianna assured her she would be able to get a tan before the wedding. But first of all, Megan worked every day until five. Her chances of getting in the sun were limited to weekends. And second, she flat-out refused to go to tanning beds. She was scared to death of them.

Once, as a teenager, she'd ventured to Forever Tans in their small hometown. She'd paid for just one visit. Donned the sunscreen and her bikini. Reclined on the bed and placed the eye protection goggles over her lids. Took a deep breath and pulled the top of the bed halfway over her body. The bulbs turned on, and she'd practically jumped out of her skin. She'd reached for the handle on the lid and realized it had closed on top of her. She pushed the thing off and jumped out. It was like lying in a cooking coffin. A tan wasn't worth it. She'd put her clothes back on, walked out, and hadn't gone back.

She peered at her reflection in the mirror. No. She'd probably look just like this when it came time to walk down the aisle ahead of her sister.

"Hurry, Megan. Everyone's already out here." Marianna's voice sounded from the runway area at the back of the store. She appreciated the relative privacy the boutique had for brides and their parties to model dresses. Sure, people could still see them if they wanted, but a person would have to be purposeful or downright rude to be able to do it.

Megan already knew what her mother would say about the dress. Sucking in a deep breath, she pushed open the changing room door and walked out to join Julie and Amber.

Marianna clapped her hands when the three of them stood side by side. "You all look beautiful."

Megan glanced at Julie and Amber. One of the seamstresses pinned the fabric around Amber's waist to make it a bit tighter. The pale yellow color harmonized with the dark skin and hair color of both of their friends. Megan glanced at her mother. Her expression spoke volumes.

She remembered one of the skits she'd watched on *Sesame Street* as a girl. Four shoes—three small tennis shoes and a great big boot—sat on the ground while some off-camera guy sang for the audience to try to figure out which of the things was not like the other, and to try to figure it out before he finished the song. Well, today Megan was the bridesmaid who didn't belong.

"Are you going to try to get a bit of a tan, Megan?" her mother asked.

Megan studied the woman. Light red hair, cut short and curly, framed her face. Her skin, much lighter than Marianna's and Megan's, would have been washed away in the pale yellow dress if she'd been the one to have to wear it. Worse than Megan. She'd have thought her mom would have a little bit of mercy on her.

But it was her mother. Mrs. I'll-say-what-I-want-when-I-want-and-make-no-apologies-for-it.

Megan sighed. "Probably not. I work until five Monday through Friday."

"Have you thought about going to a tanning bed?"

Megan shook her head.

"It's not a cooking coffin, Megan."

Megan shook her head again. She wasn't going to get back in a tanning bed. Not even for her sister's wedding. She looked at her friends with their gorgeous darker skin color then down at her own white-as-snow legs. She'd just be the bridesmaid who looked a little different. She was the maid of honor, after all. It was okay she wouldn't look the same.

"What about a spray tan?" said her mom.

"Last time I had one, I was orange. Though it would go with Marianna's colors, it's not a shade I prefer for my skin."

Marianna jumped in. "Mom, look how beautiful the style fits Megan. Her calves look amazing." She pointed toward the top of the dress and arched her eyebrows. "My sister's got a killer body."

Megan squinted at her. "We have the same shape."

Marianna shrugged. "What can I say? We both have killer bodies."

Megan, Julie, and Amber burst out laughing, and Megan noticed her mom chuckled a bit as well.

"They all look beautiful if you ask me." Her stepfather, Bill, placed his arm around her mother's shoulders. "I can't believe one of our girls is getting married."

Megan couldn't believe he sounded so sentimental. He'd been their stepfather since they were toddlers. In truth, he'd been the only father they'd known. Both of them called him Dad. He'd never been cruel, but he hadn't been overly close with them either. He worked a lot, and when he was home, he watched television.

"I can't believe it either." Her mother reached across her chest and touched his hand on her shoulder.

"Well, I can't wait," Marianna squealed. "Only sixty-three days." She swatted the air. "But who's counting."

"Obviously you are," Julie laughed. "Have you decided on our shoes?"

Marianna clapped her hands. "Actually I have. Be right back."

She raced to the shoe section of the store. Megan pursed her lips together when her sister returned with a very loud red, orange, and yellow floral high heel. She didn't know how they were twins. No way. Not in a gazillion years would Megan pick those gaudy shoes for someone to wear in her wedding.

Amber grabbed it from Marianna's hand. "Oh, they're so cool. I've never seen anything like them."

Megan agreed with her there.

Julie touched it. "Feel the texture. They're so soft."

Megan didn't care how soft the disgusting things were. Baby's bottom. Kitten fur. They were still revolting.

"I've got a surprise for you." Marianna pressed her hands against her chest. "The cost is on me. I'm so thankful y'all were willing to pay for the dresses that Kirk and I agreed to buy your shoes."

"That's so sweet." Julie hugged Marianna.

"Yes, thanks." Amber joined her. "I'm going to have to find an outfit to wear these shoes with. They are so cool. So unique."

Megan joined her friends in hugging her sister, but she wasn't feeling the same excitement over Marianna's gift. She was just thankful she didn't have to fork over the cash for the atrocious footwear.

Marianna whispered in her ear. "I know you hate them."

"I don't hate them."

Marianna grinned. "Yes you do."

Megan slid her arm through the crook of Marianna's. "You know I'll wear anything you want for your day. I'm so happy for you."

"I know that." Marianna kissed Megan's forehead. "You are the best twin sister a girl could ever have."

"Wearing this." She pointed to the dress then the shoes. "And those. Uh, yes I am the best sister ever."

Marianna laughed. "You really look beautiful. Your skin is flawless."

"Freckles?"

"Your freckles are adorable. I'm sure Hadley's uncle would think so."

Megan elbowed her sister. "Whatever! I have no interest in Colt Baker."

"You should."

Julie called from the bridal dress section of the store. "Marianna, I know your dress is still being altered, but why don't you try on the floor model so we can see all of us together?"

Their mother stood and walked in Julie's direction. "That's a marvelous idea. Here, let me help you find it."

Marianna's face lit up. "I'm coming."

She raced off the platform, and Amber and their dad followed behind. Megan stepped down and plopped into the chair her mom had left. The last thing she needed to do was encourage Colt. She still couldn't believe she'd kissed Justin yesterday.

She'd tossed and turned most of the night, fretting over how she would behave in front of him at work. Worry niggled her brain over how he would act with her. To her relief, he'd spent the best part of the day out of the office. He'd said he had court, but she had no idea who for. She logged their cases, and it was no one she knew of.

Maybe he was meeting up with some woman and he'd only been playing the part of Christian. Maybe it was all some weird act.

Shame washed over her at the ugly thought. He'd given her no reason to believe his faith wasn't genuine. She was the one who'd behaved less than appropriately, flinging herself at him at lunch after church.

She didn't want to think about Justin. Marianna was right. Colt would be a better match for her. A solid Christian. Raising his niece on a farm. Didn't seem to have a sordid past. Very protective. She couldn't imagine him disrespecting a woman.

She also couldn't imagine herself in a relationship with him. She didn't want a man. Any man. Sordid. Solid. Stable. Or surly. She didn't want to partner up with anyone.

She was destined to be single. She'd finish school and find a job as a music teacher. Love her students. Love her nieces and nephews. And one day die a contented old maid. That was her plan. And neither Colt Baker nor Justin Frasure was going to alter the plan she determined for her life.

"We found it." Marianna's face shone with delight as she made her way to the fitting room. Their mother followed close behind, and normally Megan would join to help. But she wasn't sure what her mom would say. Besides, it would be good for the two of them to have a little time together.

Dad sat in the chair beside her. She crossed her legs, twitching her foot. Not wanting to be stuck alone with her dad, she scanned the shop for Julie and Amber. They hadn't followed her mom and sister into the fitting room. But they couldn't be too far.

"How are things going, Megan?"

"Good." She continued to scan the room. It was just as she feared. He would start talking to her.

Their conversations had been limited since their blowup when she was almost seventeen. As soon as she'd graduated, she'd hightailed it out of their house and never looked back. Of course, she saw them on holidays. And on occasion, Marianna would drag her to their hometown to visit. But Megan kept to herself. Listened to conversations between Marianna and Mom. Dad usually stayed in the TV room anyway.

"You still working at a law firm?"

He was looking at her. She knew he was. Why he wanted to start a big old conversation now after all these years, she had no idea. "Yep."

"Still in school?"

"Mm-hmm."

"Finished for the summer?"

She nodded.

"So what are your plans?"

She glanced at him then studied the hem of her dress. She wasn't going to get away with not talking to him. Praying for God to give her peace and patience, she said, "Well I hope to get a job this summer so I can do my student teaching while I'm actually working. It's the only thing I have left to complete the program. And since I already have a degree, I could complete my student teaching on the job."

He nodded, and Megan was surprised to see he genuinely seemed interested. "You have any prospects?"

"I have applied for an opening in an elementary school in Lexington. I haven't gotten a call about an interview yet, but school isn't out for the summer until next week either."

"They wait until school's out to start interviews?"

Megan shrugged. "That's what I hear."

Her dad patted her shoulder, and Megan tensed. "I hope you get the job."

She looked into his face, and she could tell he meant it. "Thanks."

"Here we are." Her mom guided Marianna out of the fitting room.

Her sister was a vision in the sleeveless, sweetheart-cut dress. The fit was tight around her top and waist and loosened only a bit around her hips. It then flowed down over her legs and into a long train. Unlike the decorations and the styles she'd selected for the bridesmaids, Marianna's dress was simple elegance. It was something Megan would pick for herself.

Though that would never happen.

Julie and Amber appeared from whatever corner they'd been hiding in. They stepped onto the platform with Marianna. Megan couldn't deny the dresses flattered the wedding gown. Marianna had an excellent eye.

Her mother nudged Megan out of the chair. "Go on up there with them. Let me look at you all together."

Megan joined her sister and friends. She grabbed Marianna's hand. "You are absolutely gorgeous."

"Thank you."

Their mom waved her hands. "Okay. Stand in the order you'll be in at the wedding. Let us get the whole effect."

Megan stood beside her sister, then Julie, then Amber.

"Breathtaking," said their dad.

Mom grabbed Dad's hand. "You all look so beautiful."

They turned to look at themselves in the mirror. Megan couldn't help but smile. She still looked like the one that didn't belong, but she couldn't deny the overall picture was lovely.

Julie made her way to Marianna. She pulled back her hair to get a better visual for what it would look like in just a little over two months. "You're going to be the most beautiful bride ever."

Tears glistened in Marianna's eyes, and Megan felt such excitement for her sister. Kirk was a wonderful, godly man. He would be a good husband. One day the two of them would have a passel of children, and Megan would have the opportunity to spoil them all rotten.

Amber stood beside Marianna. "This dress flatters you so much." She turned toward Megan. "You'll have to get a similar one when you get married."

Her mother huffed. "She can't wear white."

Megan heard Marianna draw in her breath. Megan's mother might as well have jabbed a knife through her stomach. Julie and Amber didn't know the past. They had no need to know. Megan had spent eight years trying to forget. More time than usual of late.

Megan lifted her chin and straightened her shoulders. The look of confused shock on Julie and Amber's faces made her nauseous. She nodded to Amber. "Thank you. Marianna does look gorgeous, doesn't she?"

Marianna smiled. Megan knew her sister well enough to know it was forced. She clapped her hands. "I'm starving. Let's get out of these dresses and get some lunch."

Megan snuck a peek at her parents who were deep in conversation before she turned to head back to the dressing room. Julie and Amber seemed to have forgotten her mother's outburst as they giggled back to their rooms. Or maybe they'd simply decided to ignore the comment.

Megan walked into her room and shut and locked the door. A slight knock sounded. Megan stared at the door knob. "Yes?"

"Are you okay?" Marianna's voice, laced with concern, was a little above a whisper.

"Of course. I'll be out in just a minute." She sucked back the sniffle, determined not to let anyone know the hurt of her mother's words.

Silence sounded from the other side, and Megan thought Marianna had moved on. Then another whisper followed. "I'm sorry, Megan."

This time she heard the rustling of dress fabric and knew her sister had made her way to her own dressing room. Megan pulled at the thick red bow tied in the back. She turned toward the mirror. A single tear slipped down her cheek. She brushed it away with her finger. She was sorry, too.

Chapter 10

Conflict is inevitable, but combat is optional.
MAX LUCADO

Justin lifted his baseball glove and bat out of the trunk of his car. It felt good to hold the equipment again. At first, he'd been a little rusty at the practice on Sunday afternoon.

Could have been because it had been years since he'd picked up a bat. Or because of Megan's kiss. He pressed his lips together at the memory of it. They didn't have some passionate, fire-brewing exchange. And yet it had churned something inside his gut he didn't know needed stirred.

He'd pondered what it could mean. Maybe the kiss was different because he was a Christian, determined to live for the Lord and not his temptations. Or because he didn't whisk her off her feet and take her back to his place. Maybe it was because she let him know point-blank she hadn't meant it and wasn't interested.

Whatever it was, that kiss haunted him.

He'd avoided Megan yesterday at work. Spent most of the day running errands, met a few clients in a coffee shop. Today he had to go to the office. Seeing her tightened his chest. Even in a long skirt that appeared a couple sizes too big and a crazy, ruffled floral top, she'd looked so cute, he'd wanted to scoop her up and at least kiss the tip of her nose.

He shook his head. This wasn't good. Not good at all. Women were his weakness. His greatest temptation. When he'd committed himself to the Lord, he'd promised to develop and grow his relationship with Jesus for a while. Then he'd consider trying to build one with someone of the opposite sex. He hadn't been a Christian long enough. Only a few months. There was still so much he needed to learn about God and faith and trust and sacrifice. He still had too many women to seek and offer an apology.

"There you are."

Justin looked to his left. Kirk and a blond woman wearing sunglasses and a ball cap walked toward him. Justin waved. The girl looked so much like Megan. Same height. Same build. He even noted the same hair color spilling from the back of her ball cap. He needed to get a grip. He spent too much time thinking about his secretary.

Kirk motioned to the woman. "Justin, it seems like it's taken forever to get the two of you in the same place. But I want you to meet my fiancée."

"It's about time." Justin extended his hand. "It's a pleasure to meet you."

The woman took off her sunglasses, and Justin dropped the bat and glove to the ground. "Megan?"

The woman laughed, and Justin instantly realized she wasn't Megan. Megan had a dimple in her left cheek. The look-alike extended her hand. "Megan's my twin. I'm Marianna. How do you know my sister?"

Justin blinked. He hadn't known Megan had a twin. Of course, he hadn't known she sang until Sunday. The woman had worked in his office for more than half a year and there was so much he didn't know about her. Too much he wanted to know. He accepted her hand. "She works for my firm."

"You're Justin? Justin *Frasure*?" She shook her head. "How could I not have put this together before now?" A look of contempt flashed across Marianna's face, and her smile wavered, but she recovered and kept it plastered to her lips.

"Guilty as charged." Justin studied the woman's face, wishing he could ask what Megan had said about him. He'd been a scoundrel. He couldn't and didn't deny it. But he was a new man. Something in him needed Megan to know that. More than any other person on earth. What had his secretary told her sister? Had she mentioned the kiss? Didn't twins tell each other everything?

"This is great." Kirk's response broke Justin's concentration. He looked away from his friend's fiancée. "Megan is Marianna's maid of honor. You're my best man. And the two of you already know each other."

Marianna frowned. "You'd told me his name was Justin." She shoved her hands in her pockets. "You probably told me his last name. I just didn't put it together."

"No problem, honey." Kirk wrapped his arm around her shoulder. "It's great they already know each other. Especially since I took so long selecting my groomsmen." He laughed and spread his arms. "It's kinda hard to pick stand-ups when God, Marianna, youth, and video games are a guy's life."

Justin continued to study Marianna. He couldn't read her

expression. He picked up his equipment off the ground. "I'd better start warming up."

Justin started toward the field when Kirk continued, "Marianna and I will be cheering for you on the bleachers. I always rode the bench while you made all the plays anyway."

Justin chuckled at his friend. "You were a better cheerleader than any of the girls."

Kirk squinted. "Don't be comparing me to the cheerleaders."

Justin laughed and continued toward the field.

"Wonder why Megan didn't come," Kirk said to Marianna.

"She's riding horses with Colt and his niece."

Marianna's response sent prickles of jealousy through Justin. Who was this Colt fellow? Megan had never mentioned him. Course, it was nearly every day Justin learned something new about the woman who wouldn't leave his thoughts. Was she dating this horseback rider? And if she was, why did she kiss Justin, and why did she say she wasn't interested in a relationship at all?

"Oh, I don't think so."

Justin looked up and saw Amy's husband, Timmy, barreling toward him. Justin sighed. He glanced at the bleachers and for the first time noticed Amy sitting on the bottom row. Her gaze was trained on her husband, and a look of fear marked her face.

He wished he could apologize to Amy. Really apologize. One of her complaints about her husband, besides his constant infidelity, had been his volatile temper and willingness to make a scene when he was mad.

Justin looked at Timmy, who was now only a few yards away from him. The man obviously hadn't changed. Trying to settle the guy down, Justin extended his hand. "I don't want any trouble, Timmy."

Fire seemed to shoot from Timmy's eyes. His face had morphed through more shades of red than Justin thought possible. It had been a few years since Justin had to use his fists to calm a fellow down. Admittedly it was because Justin had stolen away the guy's girlfriend. But if he had to defend himself, he would.

"You don't want any trouble?" Timmy spat through his teeth. "What are you doing here?"

Justin pointed to the baseball bag. "Came to play ball."

Timmy pointed to the dark blue T-shirt Justin wore. It didn't say the church's name on it, like Timmy's did, as Justin had been late to join, but it matched in color. "Play for *my* church." He pointed to his chest. "Oh no. I don't think so."

Justin wondered where Timmy had been during the afternoon practice on Sunday. If he'd shown up then, they could have gotten past this with a little more privacy. He knew Timmy felt he should move on to another church, but he'd probably run out of places to worship if he had to avoid every woman from his past. No. He wouldn't leave. He'd sinned. There were consequences for those sins, but he'd also changed.

Amy had been willing to forgive Timmy. He didn't understand why Timmy felt what happened between her and Justin was any different.

"What's going on guys?"

Justin looked to his right. He hadn't noticed Pastor Wes stood beside him.

Timmy motioned to Justin. "He's not playing with us."

Pastor Wes nodded. "Yes he is."

Timmy squinted. "Do you know who he is?"

Justin balled his fists. He'd had just about enough. He was

trying to be patient with the guy. Understood why the man wouldn't want to hang out. Even understood why the guy didn't want Justin around his wife. But this needed to be hashed out in private. Not after a church service and not before a church ball game.

Pastor Wes nodded again. "Yes, Timmy. I do know who he is, and he's playing on our team. God's changed his life. Just as he changed yours."

Timmy's expression blanched, and for a moment, Justin thought the pastor's words had gotten through to the man. His jaw tightened and his face hardened again. He pointed to his chest. "If he stays, I leave."

"He's staying."

Timmy glared from Pastor Wes to Justin then back to the pastor. He shoved his glove under his arm. "Fine."

He stomped toward the dugout, picked up his gear, and motioned to Amy. She hopped off the bleachers and hustled behind him.

Justin frowned at Pastor Wes. "I'm really sorry about that. I could leave. He has reason to hate me."

Pastor Wes stroked his goatee as he peered at Justin. "Justin, I counseled Timmy and Amy before their divorce. I counseled Amy through the divorce. She spent nights at our house with my wife comforting her, encouraging her in the Lord. I know exactly who you are and what you've done."

Embarrassment swelled from the pit of his stomach to the top of his head. The ugliness of his own sin that Jesus washed away flooded him anew. The reality of all he'd done hit him in spurts, like when he was confronted with someone who'd hurt from his past actions. Sometimes the reality overwhelmed him. Like now.

It was the reason he studied Paul so thoroughly. Paul claimed to be the chief of all sinners. Justin would argue he was worse than Paul. Still, Justin related to the apostle from scripture. He knew what it was to be the worst of men and then be changed.

"A lot of the sin heaped on Christ on that cross came from me."

Pastor Wes patted his shoulder. "Me, too, brother. But we don't have time for a share fest." He nudged Justin toward the field. "Let's go warm up."

Justin followed the pastor to the team. They were tossing balls back and forth. This church team was not going to be anything like the last team he played for in college. Several of the players were over fifty and some well over two hundred pounds. These were just a bunch of members getting together to have a good time.

Brian, one of the guys who'd been at the Sunday practice, motioned to him. "Wanna catch?"

"Sure." Justin picked up a ball and tossed it to Brian. He caught it and threw it back.

"Heard you went to Bible study Thursday night."

"Yep."

"I'll be there this week." He pointed to two guys a ways across the field. "Rick and Mike, too. Had to miss 'cause of a make-up game. Guess you already know that."

"That's what Kat said."

Brian's face turned red, and Justin wondered if he and the teacher had a bit of a thing going. Brian changed the subject. "I'm glad you came. We need more players."

"Looks like you lost one when I came."

Brian didn't comment, and Justin wondered if he and Timmy were friends. Maybe it really aggravated him to be warming up with

Justin instead of Amy's husband.

Brian threw the ball again. "I've been praying for Timmy. He's having a hard time. Just lost his job."

Justin didn't respond, but he felt for the guy. A lot of people had been losing their jobs. Caused stress on the families. Made people angry. Course, Justin understood why Timmy was angry with him. Justin had no notion of being friends with the guy and his wife. It wouldn't be proper. Even though their divorce had been final when Justin dated Amy, he'd crossed a line that couldn't be uncrossed.

But he couldn't avoid everyone he'd ever known before becoming a Christian. He'd have to move to another state, and he didn't feel God asking him to do that. No. He'd stay in Lexington. Live his life now for the Lord. And deal with consequences of his past as they came. Like dealing with Timmy.

Something in his heart twisted, and he felt an urge to pray for Timmy and Amy. After a quick silent prayer, he inwardly committed to keep them in his daily petitions. They would never be friends, but he could still pray for them.

Brian passed the ball again. "Can you play shortstop?"

Justin threw the ball back and shrugged. It wasn't his strongest position. In fact, with all the bending and squatting involved, and having not played for years, he felt pretty confident he'd be downright atrocious in the position. But he'd do what was needed. "Sure. If that's where you need me."

Brian caught the ball and tossed it into his gloves a few times. "Well, I know you're better as pitcher, but Timmy was shortstop, and all the other guys haven't really played it or are too out of shape." Brian elbowed one of the overweight older guys beside him.

The guy, Jerry, puffed out his chest and sucked in his gut. "Who you calling overweight?" He rubbed the top of his bald head. "And I ain't old."

Justin and Brian laughed.

Jerry guffawed as he shook his finger in the air. "Your day's coming, boys." He patted his belly. "It takes years to build up this physique, but it comes just the same."

Justin laughed again. Jerry was probably the same age as his dad, and the senior Frasure was most likely in better shape than Justin. He had to be, chasing after all the women Justin's age.

A thought traipsed through his mind. If he wasn't spending his senior years chasing women, if he was settled down, would he allow himself to put on a little weight? Embrace losing his hair? Would he be happy like that?

As those thoughts weaved through Justin's mind, Jerry's wife jogged out onto the field with a cold bottle of water. The slightly plump, graying woman handed it to him then rose on tiptoes to kiss his cheek.

An older version of Megan flashed through his mind. He might downright enjoy seeing her jog out to bring him water and kiss his cheek. If she looked at Justin as Jerry's wife had looked at him, he wouldn't mind if she added a few pounds and a bit of gray splashed through her hair.

He pushed the thought away. He needed to focus on baseball. The game was about to start. Making his way to the dugout, he glanced over to the stands. He wondered if Megan attended the games. Obviously she didn't. Besides, Marianna said she'd gone horseback riding with some guy named Colt.

The idea still grated on his nerves. He needed to push this fancy toward his secretary out of his mind. It wasn't time. Maybe a year from now. Once he was stronger in his faith. He spent time in the Word every day, but he still worried he'd mess up.

He glanced at Marianna and Kirk. The woman watched him, a look of wariness in her expression. He knew she'd seen the exchange between him and Timmy. He wondered how much she'd heard. He wondered what Megan had shared with her.

He wanted to defend himself to Megan's look-alike, to tell her he was different than his reputation. That he wouldn't be unkind to her sister. That he cared about her.

He shook his head. What was he thinking? Only moments ago, he admitted he needed nothing to do with a relationship with any woman. And his constant thoughts about Megan made her an even worse possibility.

The feel of her lips against his pressed on his mind. Why it haunted him he didn't know. It made no sense. He just wanted to stop thinking about it. He looked around the field. He needed this game to get going. He watched the players from the other team take the field. If the game didn't hurry up and start, he was going to have to do something. Run around the field. Punch a wall. Something. His hands itched for movement. His feet tapped against the ground. He couldn't take it any longer.

The umpire shouted, "Play ball!"

Relief washed over Justin. He had something to occupy his mind.

Chapter 11

One of the hardest things in life is having
words in your heart that you can't utter.
JAMES EARL JONES

Colt rode his steed at a slower pace than Megan and Hadley. Thunderbolt would have been happy to ride at a faster pace, and truth be told, Colt wouldn't have minded riding alongside Megan. But he held back.

"There is this one guy."

Colt perked up at Hadley's words. She was in sixth grade. Boys should still have cooties.

"Tell me about him," answered Megan.

"He's mean to me. He pushed me into the locker. Told me I was ugly."

Anger balled in Colt's gut. A teacher should have been around to witness a boy pushing his niece. He'd have to make a trip to the middle school. He blew out a breath. School was almost out, and Hadley had gotten mad at him several times for sticking his nose in her business.

Megan laughed, and he frowned. His niece's mistreatment was hardly cause for happiness. Her voice was light. "I remember when boys used to do that. Next thing I knew they wanted to be my boyfriend."

Colt leaned back in the saddle and smiled. Now that he thought about it, he'd picked on a cute blond in middle school. Emily Watson. She'd been a full three inches taller than him and wore the same red shirt every day. He'd pinched her, even poked her with his pencil to get her attention. She'd run off and told the teacher, and he'd had to stay in during break.

"I don't think he wants to be my boyfriend," said Hadley.

"I bet he does, but since it sounds like he's not being very kind, I'd ignore him if I were you."

"I can't. He sits behind me in science."

"Ask to be moved."

Hadley shifted in the saddle. "She'll get mad at me."

"Trust me. I know the teacher. She won't."

Colt grinned as he recalled the science teacher was Megan's twin.

"You wanna race?" asked Hadley.

"Definitely."

Before Hadley could say, "Go," Megan shot off. Colt laughed as Hadley shouted, "No fair."

Colt laughed as she kicked Fairybelle in the haunches and took off after her piano teacher. Megan handled the boy discussion well. He would have threatened to call the school, and Hadley would have thrown a fit, and they'd have battled for the rest of the day. Already, the situation was nearly resolved.

He thought of Megan sitting with Hadley on the piano bench. He'd forced himself to stay close while Megan taught the second lesson of the week. The memories of Mama playing niggled at him once again, but he'd determined to keep himself inside and listen.

Hadley already loved Megan McKinney. She'd talked about little else since the lesson on Saturday. Even wanted to know what church she attended, thinking Colt might take her for a visit. The girl needed a woman in her life. He knew the time was coming when she'd have personal questions Colt wouldn't know how to answer. If he even knew the answers.

Hadley and Fairybelle beat Megan and Daisy with ease. Of course, it wasn't really a fair race. Daisy was the most laidback horse he owned. Docile. A bit past her prime.

With it being so long since Megan had ridden a horse, he didn't want to chance one with too much spunk. Though watching her now, he was pretty sure she could handle Thunderbolt if he let her. She'd been right. Horseback riding must be like riding a bike. Something one never forgot.

The girls slowed their pace, and soon Colt had caught up with them. He glanced at Megan. Her hair blew around her face, and her cheeks were deep pink and her eyes bright from the exertion of the ride. She sucked in a deep breath and looked at Hadley. "You beat me."

Hadley grabbed the reins in one hand and swatted the air. "Of course. Was there any doubt?"

Colt laughed at his niece's teasing. "I reckon it would have been a fairer race if we'd given her a horse that could hold a candle to Fairybelle."

Daisy whinnied, and Colt reached over and petted her neck. "You're a good girl, Daisy. But truth is truth."

This time Megan and Hadley laughed. Colt drank in the sincerity of Megan's expressions. She enjoyed this ride through his land.

A real country girl at heart. Someone who thrived on breathing in the land God created.

Hadley guided her horse to the left. "Let's go this way."

"What's this way?" Megan asked.

Colt didn't respond. He knew Hadley had prepared a surprise for her piano teacher. He'd been thrilled with the idea when his niece suggested it. Give him more time to talk to the woman.

"You'll see," said Hadley.

The trail thinned between trees and bushes, and Colt moved behind Megan with Hadley taking the lead. He sucked in the delicious smells of late spring. With June just around the corner, the land had been fully replenished with spring showers and mid-May sunshine.

He was proud of his land. It boasted some of the richest soil in all of Kentucky. He raised strong, healthy cattle, always turning a good profit when time came to sell. And his horses were some of the best in the nation. He'd had five make it to the Kentucky Derby, and he rarely wanted for investors to buy a filly or a steed from him.

Yes. God had been good to him. True, he'd inherited the land. It was his grandfather's father who'd done the hardest work, starting the farm from next to nothing. He had gone to an early grave, having put so much blood, sweat, and tears into this land.

But Colt had done good by the land as well. Even got his degree in agriculture. He knew what to grow, when, and how. He'd plotted the land into sections, placing cattle and horses in the best areas at the best times, all the while allowing each section a rest after a few years of labor of keeping up livestock and vegetation.

The land would be here long after him. It was his duty before God to care for it properly, and he'd always done just that. He'd been a good son to his parents. Done right. Not been a burden. They'd gone to their graves knowing the land would be cared for. Now it was Colt's responsibility to ensure the next generation took pride in the land as well.

He looked up at Hadley. She cared for the land and for the animals. But she didn't really know farmwork. She knew rodeos and barrel racing, how to care for horses. But not cattle and crops. Besides, he kinda wanted to be able to pass the farm on to a son. One who would carry on the Baker name.

To do that, he'd need a wife. One who served God and wasn't afraid of hard work. One who'd uphold the family's good name. His gaze shifted to Megan.

"We're almost there," Hadley called from the front.

He couldn't wait to see Megan's face. Confident Hadley's scheme was one the piano teacher would appreciate. The trees thickened, and he pushed a bush away from his foot. The land opened up, and he saw the clearing. An old oak tree with a swing tied to one of the strongest branches sat beside his favorite pond.

He looked at Megan, wanting to note her first reaction. Her eyes opened wide as she scanned the land. He knew it was a breathtaking sight, and the expression on her face said all he'd expected. She loved it.

Megan placed her hand on her chest. "This place is amazing."

Colt hopped off his horse and grabbed the reins in one hand. He held up his free hand to help Megan off the horse. She accepted it, and Colt felt a moment of thrill to be holding Megan's soft hand in his. She put her weight on the left stirrup then swung her right leg over the horse and stepped down to the ground.

Hadley grabbed Megan's hand away from his, and he had to bite back a growl at his niece. "Come here. Let me show you."

Colt tethered the horses, allowing them to drink, then followed the girls around the tree.

Hadley pointed to the closed wicker basket and cooler they'd brought to the spot just a bit before Megan arrived. "Colt and I made lemon cake today. Remember when we were making cookies for Colt? You told me it was your favorite. I hope it's good. Colt and I never made it before."

Colt's cheeks warmed when Megan looked at him, an expression of appreciation and awe on her face. Hadley hadn't had to do much convincing to get him to do something kind for Megan. Right now, he wanted to feel the softness of her hand in his again.

Hadley continued, "We put some pops and waters in a cooler. I didn't know what you like to drink, so there are several different kinds."

He watched as Megan took in the quilt that was already laid out on the ground. Then she scanned the view of the pond and the land around them. She shook her head. "I don't know what to say."

Hadley rubbed her belly. "Say you're ready for some cake. I'm hungry."

Megan smiled. "Sounds good to me." She walked to the wicker basket, opened it, and lifted out the cake. She popped off the plastic lid. "Mmm. It smells and looks wonderful."

As if on cue, Colt heard barking in the not-so-far distance. In the blink of an eye, Old Yeller had bounded out of the woods and made his way to Megan.

"Now wait a minute, Old Yeller." Colt smacked his thigh, and the dog reluctantly meandered to him. "You have to wait your turn." He looked up at Megan and smiled. "The dog has a terrible sweet tooth."

Megan's laugh filled the air and blew through the leaves and grass. It was a beautiful, honest sound. She addressed his dog. "Then I'll be sure to save a good-sized piece for you."

Old Yeller barked his obvious appreciation.

Hadley handed him his favorite soft drink then placed the caffeine-free drink Megan selected beside her. He took the piece of cake Megan offered him. Old Yeller sat beside him with a filled paper plate as well. His was gone before Colt had time to get the fork to his mouth.

Megan swallowed a bite. "This is really good." She looked from him to Hadley. "I'm impressed."

Hadley beamed. "Thanks."

Colt took his bite. It was pretty good. Moist like it should be. The icing wasn't homemade, but it was a good brand. He wasn't a big fan of lemon, but it tasted like it was supposed to.

Hadley swallowed a bite. "So what do you think of this place, Miss Megan?"

"It's the most beautiful place I've seen since moving away from home."

"Where did you live before?" Hadley asked.

"I lived in a small hollow in Pike County." She lifted her hands in the air. "The trees grew every bit as big as this one. The hills rolled all around us. There were ponds and trails and perfect hiding places around every nook and cranny." She focused on Hadley, and Colt drank in her enthusiasm. "Marianna and I even found tombstones dated all the way back to the mid-1800s."

"Sounds like a neat place to grow up."

"It was a lot of fun."

Hadley had a quizzical look on her face. "So why'd you move?"

Colt watched as a flash of pain raced through Megan's eyes. She missed her mountains.

Megan twisted a paper towel in her hands. "Marianna"—she nodded to Hadley—"Miss McKinney, and I had to go away for college."

She nodded and averted her gaze for a moment. It was more than that. Colt could tell it was. He wondered what had happened that she'd left her beloved country, but now wasn't the time to ask. She obviously didn't want to share the whole truth with Hadley.

As usual, Hadley's interest shifted, and she hopped to her knees and looked at Megan. "I'm going to go swing. Wanna go with me?"

Megan pointed to her plate. "I'm going to finish your delicious cake first. You go on over there."

Hadley scurried off, and Colt felt a mixture of relief and trepidation to be alone with Megan. He searched for what to say. He could ask her about school. She'd said she had attended college. Maybe ask about her church or her hobbies or. . .

"Hadley is a total sweetheart."

Colt nodded as he looked at Megan. Hadley was definitely a safe way to start a conversation between them. "She is."

"She's picking up the piano super fast."

"Yes. You said she would." Colt gnawed on the inside of his cheek. His stomach turned, and his hands clammed up. Hadley should be an easy subject. But she was a woman, and his one-on-one experience with women was a list about as long as his fingers. Nope. Not that long. It included Hadley and his mom. And maybe Emily Watson. She had agreed to go with him to their eighth-grade dance.

He wanted to talk about more stuff with Megan. Get to know her. He wiped away the sweat beading on his brow. But talking to a woman was hard.

Maybe he should just be honest. Throw himself out there. He hadn't really thought about needing a woman in Hadley's life before, but he must not have had his eyes open wide enough. Hadley needed a woman. He swallowed. He'd just come out and ask about her passions and dreams. How she'd feel about living on a farm again. His farm maybe.

Whoa, Colt. Now let's slow down those thoughts. Get to know the woman a bit first.

He cleared his throat. "Didn't you say you were in school to be a music teacher?"

She nodded.

"I'm assuming you're done with classes for the summer."

She nodded again and swallowed down a bite of cake. He watched her wipe her mouth and take a quick drink of pop. "Yeah, I am. All I have left is student teaching, but I can do that on the job. In fact, I have an interview on Thursday for an elementary school." She wrinkled her nose. "I haven't told Justin yet, and I listed him as a reference. I better do that tomorrow."

A flash of heat skidded through his veins. "Justin?"

Megan shoved her empty paper plate into the bag they'd brought for the trash. "He's my boss."

Colt nodded in understanding, but something about her calling the man by his first name upset Colt. He tried to shake the feeling away. For all he knew, Justin was a fifty-year-old married man with a passel of kids and grandkids. "I forgot where you said you work."

"Frasure, Frasure, and Combs Law Offices in Lexington. I've been there about seven months. Planned to stay longer. I didn't know I could work and complete my student teaching at the same time."

She wrinkled her nose again. "They'll probably be a bit bummed if I get the job."

Colt had a questioning look on his face. "Why?" He realized his query could be construed that he didn't believe her to be a good employee. He opened his mouth to explain, but she'd already started to answer.

"They've had several secretaries come and go."

"They're hard to work for?"

Colt remembered his first farming job that wasn't on this farm. His dad had wanted him to see what it was like to work another man's land. The guy was a bear to work for, demanding, never satisfied. He'd worn Colt plum out. Looking back, he wondered if the old guy and his dad planned it that way to ensure Colt wouldn't be a difficult boss when the day came for him to hire help.

Megan shook her head. "No. The work isn't bad. It's just that. . ."

Megan paused, and Colt's interest piqued. He could see she fished for the right thing to say. He appreciated she wasn't someone who just sought out ways to bad-mouth her boss. Still, Colt wanted to know more about this Justin guy.

Megan clasped her hands. "In the past, there have been a lot of girls."

"Girls?"

"Well, women really. I mean, Combs is married, so not him, but. . ."

Colt felt his blood pressure rise. What was Megan trying to say exactly? "And this Combs fellow? He's Justin?"

She shook her head. "No. Justin is one of the Frasures. He's the son. He and his dad aren't married, and they. . ."

Megan clapped her hands together and sat up straighter. "You know what, let me tell you about Justin. He's a new Christian. He seems to be very genuine in his faith. He's even joined the Bible study I attend at my church. That's Justin." She stood, and a smile split her lips as she motioned toward Hadley. "I think I'll join her on the swing."

Colt watched Megan leave. So, Justin was a womanizer who'd suddenly found faith and decided to join Megan's Bible study. Colt wasn't an idiot. He knew how men think. Megan was a sweet, innocent, beautiful woman, and Justin wanted to take advantage of her. He just might have to look into this Justin Frasure.

Chapter 12

Never be afraid to trust an unknown future to a known God.
CORRIE TEN BOOM

Megan's heart raced as fast as a filly straight out of the gate at the Kentucky Derby. She'd hoped. She'd prayed. She'd even procrastinated the last two hours of work on the chance the senior Frasure or Mr. Combs would walk through the office front door. Didn't they have work that needed to be finished? Where could they be at all hours of the morning?

She looked up at the pewter-finished antique clock on the wall. Her interview was scheduled for 11:30. She still hadn't told her bosses about it, hadn't asked if she could take her lunch half an hour before her regular time.

Normally this type of hesitation would be the action of an irresponsible employee, one who didn't care or take pride in her work. That wasn't the case for Megan.

She had no choice. She had to avoid Justin.

They'd said only a few passing words since their Sunday afternoon lunch in which she had plastered a big one on his lips. Heat warmed her cheeks. She still couldn't believe she'd done that. Not that it hadn't been delicious. Mind consuming. Toe curling. But what kind of weird entity had momentarily taken over her body and caused her to act so out of character?

She glanced at his closed office door. He hadn't come out, and no one had gone in since he'd arrived at 8:00. It was now 10:30, and she really needed to be on her way in around thirty minutes.

Perspiration dotted her upper lip. She was being ridiculous. Nearing a panic attack over speaking with a man she wasn't supposed to like and didn't want to have anything to do with. *Though he does seemed to have changed.*

She pounded her fist against the top of her thigh. It was that kind of thinking that kept getting her into trouble. Shaking her head, she jumped to her feet and pushed away from her desk area. She had no more time to waste.

He probably wouldn't want to discuss her momentary lapse in judgment anymore than she did. In fact, it was probably the reason he'd holed himself up in the office all morning.

Lifting her shoulders and chin, she made her way to the door and knocked. She could do this. She was a grown woman. Who had a degree. Who paid her own bills. Who didn't need a man in her life.

"Come in."

Justin's voice was entirely too delicious. Deep as a bass drum. Confident as a steady rhythm. Her knees weakened, and she touched the doorjamb to ensure her vertical position. She opened the door then bit the inside of her cheek to keep from swooning over the lamination of his pearly whites.

"Do you need something, Megan?"

"Uh. . .well, yes." She cleared her throat. The mixture of

embarrassment over their last meeting and the anxiety over telling him about the interview nearly overwhelmed her.

He pursed his lips and folded his hands together, placing them on his desk. "We need to discuss Sunday. I haven't spoken with you, because I didn't want you to feel uncomfortable."

Megan waved her hands. "No." She shook her head. "That's not what I came here to talk about." It was the absolute last thing she wanted to talk about. Though she'd enjoy thinking about it later.

He leaned back in his chair. "Okay. What is it?"

The motion tightened the button-down shirt against his entirely-too-bulky chest. She blinked several times. What was happening to her? An alien with a crush on dark-haired lawyers had slipped into her room in the middle of the night and slithered into her body and taken over. It was the only explanation she could think of.

Megan looked above the man. She studied the framed diploma on his wall. "I need to take an early lunch today. Leave at eleven, and I won't be back until one. I should have asked earlier, but. . ."

What could she tell him for the "but"? But I was waiting for your dad or Mr. Combs to come into the office? I didn't want to talk with you because the kiss that you *didn't* give me, but I slobbered all over you, haunts me during the night and a good part of the day. She stood with her mouth agape. She had no answer for the "but." None she was willing to voice anyway.

Justin waved his hands in front of him. "You don't have to explain."

She clamped her mouth shut. He'd saved her from the horror of whatever explanation she'd have tried to come up with.

Justin studied her, his expression full of interest and concern. "However, may I ask what's going on?"

She swallowed again. She had to tell him anyway. He may be getting a call in the next few days. In fact, she hoped he would. "I have an interview."

"What?" His face twisted into a myriad of shock, concern, and regret. "Why? Because of the kiss?"

Megan waved her hands. She really didn't want to talk about the kiss. She'd already said she didn't want to talk about it. Didn't want to think about it. Couldn't the man take a hint? "It has nothing to do with that. You know I've been taking classes to get my certification to teach music."

Justin nodded.

"I have an interview for a music position at an elementary school."

His eyebrows drew together in a straight line. "I didn't think you were finished with classes."

"Technically I'm not. However, I am allowed to complete my student teaching while on the job. If I'm hired."

He lifted and lowered his chin in slow motion as if filtering the information through his mind. He didn't look happy. She knew it was because it would be a nuisance to train a new assistant if she left. But a part of her wanted him to be upset it would be her leaving.

He turned back to his computer. "Of course, you can take a longer lunch."

His tone was gruff. He was more than just upset. He was mad at her. But surely he understood her goal was to get a job as a teacher, and she'd have to try for opportunities as they presented themselves.

In fact, he had no right to be angry. As long as she gave a good notice, it was her life. He had no part of it. Even if he had been trying to take up residence in her brain.

She bit her lip. He was one of her references. Crud. She still hadn't told him. She'd listed all of the lawyers, as she wasn't sure which would be available to answer a reference call. It wouldn't do her any good if Justin answered it all cranky because he didn't like the thought of replacing his secretary. The very thought of her missing out on a job opportunity because Justin gave her a bad reference. . .

She shook her head and inwardly groaned. Just tell him already. "I also listed you as a reference."

She clasped her hands together, willing herself not to fidget as he turned back around to face her. His brows rose, and a mischievous smile spread across his face. "Does that mean I could give you a bad reference to keep you from getting the job?"

Megan gasped. Justin was a scoundrel. Surely he wouldn't do such a thing. She'd been a good employee the last several months, taking almost no time off, finishing work on time or early. She even kept the office straightened up and clean, even though a woman came in to clean thoroughly once a week.

Justin winked. "I'm just teasing you, Megan. I couldn't possibly give you a bad report. You're an excellent employee."

His praise warmed her all the way to the soles of her feet. "Thanks, Justin."

He lifted one eyebrow. "No Mr. Frasure, huh?"

"I—well—" He was Mr. Frasure. It was the way she should think of him. The way she wanted to think of him, and yet *Justin* repeated itself over in her mind. Especially when she thought of his lips against hers.

"I'm still just teasing, Megan." His face shifted to a more serious expression. "I want you to call me Justin."

She nodded. She didn't trust herself to respond. She walked out of the room and scooped her purse out of the drawer. She needed out of the office. It didn't matter that it was seventy-five degrees outside and a cool sixty-eight in the building. His office was entirely too hot.

"Where are you?" Megan yelled as she threw open the front door of the apartment. She tossed her purse and briefcase on the couch. "Marianna!"

Marianna walked out of the kitchen, wiping her hands on a dish towel. "What is it?"

Megan opened her hands and twirled in a circle. Her heart felt as if it would burst through her chest. She envisioned her classroom filled with children looking at her, their expectant gazes waiting for instruction.

Okay, so maybe Marianna's classes had never behaved in that way the times Megan visited, but elementary kids would be different. She wouldn't have paper wads and rubber bands hurling across the room. She inwardly chuckled. It would be their bodies flopping all over the place, probably.

She pushed the thought away. Only happy thoughts at this moment. "I think I nailed the interview."

Marianna wrapped her in a hug. She released her and squeezed Megan's arm. "I knew you would do great. There was no doubt."

Megan noted the fingerprint of flour on her sister's face and knit her eyebrows. "What are you doing?"

"Making fried chicken." Marianna ducked her chin. "Or something like it."

"*You* are cooking?"

"I'm trying. Kirk loves his mom's fried chicken, so I got the recipe from her, and. . ."

Megan pointed at her sister. "And you're trying to make it."

Marianna rolled her eyes. "I've got to learn to cook sometime. Kirk won't marry me if he finds out how pathetic I am in the kitchen."

"He already knows you're a wretched cook."

"I know. Isn't he wonderful?"

Megan laughed. "Is it edible?"

Marianna looped her arm around Megan's. "Everything is ready, so let's go find out. You can tell me about the interview while we eat."

"I'm going to change first."

Megan walked to her room and changed into a pair of gray stretchy shorts and an old I Love New York T-shirt. She washed her hands before joining her sister in the kitchen/dining room. She had to admit the food actually smelled delicious. She was starving, so she hoped her senses weren't being deceived.

Marianna pulled a plate from the cabinet and handed it to Megan. "Tell me all about the interview."

Megan dipped mashed potatoes from the stovetop onto her plate. "I think I answered the questions well. They asked why I wanted to be a music teacher, and I told them about my love for music and getting to work with you."

Marianna nodded, and Megan spooned a good helping of green beans from the pan. "The principal had already spoken with your principal. Remember I listed her as a reference?"

"You're kidding? They must have looked into you before

you even got there."

Excitement bubbled up inside her. "That's a good thing, don't you think?"

"Absolutely."

Megan speared a piece of fried chicken and put it on her plate. It actually looked pretty good. Her sister may have started to develop some culinary abilities after all these years of living on their own. She walked to the table and sat across from Marianna. "Justin acted a little weird when I told him I had an interview. But I expected that. I wanted to speak with his dad or Mr. Combs."

"Justin?" Marianna squinted. "You mean Mr. Frasure?"

Heat blazed up Megan's neck and cheeks. She hadn't wanted to call her boss by his given name, and she'd been adamant about keeping their relationship on a professional level. Until she kissed him. Even though it hadn't meant anything, she couldn't seem to go back to thinking of him as Mr. Frasure.

Megan shoved an oversized bite of potatoes into her mouth, hoping to mask the blush she knew was forming on her entirely too-white skin. "Yes. That's who I mean."

"I met Justin."

Megan's interest piqued, and she looked at her sister. "You did?"

"You'll never guess who he is."

"Who?"

"Kirk's best man."

Megan choked on the mashed potatoes. She coughed and patted her chest then took a long drink. "The guy from high school?"

"Yep."

Megan's hands grew clammy as she thought of spending so much time with the boss she wanted to avoid. He was Kirk's best man. She was the maid of honor. They'd see a lot of each other in the next two months.

Marianna was staring at her. Megan wanted to believe she had no idea why, but the girl was her twin. Since birth they'd been able to sense things about each other.

Marianna shook her head. "You can't like him."

"I don't like him." Megan dabbed her mouth with the napkin. She was determined not to like him.

"You wanna know where I met him?"

Megan shrugged, feigning indifference. "I don't care."

"I met him at the church softball game. Kirk wanted to go to support him. He's encouraging him in his new faith."

"That's terrific. He's been coming to our Bible study."

Marianna continued to study her, and Megan knew her face had to be the same color as the fire hydrant in front of their apartment. "Timmy was there, too. For a while."

Megan cringed. She'd seen Timmy try to confront Justin at church. She wondered how much worse it may have been on the ball field, but she didn't want to act overly interested either.

"Timmy and Amy left, and I think you know why."

"Yes, I know why."

Megan tried to act as if her sister's words didn't bother her. She shoved a bite of green beans into her mouth and forced herself to chew them. She didn't want to be attracted to Justin. Didn't want to think about him all the time. The only time she wasn't thinking of him was when she was with Colt and Hadley. She'd have to find a way to spend more time with them.

"Megan, you can't fall for him."

Megan smacked her hand on the table. She did not want to have this discussion with her sister. "Have I said one word to make you believe I like Justin Frasure?"

"You don't have to. Remember we had concerns about Clint, and—"

Megan stood, pushing the chair away from her so hard it fell to the floor with a thud. "I remember Clint every day of my life." She clenched her fists. "Every day. Do not mention him to me."

Marianna opened her mouth to speak. Megan noted the apology in her sister's eyes, but Megan didn't want to hear it. She lifted her hand to silence her sister and stormed to her room.

She shut the door and locked it then fell on top of her bed. How could Marianna say that? She knew what happened with Clint. Knew what he took from her. Even knew Megan had kept the shame to herself for three long months until Clint was killed in a car accident. Marianna knew the horrible things her parents said when Megan finally told.

Tears welled in Megan's eyes. She'd spent too many days of her life wrapped in sorrow over that man. He wasn't even a man. He was a sixteen-year-old boy.

Justin was wrong in every way. She didn't want a man in her life. She wanted to be free, to be safe. She would never feel safe with a man.

Megan sat up in her bed and wiped the tears from her eyes. She'd had eight years to cope with it, and she would not allow herself to go to that wretched place of hopelessness again. No. She was stronger than that. God made her stronger. She would not think of Clint or Justin. A relationship was the last thing she wanted.

Chapter 13

Trials, temptations, disappointments—all these are helps instead of hindrances if one uses them rightly. They not only test the fiber of character but strengthen it.

JAMES BUCKHAM

A relationship was the last thing he wanted. Justin shoved the gearshift into PARK and hopped out of the car. He couldn't stop thinking about Megan's interview. Wondering how it went.

He didn't want her to get the job, but he should. He should be happy she might be able to do what she'd been working toward the whole time he'd known her. But the thought of walking into work and not seeing her—a growl escaped his lips.

This attraction he felt wasn't good. He'd promised to spend time, months of time, building his relationship with the Lord, resisting his greatest temptation—women. But Megan was different. He didn't simply want a physical relationship with her. He enjoyed talking to her. Something inside him turned when he listened to her sing. He wanted to understand what she was thinking. He wanted to know she was thinking of him.

He shook his head. Thoughts like this were dangerous. He

didn't need a woman in his life, and she deserved someone who wasn't him. He'd mistreated too many women to deserve someone so purely devoted to God.

He spied Kirk through the gym window and waved. Walking inside, he nodded to the young woman at the desk. What was her name? Bridget? Brittany? Brandy. That was it. He looked away from her. A knockout from head to toe, she was the kind of woman he'd always gone after. Someone he appreciated physically but cared nothing about in any other way. From the way she looked at him, the feeling seemed to be mutual.

He looked away from her and headed toward Kirk who'd already started his workout on the treadmill. Justin noted his friend had a full twenty minutes on him.

Kirk pointed to his watch. Sweat rolled down his forehead as he panted through his words. "Gotta get done quick tonight. Taking a shower here. Marianna's picking me up at six."

Justin programmed the machine for the workout he wanted. "I wondered where your car was."

"She dropped me off. We're going to dinner then back to her place to stuff invitations." Kirk ducked his chin and scowled.

Justin wrinkled his nose. "Sounds like a lot of fun."

"It'll be a blast."

Justin laughed at his friend's sarcastic tone. "Better you than me, friend."

The workout on the treadmill picked up, and Justin's heart rate accelerated. It felt good to get his blood pumping. Took his mind off watching Megan walk out that door and head to an interview.

"Your day will come," Kirk said. "But I'm glad you're focusing on God first. How's Bible study going?"

"Terrific. It's great to study scripture and make friends with people who want to encourage my faith." Justin didn't mention his favorite part of the study was being able to see Megan. She knew so much about scripture. She felt everything they studied to the depth of her being. Her passion for God and for learning more about Him drew Justin. He wanted to learn more about her. Discover when it was she became so impassioned about deepening her walk with the Lord.

He wanted what she had. But he also wanted her.

The kiss traced through his mind. How many times had he thought of it? The kiss played constantly on a loop that tracked through his mind, and it didn't make sense that he pondered it more than he remembered his various escapades with multiple gorgeous women. It was the simplicity, the honesty, the sincerity of Megan that made him keep going back to that one moment.

Kirk tapped his arm. "You still with me?"

Justin looked at Kirk. "Yeah, just got caught up in thinking about Bible study." Well, that was partly true.

"I said I was glad you're finding more accountability partners."

"Yeah, after all the beat downs I'm getting from confessing my sins to every woman I've ever known"—Justin blew out a breath— "I've needed the encouragement."

"What are you studying?"

"Paul, which is terrific for me. I feel like a modern-day Paul."

"How so?"

"I'm the worst of sinners whom God mercifully chose to save."

Kirk's workout slowed to the cool-down stage. He grabbed his towel off the side of the machine and wiped his face while he slowed to a walk. "That's true for a lot of us. Not just you."

Justin nodded. His workout accelerated, and he pushed through the programmed mountain climb. He tried to focus on the workout, keep his mind off his secretary.

Kirk's machine stopped. "I'm going to go ahead and start lower-body strengthening. We'll work on upper-body when you finish."

"Sounds good." Justin focused on the workout. He wished it was Thursday. He'd be able to see Megan at Bible study. He could ask how the interview went.

"Hey, Justin. How's it going?"

He looked beside him. Brandy had gotten on Kirk's treadmill. She walked at a leisurely pace. He noticed the flirtatious smirk on her face. *Give me strength, Lord. I'm feeling weak.*

Justin acknowledged her then turned his attention back to the workout. He tried to recall the 1 Corinthians scripture he'd determined to memorize. "*Do you not know that in a race all the runners run, but only one gets the prize? Run in such a way as to get the prize. Everyone who competes. . .*"

He always forgot the exact wording at that point. It was something about going into strict training for a crown that would last. He closed his eyes. He'd read the passage again when he got home. It was the strict training part of the passage that drew him. He knew he'd have to be disciplined, very determined, in order to win his battle with the flesh. Kirk warned him he may always fight the temptations, but the longer he was obedient, the easier the fight would be.

God, I'm counting on that.

"So, how have you been Justin? Work going okay?"

Justin glanced at the bombshell beside him. Is this some kind of joke from You, Lord, or a playing of the devil? Justin knew the answer. God didn't play jokes. Situations like these were something else Kirk warned him about. As long as Justin was trying to live for Christ, the enemy would throw in distractions to dissuade his faith.

Justin sighed. It would be rude to outright ignore her. He glanced down at the time left on his workout. The cooldown started in two minutes. He'd be off this machine and working on strength and tone in only six minutes. He could make it that long. He looked at Brandy. "It's been a good week. Everything's fine."

"Great. It's been busy here. Everyone wanting to shrink a few inches before heading to the beach." She leaned toward him. "Not going to happen for most of our clients. You gotta put down the doughnut if you're going to lose the weight." She nudged him with her elbow. "Know what I mean?"

Justin cringed at her critical attitude. Though he knew only months ago he would have laughed and added his own sentiments to the comment.

He focused on the machine. Four minutes left. Maybe if he didn't talk to her, she would go away. He almost chuckled aloud. That sounded like his philosophy for finishing his math homework when he was a kid. It never worked.

"I get off at six." Brandy's voice was sultry. Way too enticing. "Would you like to grab a bite?"

Justin blew out a breath. He didn't need to finish his cool down. There was only three minutes left anyway. He glanced at Brandy. Wow. The woman's hair fell in cascades over her shoulders. It looked so soft and silky. And the expression in her eyes. A welcome invitation. Justin swallowed back the knot in his throat. He shook his head. "Sorry. I have plans tonight."

It was true those plans involved picking up a deli sandwich and heading back to the house to watch whatever was on the television. But he didn't need to go into those details. He needed to get away from her. He stepped off the machine and headed toward Kirk.

Justin jingled the car keys. He hadn't completed the workout he'd planned, but he didn't want to stay at the fitness center once Kirk left. Not with Brandy working today. Kirk was finishing his shower, and Justin had already called good-bye to him.

Walking toward his car, he spied Megan sitting in her vehicle in the parking lot. He shook his head. That wasn't Megan. It was Marianna. Kirk's fiancée. Justin still couldn't get over his best friend's future wife was Megan's sister. It was going to be a tough couple of months trying to keep his thoughts on friendship while working with Megan.

"Hey." He waved to Marianna then made his way to the car.

To his surprise, she got out and headed toward him. She wore a smile, but it was forced, and Justin could see the look of disapproval in her gaze. She gripped the strap of her purse once she stood beside him. Justin wiped his still-sweaty forehead with the palm of his hand.

She glared up at him. "I need to talk to you."

Justin studied her. "Okay."

"My sister works for you."

"Yes, I know." His brow wrinkled. He thought they'd already discussed this. Her lip trembled.

"Amy and I were good friends."

His stomach twisted. So that was what this was about.

Marianna continued, "When she remarried Timmy, she kinda stepped away. We don't talk as much."

Justin didn't respond. He knew where this was going. She might as well get her feelings out now so they could make it through the wedding preparations in relative peace. He hoped.

She shifted her feet as her voice became stronger. "She confided in me about things. Lots of things."

That was it. Just as he figured. She knew all about his darkest hour. Sure, he'd dated many women with whom he'd been their divorce attorney, but Amy was by far his lowest moment.

"I'm not the same person."

She lifted her hand to stop him. "I know God changes people. I don't deny that. Kirk says your faith is real." She squinted as she crossed her arms across her chest. "You can be as real and as Christianlike as you want. Change the world. Write books. Speak in schools about how God got ahold of your life and made you a better man."

She paused, and her nostrils flared. "Just stay away from my sister."

Aggravation swelled inside him. He'd just spent the last hour working out in the presence of a beautiful temptation, and he'd walked away from her. Besides the fact he hadn't made the first move on Megan McKinney. Although it was probably a good thing her sister couldn't read his thoughts.

He thrust out his chin. This woman had no right to talk to him in such a way. She knew only what she'd been told about him— which was probably largely true. Still, she didn't know the person he'd become. He'd only seen Marianna twice. And from what he knew of her from Kirk, she was supposed to be this amazing

Christian woman. The expression on her face at that moment was anything but Christian.

"Marianna, you don't know me."

"I know enough."

Justin bit the inside of his lip. He wanted to light into her. To use a few choice words to tell her she needed to mind her own business. A few months before, he'd have waylaid her with a verbal fury that would have sent her home crying. *God, calm my thoughts. Guide my words.*

It was good she was protective of her sister. A quality he admired in people. He cleared his throat. "I can assure you I have the utmost respect for Megan."

She glared at him, and he knew she wanted to hear more. She wanted to hear he didn't like Megan, that he didn't think about dating her or kissing her at all moments of the day. Again, he realized it was a good thing she couldn't read his mind.

"She's dealt with enough, Justin. Her last boyfriend had 'changed.'" She put up her pointer and middle fingers on both hands and made quotation marks. "It was a lie. He. . ."

She paused, and Justin found himself needing to know what the guy had done to Megan. Marianna shook her head. "He hurt her. She hasn't dated since."

He puffed out his chest. Whatever happened in the past had nothing to do with him. She had no right to judge him when she hadn't bothered to give him a chance. "Not that it is any of your business, but I can assure you. . ."

Her expression softened, and her eyes took on a pleading look. "That was eight years ago, Justin. She hasn't even gone out on a date since she was sixteen."

"That's got nothing to do with me."

"You don't know my sister."

"But—"

"Heed my words. Stay away."

Justin felt as if he'd been punched in the gut. Questions that needed answers swirled through his mind. What could the guy have done that she'd stopped dating completely? He remembered her words at the restaurant of not being interested in ever dating. But why had she kissed him? Was he the first guy she'd kissed since she was in high school?

Kirk walked out of the fitness center, and Marianna pierced Justin with a pleading look not to share what they'd been discussing. It wasn't the first time a woman wanted him to keep his mouth shut when her fiancé, husband, boyfriend, or whoever caught them talking.

Marianna didn't have to worry. He wouldn't tattle that she'd just slammed his character, and he had no desire to talk about Megan. Even though he did want to know what happened to his secretary.

Kirk wrapped his arm around Marianna and planted a quick kiss on her forehead. "She talking your ear off about the wedding?"

Marianna giggled and punched his arm. "You're the only one I do that to."

Kirk let out an exaggerated sigh. "Don't I know it."

She punched him again, and he laughed.

Justin motioned toward his car. "I'd better get going. You two have fun licking invitations."

Kirk groaned and looked at Marianna. "You did get the wet pads, right?"

"Of course I did. We can't really lick over two hundred invitations."

Justin slipped into his car, thankful he didn't have anything to do with a wedding. The very idea of being dragged around from one frilly place to another to pick out dresses, flowers, and fancy cards made his stomach ache.

He thought of Megan. She was the only woman in the world he could imagine being willing to do such awful things with. She'd be simple but elegant, and she wouldn't get all bent out of shape about things that didn't matter.

Marianna's words flooded his mind. Someone had hurt Megan. A primal urge to find the man and rip him to shreds welled up within him. He didn't know how the guy had hurt her. Broken up with her just before prom? Cheated on her with her best friend? Whatever it was, he couldn't stand the idea of someone hurting her. But who was he to talk. . . ?

He pushed the ridiculous notions from his mind. The last thing he needed was a relationship. Unless it was with God.

Chapter 14

The weak can never forgive.
Forgiveness is the attribute of the strong.
MAHATMA GANDHI

Megan tried not to think about the job interview as she drove the scenic route to Colt's house. Only a few days had passed. It would be at least a week more before she heard anything.

And yet each day she found herself growing more anxious. She wanted the job. More than she realized.

She drove down the long lane leading to Colt's house. She hoped Hadley would enjoy the new music book she'd brought with her. The preteen was nutty about the latest teen Nickelodeon shows, so Megan brought one of the more popular current tunes to play on the piano.

She parked the car, but Hadley shot out of the front door of the house before Megan had time to get out of her vehicle. The girl's eyes were swollen, and tearstains streaked her cheeks. She yanked open Megan's door and shoved a partially wadded letter in Megan's face. "Look at this. Read it."

She dropped the note in Megan's lap and covered her face with both hands. "I hate Uncle Colt. I hate him." She raced away from the car and toward the barn.

Megan sat, flabbergasted, as she picked up the note and read it. The sound of horses' hooves caused her to look up and see Hadley riding Fairybelle toward the pond at a pace that made Megan's stomach twist.

She skimmed through the letter. Pain for the girl who was so much more to her than just a student laced through her heart. Today they wouldn't get much piano playing accomplished, but Megan would be a shoulder for the girl to cry on when she returned. But why did Hadley say she hated Colt? It wasn't her uncle's fault.

"Shouldn't have let her check the mail today."

Colt's slow, sad voice made Megan jump. She placed her hand against her chest and got out of the car. "You scared the life out of me."

"Sorry." Colt took the paper from Megan's hand.

Megan felt instant compassion for the blond-haired giant. A true, rough-around-the-edges farmer, Colt was doing his best by his niece, even though it was painfully obvious he had no idea how to handle the pain in this letter.

She grabbed his hand in hers and squeezed. "It's not your fault her father died." Sadness welled inside her. He had been Colt's only sibling as well. "He was your brother, too. I'm surprised Hadley hadn't mentioned it. The child is so open, and the letter said he died a month ago."

"She didn't know."

Megan frowned. "Hadley didn't know?"

Colt nodded.

Megan tried to figure out what he meant. She must have missed some crucial information. "But her mom's letter said you'd taken care of all the arrangements and—didn't Hadley go with you?"

Colt shook his head. "No. I didn't want her to know. Didn't want to upset her."

What a ridiculous thing to think. Did he plan to protect her from life? The child couldn't hide from heartache. Especially pain that directly affected her. At some point, she had to learn to cope with hard things.

Megan looked in the direction Hadley had raced off on her horse. How could Colt not tell her? Not give her the opportunity to say good-bye? No wonder Hadley was so upset with her uncle. Megan peered up at the man. "Well she's upset now."

"I should've checked the mail."

Megan's mouth fell open. He still wanted it to be a secret. So he planned never to tell the child her biological father was dead. Even if the man had never uttered a single word to Hadley, he was her father, and she would always be tied to him. "You just weren't going to tell her?"

Colt looked down at her, his gaze ablaze with anger and frustration. "The last time her dad, my brother"—he pointed to his chest—"saw Hadley was when she was four months old. He stayed long enough to beg my parents for cash and didn't even so much as look at his daughter. So, yes, I didn't tell her because I didn't want to upset her."

Megan searched for the words to say, to help him understand that even though the man hadn't been a part of Hadley's life, he was still the girl's biological father, and she'd want to know. An old wound peeled open inside Megan's heart when she thought of her own father. The one she hadn't seen or heard from since she was in kindergarten. Megan's words were little above a whisper as she tried to keep her own emotions at bay. "She would still have wanted to know, to have gone with you."

Colt shook his head. His eyes blazed with contempt, and his jaw was set tight. "Hadley's mother, if that's what you want to call her, never should have sent this letter. She's a no-good alcoholic and drug addict. Maybe worse than my brother. Do you know how he died?"

Megan shook her head.

"It's disgusting. Vile."

Megan bit her bottom lip. Colt was angrier than she'd ever seen. His hands shook with the fury inside him. She didn't answer, but she knew the dam of his attempt at control was about to break, and she'd learn more than she probably wanted to know.

Colt twisted the ball cap Megan only just realized he'd held in his hand. "Hadley's father got so drunk and high on pills he went into the bathroom to vomit. But he passed out and drowned in the commode."

Megan's stomach turned at the mental image. She noted Colt's fury was quickly turning to a deep-seated sadness. A hurt that he'd carried alone for over a month.

"Colt, I'm sorry."

He raised his hand. "Now, you think I should have told Hadley all that?"

"Not all that, just. . ."

He pierced her with his gaze. "Not any of it. It's my job to protect Hadley. I've made a commitment to my parents and the Lord to raise her in Him, to shield her from the filth that was"—

he lifted up the letter—"and still is, her biological parents."

Megan felt deep sorrow at his arrogance and unforgiveness, and yet she knew his heart's intention was to protect Hadley. And she didn't know what it was like to deal with a drug addict as such a close relative, but she did know what it was like to wonder about an absent biological father.

Megan cleared her throat. "You're a good uncle, Colt. God has blessed Hadley with you, but you should have told her that her father died."

Colt started to say something then clamped his lips, wadded the letter in his hand, threw it down, and walked back to the house. Megan picked up the note and read through it again. Hadley's mother, Tina, said she'd written once before and asked if Hadley would contact her.

Megan's heart constricted. Another reason for Hadley to be mad at Colt and for Colt to be worried about Hadley. Megan knew contact with her biological mother could be detrimental for the preteen. Especially if the woman was still abusing drugs and alcohol. Colt probably had every legal right to keep Hadley and the woman away from each other. And Megan would not try to encourage him to allow a relationship that would be unsafe for Hadley.

She glanced back down at the note. The woman's pleadings seemed so honest and genuine. It was no wonder Hadley felt so much anger toward her uncle. But the woman's true emotional and physical state couldn't be observed through a letter.

Megan closed her eyes and lifted her face to the heavens. *Oh God, help Colt and Hadley. What a hard situation. Give Colt the ability to put away past hurt. Show him how much, if any, relationship he should allow for Hadley and her mom.*

The old wound that had only been superficially closed rubbed against her insides. *And God, be with my dad wherever he is.*

More than an hour passed, and Hadley still hadn't returned from the pond. At least Megan assumed that's where she'd gone. Colt tried to pay her for a piano lesson that didn't happen and send her on her way, but Megan would have no part in it. The man had said precious little to her since their discussion when she'd first arrived, but in her spirit, she knew she couldn't leave.

He felt he'd done the right thing by keeping his brother's death from Hadley. And she loved that he had such a protective nature toward his niece. But Megan agreed with Hadley. He should have told her.

She clasped her hands. "Colt?"

"What?"

"I want to go find Hadley."

"Why?"

"To talk to her."

"She's okay."

Megan placed her hand on Colt's shoulder. He acted like a little boy who wasn't willing to share his favorite toy with a friend. Well, she had news for him. Hadley was not a toy. "Colt, she is not okay."

"She should be. I was protecting her from them."

"I know you think you were protecting her, but you should have told her the truth."

Megan held her breath when Colt turned and peered at her. He was going to throw her out, but she determined she would fight to stay. Hadley needed her, and Colt was acting like a spoiled brat.

"Fine," he muttered as he looked away.

Megan patted his shoulder before she walked out of the house and headed to the barn. Once she had the saddle on Daisy, Megan hefted herself onto the horse and nudged her in the flanks. Not the most excitable of animals to begin with, Daisy simply did not feel the same compulsion to check on Hadley.

Finally reaching the clearing, Megan breathed a sigh of relief when she saw Fairybelle tethered to a tree. Hadley sat beside the pond's bank, her legs folded up against her chest, her chin propped on her knees.

Megan hopped off the horse and approached her young friend. Hadley didn't move, but Megan noted the darkened tear streaks trailing down her dirty face. She sat beside her young friend and waited for Hadley to talk.

Megan drank in the serenity of the place. It was a good place to clear her head. The calm water and just an occasional *kerplunk* of a fish or frog or some small creature moving around in the water. Birds chirped overhead, and crickets sang on the ground around them.

"I thought you'd have left by now." Hadley's voice was low. She sounded like a wounded cat who'd barely managed to escape a fight with her life.

"No. I was waiting for you."

"I don't want to play today."

"I don't blame you."

Hadley didn't respond again, and Megan waited. She prayed God would give her the right words to say. Words that would comfort. That wouldn't encourage Hadley's anger toward Colt. Misguided as Megan believed he was, she appreciated his want to protect his niece. His motives were correct, and in truth, Megan didn't know the whole situation. She only knew how desperately she'd always longed to know her own biological father.

"He should have told me."

Hadley sounded more tortured than angry, and Megan still waited. She inwardly begged God for wisdom in how to speak. With no answers coming, she stayed silent.

"I don't even know how he died." Hadley turned toward Megan. The pain etched across her features stabbed at Megan, and she grabbed the preteen's hand in hers. Hadley went on. "I know when it was though. Last month Colt said he had to take care of some business with the farm. He let me stay with my friend Callie. I was so excited to stay with her for three nights in a row. If I'd have known. . ." Hadley made a fist and punched the ground.

"I don't have all the answers, but I know this for sure"—Megan stroked the girl's long, matted hair—"Colt loves you. He had the best of intentions. He wanted to protect you."

"Uncle Colt always wants to protect me, and I know he loves me. But sometimes he's just too proud to tell me the truth about things." Hadley looked at the ground. "My dad was an embarrassment to the family. But he was still my dad."

Megan sucked in her breath. The child understood things well beyond her years. Probably because she was left by her parents. She'd been raised in the most loving and caring environment possible, but the knowledge that her biological parents had left her still stung to the depths of her heart.

Megan looked out over the water. "You know, I don't know my dad either."

"I thought your mom and dad lived out in eastern Kentucky."

"Mom and stepdad."

"Oh."

Hadley was quiet, and Megan knew the preteen studied her and tried to figure out what Megan was thinking. Megan turned toward her young friend. "It's hard when someone who should care about you isn't a part of your life."

Fresh tears swelled in Hadley's eyes, and she looked back at the ground. "That's why I should have been there to say good-bye."

"Maybe you should have." Megan wrapped her arm around Hadley's shoulder. "You need to talk to Colt. Not yell. Talk. He loves you." Megan cupped Hadley's chin and lifted her gaze to hers. "And you need to forgive Colt."

A wave of realization washed through Megan, and she knew she needed to heed her own advice. It was time to forgive her mom and stepdad for their reaction. They'd been wrong, just as Megan knew Colt had been wrong, but Megan still needed to forgive them.

Just as Colt might not realize Hadley needed the opportunity to say good-bye to her father, her parents may not realize their reaction had been wrong. But what they thought or believed didn't matter. What mattered was that she needed to forgive. Truly forgive.

Megan bit her bottom lip. The thought of it weighed on her heart. There was a ridiculous comfort in carrying the unforgiveness within her. It gave her reason to be angry with them, to keep their relationship at a distance. Forgiveness would make her vulnerable. It would tear down the wall.

And yet God required it.

And the wall hurt. It was heavy.

To the depths of her soul, she knew whatever God required, He would provide what was needed to make it through. He would help her vulnerability. He would make something beautiful in place of that wall. If she'd let Him.

God, help me let You heal me. I'm like the father in scripture who begged for help with his unbelief. Release me from my need to stay safe behind the wall of unforgiveness. Help me to forgive.

"She didn't tell me she loved me in the note."

Hadley's quiet words interrupted Megan's thoughts. Megan nudged closer to Hadley and wrapped both arms around her. She'd noticed that as well. She'd even reread the note a couple of times, hoping she'd simply missed the words. "I'm sorry, Hadley."

Hadley lowered her head against Megan's shoulders. A new stream of tears flowed, wetting Megan's shirt. She was quiet while the young girl cried. Megan simply stroked Hadley's hair and rubbed her back. After several moments, Hadley sat up and wiped her eyes. "I'm ready to talk with Uncle Colt."

Megan nodded and stood to her feet. She helped Hadley up as well. She prayed that Colt would be ready and willing to talk with his niece.

Chapter 15

Sometimes the heart sees what is invisible to the eye.

H. JACKSON BROWN JR.

Megan dropped the pen and stretched her fingers. Her sister's wedding was going to kill her. She wasn't sure she could make it through the next several weeks of preparations. Marianna and Kirk were supposed to have finished the invitations more than a week ago. They should have been in the mail, yet here Megan was helping her sister write out addresses.

Marianna put her cell phone on the table. "Kirk's going to be here to help in fifteen minutes."

Megan nodded. She hoped the guy would hurry up. She'd written her parents' address and the addresses of various potential guests on fifty envelopes, and now her fingers felt as if they would fall off.

"He's bringing Justin," Marianna added.

Megan's heartbeat sped up, and she inwardly chided herself. The man had really begun to get under her skin. He was attentive in Bible study, asked questions, and made valid points. His prayers seemed heartfelt and honest.

Even at work, he'd taken on an ethical persona Megan never would have dreamed possible. It wasn't as if he wasn't a decent lawyer before. He was good—if a person defined good as someone who got you a healthy sum of money from the spouse you were ditching. But now, as an adoption lawyer, he showed compassion for the soon-to-be parents and a diligent tenacity to help them find a child to adopt.

She'd found herself more drawn to him than ever, which meant she avoided him every chance she got. She knew a man could change. Scripture was full of changed men. But she didn't want a man, let alone one with a past that required a change.

Marianna sat beside her and placed her hand on Megan's. "He wouldn't be good for you."

Megan pulled her hand away. "Why do you keep saying that? I have never said I like him. I don't want a man in my life. No man."

Marianna didn't move. She stared at Megan, and though she didn't want to, Megan shifted under the scrutiny. "When Clint said he'd changed, we all believed him."

Megan smacked her hand against the tabletop and peered at her sister. "Really, Marianna. You're going to bring him up today of all days?"

She stood and turned toward the bathroom. She saw Marianna glance at the calendar on the wall. Megan heard Marianna's gasp, and she knew her sister understood.

Megan shut the bathroom door and turned on the faucet. She could hear Marianna's apology from outside the door, but she didn't respond. This was the hardest day of the year. Every year. In the past, she'd spent the day curled up in a blanket in her bedroom, watching hours of television. Of course, she'd make sure it was stupid programs that would never remind her of the anniversary of that day.

She cupped her hands under the water then splashed her face. Today she'd determined to get up, to get dressed, to spend the day with her sister. To forget. It had been eight years. It was time. Way past time.

She'd tried to call her parents a few times since the evening she'd spent with Hadley. Her own advice nipped at her conscience, and she needed to attempt to make things right. Each time the answering machine blared back at her. They'd returned her calls but when she was at work and unable to answer. Tears filled her eyes, and she stared at her reflection in the mirror. "God, it's over. It's been over. Help me not to go there again."

As soon as the words left her mouth, she relived Clint's hand gripped around her arm so tight she'd had bruises for several weeks. The remembrance of his breath against her mouth sent a shudder through her body, and she splashed water on her face again.

Marianna pressed against the door. "I'm sorry, Megan. Let me in."

Megan didn't respond. She couldn't. She swallowed and squeezed her eyes shut, willing the smells and visions from the past to leave her mind. Maybe she wasn't ready to join the living on this day. Maybe she needed to slip into her pajamas and get in bed. Sleep away the memories.

Marianna's voice sounded against the door again. "Kirk and Justin are here."

Megan opened her eyes. She had to collect herself. How would Marianna explain her sister locked up in her bedroom? She didn't want her to explain. Didn't want anyone to know. Past was past.

And she was over it.

She patted her face with a towel then grabbed the makeup from behind the sink. While taking deep breaths, Megan reapplied mascara and added some blush to her cheeks. She ran the brush through her hair. If she just pretended today was any other day, she'd be fine.

After taking several deep breaths, she walked out of the bathroom. She could hear Justin's deep laugh from the kitchen. A chill swept through her. She didn't understand why he seemed to suck her under his spell. Today was the worst of all days, and yet the sound of Justin's laugh charmed her like a cobra out of a wicker basket.

She wouldn't think about it. She would ignore him, and when everyone left, she'd slide into her jammies and enjoy an evening of chocolate and television. She was pretty sure she'd saved several episodes from Shark Week.

Plastering a smile to her lips, Megan walked into the kitchen and waved. Justin had taken the seat beside hers. Of course. Acting nonchalant, she sat down and started addressing an envelope.

Justin smiled at her. She hated his straight, white teeth. "How are you doing today?"

Megan didn't look at him. "I'm fine."

She was as fine as a haunted person could be. Her cell phone rang, and Megan excused herself. She walked into the living room. She didn't recognize the number on the screen. "Hello."

"Hi, Megan. This is Tammy Carey, the principal at. . ."

Megan's heart beat in her chest. She tried to understand what the woman was saying. *God, please let me get this job. I gotta get away from Justin.*

She frowned at the ending thought of her prayer. She wasn't sure God would approve of her last petition. Justin had been only gentlemanly to her. It wasn't his fault he made her act cuckoo.

"I'd like to offer you the position if you're still interested."

"Really?" Megan's voice raised two octaves higher than normal.

"Really."

Megan grabbed a paper and pen off the end table and wrote down all the information she needed about signing contracts and new teacher induction and contacting people at the board of education. She could hardly believe it was happening. She was actually going to be teaching students in the fall.

"Thank you so much, Mrs. Carey. I'm really excited about this opportunity."

"We're pleased to welcome you aboard."

She said good-bye to her new boss and pressed the paper with the information of all the things she needed to do against her chest. For the first time in eight years, this date had something good connected to it.

She closed her eyes and pushed out her chin. "God, it's a new start. The perfect day for a change."

Megan walked back into the kitchen, her heart drumming a rhythm of a new start. She placed her phone on the counter. "That was Principal Carey. I got the job at the elementary school."

Marianna jumped out of her chair and raced to Megan, wrapping her in a hug. "I just knew you'd get it."

Kirk extended his hand. "Congratulations."

Megan watched Justin. He smiled, but she could tell it didn't fully reach his eyes. His chest rose and fell in a long breath. "Well, that's call for celebration."

Megan sat beside him and lifted up an envelope. "I've got an idea. We'll address envelopes."

Marianna giggled. "Sounds like a lot of fun to me."

Justin shook his head. "I know you ladies already made dinner in the slow-cooker, but why don't I treat all of us to dessert?"

Kirk wrinkled his nose. "No can do, man. Marianna and I start our couples' counseling tonight."

Megan watched as Justin raised his eyebrows. He'd obviously not heard of counseling before the wedding.

Marianna said, "The pastor requires it for every couple before they get married."

Kirk added, "We'll discuss what we both expect from the marriage. Who pays which bills. Who cleans and does laundry." He shrugged. "We talk about expectations before the vows. Doing that limits the after-the-honeymoon surprises."

Megan watched as Justin chewed on the information. He started to nod. "That sounds like a terrific idea." He turned toward Megan, and she held her breath. "I could still take you out for dessert."

She noticed her sister's warning look from across the table. Megan jutted out her chin. Marianna had no right to pass so much judgment on Justin. He'd been in no way inappropriate toward her. If anything, Justin should be afraid of her. She was the one who smacked a kiss on him.

Besides, she wanted to celebrate. To wrap herself around a new reason to remember this day. God was blessing her with a teaching position even before she had her full credentials. A dessert and maybe a coffee sounded wonderful.

She looked at Justin. "I would love to." She scrunched up her nose. "It's going to be hard telling my boss about my new position."

Justin pursed his lips and nodded. "It's going to be hard for your boss to hear the news. Wonder how long you'll stay with your office."

"August 1st."

"A little less than two months."

Megan saw sadness etch his features. Was he simply sad he'd be losing a good employee, or was it more? She didn't want to admit it. Berated herself for it. But a part of her wished it was something more.

Her mind knew life was easier, safer when she kept relationships at a distance. But there was something about Justin. He drew her.

Me and every other single, and married, woman in Lexington.

She didn't want to think of Justin in that way. She just wouldn't think about it at all. She addressed another envelope and stuck the invitation inside. She knew Marianna stared at her, waited for her to look up so she could scold her acceptance of the offer with her eyes. Well, she wasn't in the mood for Marianna's scolding.

They finished the envelopes and ate the slow-cooker lasagna. Marianna had found the recipe online. Megan had been sure it would be disgusting, but to her surprise it wasn't too bad. As she placed her plate in the dishwasher, Justin touched her arm. "Are you ready?"

Megan nodded. For a moment, she wished she'd declined Justin's offer. Part of her longed for her jammies and chocolate. But she'd told him she'd go. She waved to Kirk and Marianna, making sure to avoid eye contact with her sister.

Justin touched the small of her back as he guided her to the car, and a mixture of trepidation and pleasure washed through her. She listened as Justin talked nonstop about a couple he was working with who were about to receive their baby from Ukraine. They reached the quaint café, and Justin made his way to open the car door for her before Megan even realized what he was doing.

It felt an awful lot like a date. Not a friendly celebration. She wished she'd driven her own car. There was comfort in knowing she could leave anytime she wanted. She looked up at Justin, and the kindness in his expression settled her.

They walked inside, ordered their desserts, then made their way to a small table in the corner. Megan watched as Justin's expression changed when he saw a woman at a table a little ways from theirs. She tried not to consider who the woman could be and opted to try conversation. "Thanks for bringing me."

Justin's gaze softened. "I'm happy for you. Even if it's bad for me."

As he fidgeted with his napkin, Megan caught him sneaking another look at the woman. A long sigh slipped from his lips. "Megan, I'll be right back."

Her forehead creased with concern as she watched him walk toward the woman. The woman didn't look pleased to see him. As Justin spoke, confusion wrapped the woman's face. She shook her head. The woman wanted Justin to leave. It looked like the woman said, "Fine," before Justin walked back to Megan. The woman watched him and scowled when he sat across from her. The disgust in her expression was apparent, and Megan shifted in her seat.

"What was that about?"

Justin studied her, frustration etching his brow. "You really want to know?"

Megan nodded, though she wasn't sure she did.

"I'm not the man I used to be." He traced his finger along the brim of the cup. "And one of the things God wants me to do as a new creation is apologize to those I've hurt."

Megan studied her chocolate brownie à la mode. She knew what he meant. It sickened her. "The women?"

"Yes."

Justin's voice was barely above a whisper, but she felt the force of it like a tornado wreaking havoc on a town. What was she doing having dessert with this man? He was the last man in the world she should ever sit with at the same table.

She sneaked a peek at the woman, who boxed her dessert in a Styrofoam container. Being in the same room as Justin must prove too much for her.

Megan chewed the inside of her cheek. The woman was gorgeous. Like breathtaking. Sickening. Long, straight blond hair. A body that required a lifestyle of diet and exercise. Megan wondered what dessert the woman could possibly be eating that would allow her to look so beautiful.

"Most of them aren't accepting my apology."

Megan looked back at Justin. He twirled his fork around his cheesecake. He gazed across the table at her. "I'm sorry to have done that in front of you. I haven't been able to get in touch with her. She was the last woman I needed to speak with, except Amy, but we both know how that's going."

He stopped and locked her gaze with his. He probed her mind for her thoughts, for her opinion of him. She averted his gaze. Knowing he'd held so many women twisted her insides. Saddened her more than it should.

"When I saw her," he continued, his voice just above a whisper, "I knew the Holy Spirit wanted me to ask forgiveness. It's hard. . . ."

He stopped and shoved a bite of his cheesecake into his mouth. Megan felt too sick to try hers. "So, there have been a lot of women?"

"More than I'd like to admit."

"Why?"

"Would you like the honest answer?"

Megan blinked.

"I wasn't a Christian, Megan. Even Christians struggle with sin, but when you aren't saved. . ."

Nausea twirled in Megan's gut. She didn't want to hear the answer. Couldn't stomach the words. She excused herself from the table and walked to the bathroom. The sickness she felt earlier. The memories. They swarmed her as she stared at her reflection. She grabbed a paper towel out of the dispenser and wiped her face. *God, get me out of here.*

Chapter 16

Love me when I least deserve it, because that's when I really need it.

SWEDISH PROVERB

Megan opened her eyes and stared at the ceiling. Somehow she'd made it through the rest of the dessert date with Justin. He'd taken her home, she'd slipped into bed, and mercifully God had allowed her a romp through dreamland.

Turning over in bed, she tucked her arm under her head. The bright sun sneaked through the cracks of the blinds. It was Saturday, and her only plans for the day were to clean the house, do some laundry, and study her Sunday school lesson. The apartment complex's pool had opened a few weeks ago. Maybe she'd slip down there and try to get a bit of a tan before Marianna's wedding.

The awful June date was behind her for an entire year. She smiled when she realized now she had something different to connect to the date. She'd gotten the job as an elementary school music teacher. Thankfully she had the whole summer to seek advice and plan her lessons and discipline tactics. She had plenty of time to study several of the books she'd read over the last few years. *I will need to call the university Monday and find out how to set up on-the-job student teaching. And I need to write a resignation letter.*

Her insides clenched as a wave of regret washed through her when she remembered Justin's reaction. He'd tried to act as if he didn't care, but she had seen the disappointment in his eyes. She was a hard worker, efficient. But she wondered if it could be something more. Berated herself that part of her hoped it was.

She thought of Justin's expressions when he returned to the table after speaking with the blond at the café. His reaction to her questions repulsed her.

She released a long breath and pulled herself up from the bed. Today was not a day to think such things. It was a new start. The past was gone, and she could dwell on things to come. Positive things. A bright outlook.

Marianna flung open Megan's door, her expression full of sadness and concern. "We have to go to Pike County. Now. Get dressed."

Megan scratched her arms. The last thing she wanted to do was make a trip to see the parents. Sure, she'd tried unsuccessfully to get in touch with them, but today was not the day she planned to focus on that. "What? Why?"

"Apparently Dad is sick. Really sick."

Megan squinted. "What do you mean?"

Tears welled in Marianna's eyes. "Mom called. He has cancer. Liver cancer. They didn't tell us because they hoped he'd make it past the wedding. They didn't want me to worry while I planned. . ." Marianna flopped onto the edge of the bed and placed her face in her hands.

Megan walked to her sister and wrapped her arms around her shoulders. His coloring had seemed a bit off when they visited for the fitting. In fact, Megan remembered thinking it kind of weird he wanted to be there with a bunch of girls for it. And she'd been surprised at how kind he'd acted.

Megan's heart beat faster, and her head began to ache. She and her sister's relationship with him had grown strained after Clint. It had been the same with their mom. Now that she thought about it, Megan remembered her mother seemed especially weary at the fitting. Megan swallowed back emotion. "What did Mom say?"

"He's not going to make it to the wedding." Marianna looked up at Megan. "And she was crying."

Megan scrunched her eyes closed, willing the tears to stay inside. She knew their mother. The woman held things inside. She didn't show pain. Or worry. She was stoic. Emotionless. Which meant their stepfather might not make it through the day.

Megan opened her eyes and gazed at her sister. She brushed a tear away from Marianna's cheek. "We need to get out of here as soon as possible."

Marianna nodded and raced to her bedroom. Megan got ready quickly. She threw on a comfortable pair of capris and a T-shirt then packed an overnight bag. By the time she grabbed a few snacks, Marianna was already waiting at the door.

The ride home was a quiet one. Megan appreciated that her sister didn't want to talk. All she could think about was her stepfather's lack of faith. He'd hurt her. He and her mother. But the thought of him spending eternity separated from God made her sick to her stomach. She wouldn't wish that on anyone. Even Clint.

The realization sparked a notion that maybe she could forgive. Possibly God had been working on her spirit bit by bit over the years to allow her a compassion for her past boyfriend and her parents she hadn't realized was growing.

She couldn't say anything to Clint. Couldn't offer forgiveness. Couldn't share her faith. He was gone. Died before she'd had the chance to emotionally heal from what he'd done to her. But she could talk to her mom and stepdad. The only dad she'd ever known.

Marianna pulled into the hospital parking lot. A fleeting thought that they should have gotten flowers flashed through her mind. No. He didn't need flowers. He needed Jesus. He needed a Savior before he left this life and journeyed into eternity.

Marianna parked the car and then grabbed Megan's hand. "We need to pray."

Megan looked at her sister. The concern etching her brows mimicked what Megan felt. Her sister shared her worry for their dad's salvation. Megan nodded, and Marianna spoke quietly and quickly. Her sister's fervent pleas twisted at Megan's heart, and she knew her sister's burning desire for her parents to know the Lord echoed her own heart's longing. The wrong they'd done to her was nothing compared to an eternity separated from God.

Marianna finished the prayer, and they jumped out of the car and rushed inside. When they reached his room, Marianna walked right in and grabbed his hand. Megan felt glued to the floor in front of the doorway.

She hadn't expected him to look so sick. So frail. Tubes were hooked up to him everywhere. His skin was yellow. He looked more than gaunt. It was like someone had sucked all the juices from his body and left little more than a barely breathing corpse. How had he gotten so sick so fast?

Megan made eye contact with her mother who sat on the opposite side of the bed. The woman sat like a statue. No visible signs of hurt or worry. She'd stood strong when one man chose to leave her with two small children. Megan could tell she determined to stay just as strong when another left her, even if it wasn't by choice.

Marianna's voice squeaked when she started to talk. "Dad, you've got to listen to me. I've been praying all the way up here. We don't have any time to waste. You need to listen now."

Megan couldn't move. She'd determined to walk confidently in the room, proclaim to her stepfather his need for the Lord. To be bold in her faith. To not take no for an answer from him. To not be concerned with the pain his words had caused in the past. The ugly name he'd called her. The accusation she'd lied.

She couldn't move.

"God loves you, Dad. The Bible says He loved you so much He sent Jesus to die for you. You believe in Jesus, don't you, Dad?"

Marianna's voice grew stronger with each word, and Megan's knees weakened. She needed to be in there beside her sister. Why couldn't she move?

"The Bible says you've sinned. Done wrong. You know that, too. We've all done things we shouldn't have done. All of us."

From the door, Megan watched her father's strained nod. The pain etched across his features ripped at her stomach. Did he hurt from the cancer only or also from the realization of the sins of his life?

She still couldn't believe he looked so sick. It had been only a few weeks since he'd sat beside her in the bridal boutique. He'd tried to talk with her, and she'd been so uncomfortable. Still, he'd said he hoped she'd get the job. She'd gotten it. She should go in and tell him. He'd want to know.

She couldn't move.

Marianna continued. "Just tell Him here." She touched their father's chest. "You don't have to say the words aloud. Just tell Him you're sorry for the sins you've committed. Ask Him to come into your heart. He'll do it, Dad. He promises He will."

Tears filled Megan's eyes. The man who'd raised her since she was just a tiny girl could barely breathe. He didn't even try to speak, but she knew he heard everything Marianna said by the expressions crossing his face. He didn't have much time.

Megan watched him so intently she hadn't noticed her mother stood beside her. "I'm surprised you came."

Megan startled then looked at her mother. "Why?"

Vulnerability flashed across her mother's features. "You hate us."

Megan furrowed her brow. She'd never seen her mother so unsure. "I don't hate you. Either of you."

Her mother didn't respond. A war raged within Megan. She should tell her mother she loved her. It was true her mother hadn't said the words since before the fight that had been etched in concrete in her mind. But God wasn't worried about what her parents did or didn't do. He wanted Megan to forgive. She knew it to the depths of her soul. She couldn't move on until she did.

Her mother straightened her shoulders. She lifted her chin and bore Megan with a look of contempt. "You should have obeyed us. We knew better. And you didn't listen. And nothing has been the same."

Megan sucked in her breath as her mother walked back to the chair beside her husband. No mercy. No compassion. If only Megan could take back that decision to go out with Clint against her parents' wishes. She wished to the core of her being she had listened and obeyed.

But what he did was not her fault. She'd blamed herself for too long. Spent years trying to forgive Clint and her parents.

What about yourself?

Tears spilled down her cheeks. She didn't even try to stop them. Had she ever forgiven herself? She'd been a foolish teenager caught up in the belief that Clint was the boy of her dreams. If she'd listened, that night never would have happened. But she didn't. She'd messed up, and she was sorry.

Closing her eyes, she thought of God's servant David. A man after God's own heart. He'd messed up. Badly. Had sex with Bathsheba. Got her pregnant. Then had her husband killed on the battlefield. His prayer to God after the prophet Nathan confronted him slipped from Megan's lips, "'Cleanse me with hyssop, and I will be clean; wash me, and I will be whiter than snow.'"

She opened her eyes and looked at her father lying in the hospital bed dying. Her sister sat at his side, leading him to an everlasting faith in God. Megan looked up at the ceiling and whispered, "Restore the joy of my salvation. Give me a willing spirit. Sustain me."

Forgive herself. She'd spent years trying to forgive others, but she hadn't realized where the forgiveness needed to start. From within.

Her feet moved. She walked to her father's bedside. Marianna still clung to his hand. His eyes were closed. He hadn't spoken the whole time Marianna prayed with him. But despite the labored breathing, his countenance looked at peace.

Megan placed her hand on her sister's shoulder. She looked at her mother whose expression was deader than it had been when Megan and Marianna arrived. The woman needed the Lord. How could she get through this without Him?

Megan looked back at her father. He opened his eyes and saw

her. A slight smile spread across his lips. He pressed the back of his head against his pillow and sucked in a deep breath. His words came out just above a whisper. "Forgive me."

Megan gasped as a fresh set of tears washed down her cheeks. She grabbed his hand in hers. She didn't have to think. The words slipped from her lips with a truth that was more than she felt. "I do."

He smiled fully and closed his eyes. Only a few more moments passed before the laboring of his lungs slowed. He took one last gasp of breath. A smile spread his lips, and he was gone.

A sob escaped her mother's lips and Marianna jumped up, rushed to the other side of the bed, and wrapped her arms around their mother. Despite feeling unsure about what her mother might say, Megan followed her sister and hugged her mom.

Words she hadn't said in more than eight years spilled from her mouth. They brought healing hope, and Megan knew she meant them. "I love you, Mom."

Chapter 17

It is difficult to know at what moment love begins;
it is less difficult to know that it has begun.
HENRY WADSWORTH LONGFELLOW

Justin placed the wrapped box on Megan's desk. He fixed the bow once more then inwardly scolded himself for acting like such a whipped pup. What reason would he have for acting that way anyhow? He was simply getting a really good secretary a going-away present. Just because she'd still be there for over a month longer, and just because he talked his father and other colleague into spending more money than either ever would have considered—it meant nothing.

His dad crossed his arms in front of his chest and lifted his left eyebrow. Justin knew that look. He found Justin's actions humorous and ridiculous. Sneaking a peek at Mr. Combs, Justin noted the eldest lawyer of the firm seemed oblivious to everything except the homemade cinnamon bun his wife gave him each morning. One look at the man's expanding waist, and Justin wondered how long it would be before Combs would move into the next size suit. Again.

Justin took his handkerchief from his suit pocket and dabbed at the water that had spilled from the flower vase onto Megan's desk.

"Son, it looks fine." His dad's voice was laced with humor and a touch of something Justin couldn't quite put his finger on.

"I know." Justin stood to his full height and adjusted his tie.

His father studied him. "Is there something going on between you and Megan?" He lifted his hands. "Not that I mind. It's just that I didn't know."

Justin shook his head. "Absolutely not. Megan is a friend. Her sister is marrying Kirk. We go to Bible study together."

His father harrumphed. He didn't understand Justin's new-found faith. Justin prayed for his dad and that he would be a living example of Christ before his dad. But Justin understood his father all too well. It would take time, and a miracle, for him to see that living a life filled with money and women was no life at all.

And yet living for Christ wasn't easy. The girl from the gym still made advances at Justin. Brandy was gorgeous, and Justin knew how a night out with her would end. He couldn't deny the temptation. But his relationship with Christ had shown him he wanted more. He wasn't willing to compromise for less than God's best in his life.

The front door opened, and Justin found himself smiling at the secretary's surprised expression. Megan's presence stirred something within him. It was a cliché statement—one too often quoted from a popular movie from the nineties, but the truth was Megan made him want to be a better man. He wanted to be more than himself. He wanted to be all that he could be in Christ.

He wanted to be worthy of her.

The thought caught in the back of his brain. His goal had been to work on his relationship with the Lord. To abstain from women who would distract his growth. He needed to stay the course, to find what God wanted from his life.

Megan, he realized, didn't distract his growth in the Lord, but encouraged all those good things in him. He drank in her light blond hair that fell just below her shoulders. Her deep blue eyes spoke of a depth deeper than the ocean.

When had he fallen in love with her?

She smiled as she walked toward them. Justin realized the smile didn't quite reach her eyes. She bent down and sniffed the rose and daisy arrangement then picked up her card. "What's all this?"

Justin's father put his arm around Megan's shoulder and kissed the top of her head. "You're going-away-slash-starting-a-new-career present."

"I haven't even written my resignation."

Mr. Combs swallowed the last bite of his cinnamon bun and wiped his mouth with his fingertips. "Justin told us about your job as a music teacher in the fall. We're very proud of you."

Her eyes glimmered, but Justin noted a small hint of sadness behind them. She hugged his dad and then Mr. Combs. She turned toward him, and Justin sucked in his breath. It was his turn. He would get a hug. Hesitation washed across her features before she halfway wrapped her arms around him and patted his back as if he were a leper whose skin was falling off and who hadn't had a bath in weeks.

His father looked at him, and his left eyebrow rose again. It took every ounce of restraint within him not to tell his father to buzz off. He didn't need his humor-filled, knowing glances.

Justin motioned toward the present. "Open it."

Megan looked at each of them. "You really didn't have to

do this."

Justin's dad pointed at the gift. "Open it. Combs and I don't know what we've done."

Justin's face warmed. He didn't want her to know the whole thing had been all his idea. He definitely didn't want her to know that left to his father and Combs, Megan would have quit with little more than her last paycheck.

Megan grinned at him. She unwrapped the gift then gasped when she realized it was a laptop.

Justin opened the box and turned on the machine. "I had the clerk install several different kinds of music software programs. Stuff I thought might help you with your new job."

"Very nice gift." Mr. Combs patted Justin's back. He grabbed Megan's hand in his. "It's been a real pleasure having you with us. We'll miss you when you're gone." He pointed to his office. "But it's time to get to work."

With that, he nodded and walked away.

"I have to agree." His dad grabbed Megan in a bear hug. "You've been the best secretary we've had. I'll miss you." He released her and held both her arms in his grip. "I mean that."

Justin realized he did. Megan had not only been the ideal woman for him, but she was the perfect secretary for his dad as well. He couldn't fathom how they would ever replace her. Again, he realized how much he didn't want to let her go. And not just as a secretary.

Megan looked up at him, her eyes glistening with the threat of tears. "I can't believe you did this. It's more than kind."

With the last words, a lone tear slipped down her cheek, and Justin couldn't stop himself. He wrapped his arms around her and pulled her against his chest. To his surprise, she melted into him, and he had to hold her tighter.

"Thank you, Justin."

The sound of his whispered name from her lips sent trails of delight through him. Feelings he'd tried to hold at bay.

A moment passed, and he felt warm wetness against his chest. The gift shouldn't cause such tears. Something else was going on. He pulled her away from him and studied her expression. "Megan, what's wrong?"

She inhaled a long breath. "My dad died on Saturday."

"I'm so sorry." He pulled her to him again.

"It was hard."

She welcomed his embrace, and he tried not to think about how perfectly she fit against him and how he wanted to always protect her from pain.

She pulled away and grabbed a tissue from her desk. "But he accepted Christ. Just before he died. Thanks to Marianna." She dotted her eyes, and her lower lip quivered. "Our relationship was strained."

"When's the funeral?"

"Not until Friday. His cancer moved so fast the doctors wanted to look at. . ." She stopped and shook her head.

"I'll go with you."

She looked up at him. "You'd do that?"

Justin swallowed. Never before would he have considered attending a funeral with a woman. Doing anything for a woman that would cause even an inkling of discomfort to him. But everything changed when it came to Megan. "Absolutely."

Megan didn't respond. Instead, she looked at her desk and pointed to the card leaning against the flowers. "I didn't see the card."

She picked it up, and Justin took it from her. "It's probably not a good idea now."

She cocked her head. "What is it?"

With a sigh, he handed it back to her. She opened the card and pulled out the two tickets to the Lexington Opera House. Though it was something he'd never consider doing on his own, he thought she might like to see the Southern quartet that was performing there tonight. He'd bought them on a whim. Now he wished he'd simply stuck with the laptop.

She lifted the tickets. "I've never heard of this group."

Justin shrugged. "Me neither. I just figured you'd like southern music, and when I saw them, I guess. . ." Justin cleared his throat. He couldn't remember the last time he'd fumbled all over himself inviting a woman out for an evening.

She smiled up at him. "I think it will be good for me. I'm assuming the second one is for you?"

Justin nodded. "I'd like to treat you to dinner as well."

Megan bit the inside of her lip, something he realized she did anytime she wasn't sure of a situation. She nodded. "Okay."

Justin sucked in a deep breath. It had been a long time since he'd been so excited about a date.

Justin leaned against his new black sports car. He crossed his arms in front of his chest. "That show was definitely not what I expected."

Megan doubled over and laughed for what seemed the millionth time that night. She stood back up and wiped her eyes with the back of her hand. "Your expressions to their jokes alone were priceless."

"Don't get me wrong. I like Gene Autry and Roy Rogers just fine. I just hadn't expected. . ."

"The quartet was a lot of fun."

Justin nodded. He had to agree with her. Dinner had been terrific, but the show had been an unexpected surprise.

She sobered as she let out a long breath. "I needed those laughs. Thanks, Justin."

She had no idea how much her laughter, her genuineness, drew him. She was like no other woman he'd ever met. He didn't want to take her home for a nightcap and an awkward morning. He wanted to take her home for good. The truth of it scared him.

"I meant it about going with you to the funeral."

Megan shook her head. "That's awfully sweet of you, but as your secretary, I recall you have court on Friday."

Justin frowned. She was right. He did. "I can see if Dad will cover for me."

She lifted her hand. "I'll be fine."

She looked up at him, and he found himself swallowing hard. He wanted her to kiss him again. Maybe he should kiss her. But what would she think? In his heart, he knew she wasn't ready. He didn't know why, but he could tell it wasn't the time.

He didn't deserve a woman like Megan. She deserved a man who didn't have to apologize to half of the women he'd ever met. He wondered how many years it would be before he'd walk in a restaurant or church building or department store without seeing a woman he'd known in his past. Maybe that day would never come. His sins had been forgiven, but consequences had a way of hanging on.

She picked at her fingernails. "How many more apologies?"

She must have read his mind. He looked up at the heavens. The stars were especially bright. Not a cloud in the sky. A man should be admiring God's natural wonder with his date, not discussing the women he'd wronged.

"Believe it or not, I'm done. Remember, I told you at the café."

"That's right. I forgot."

He stared at her. He was attracted to Megan as he'd never been attracted to another woman in his life. And he wouldn't lie to her. Wouldn't sugarcoat things. She knew what he was. One day maybe she would want to know who he was becoming in Christ. He cleared his throat. "Not everyone was forgiving. Not that I can blame them."

Megan rubbed both of her arms as if brushing away goose bumps, but the air was warmer than usual for June. "Forgiveness is a tough thing."

"This may sound a bit corny, but you like music, so maybe you'll appreciate it."

He pulled his wallet out of his back pocket and opened it. He took out the small folded paper he'd put inside. "I found this old hymn." He cocked his head. "Actually it was by complete accident. Written by this woman, Elizabeth Clephane. It talks about the cross and how it's safety and shelter, and then about the grave just beyond the cross."

He looked at her to see if he was boring her with his nostalgia about some hymn he'd found on the Internet. Her gaze seemed to search him. She wanted to hear the words of the song as much as he'd wanted to know the depths of their meaning. He looked back down at the paper, away from the intensity of her gaze.

He continued, "The song goes on to talk about seeing the form of the One who died there for me." He placed his hand against his chest, feeling the words anew in his heart as he quoted, " 'And from my stricken heart with tears two wonders I confess; the wonders of redeeming love and my unworthiness.' "

Emotion threatened to well up and spill out from within him. He cleared his throat and sneaked another peek at Megan. She studied him as if she longed to take a scalpel and pry him open to see if all he said was true. He wanted to be true. To be honest and upright. He didn't want to be the man he once was. He was unworthy. Forever unworthy. But his unworthiness had been redeemed by God's love.

He wanted to start fresh. Again. The apostle Paul had been the best and most educated among Pharisees. Yet, he met Jesus on the Damascus road and was forever changed. It could be true for Justin. He had to believe God would take the mess he'd made of his life and make him into a man who didn't need to be constantly reminded of his great wealth or need the admiration of the most beautiful of women.

She whispered, " 'Beneath the Cross of Jesus.' "

He looked at her questioningly.

She pointed to the paper. "That's the name of the song."

"Oh. Yes. That's right."

He looked at her. She looked as if her mind raced with a million things at one time. When sadness stole over her expression, he clapped his hands. "Enough with the heavy. I had a lot of fun tonight. I thought I'd fall out of my seat when that guy brought out an accordion and they started yodeling."

A smile spread across Megan's face. "I was pretty sure you weren't expecting that. What did you think of the song about learning to yodel?"

Justin shook his head. "I didn't know sounds like that could come out of a man."

Megan laughed. "You wanna try?"

"No!"

Her laughter bubbled out again, gracing him with her inner joy. "You'd better get me home. I gotta work tomorrow." She winked. "Wouldn't want the boss to be mad at me for being tired on the job."

Justin shoved his wallet back into his pocket. He had to do something to keep himself from kissing the wink off her eyelid. And her other eyelid. And her. . . "I suppose you're right."

He opened her car door for her, and she slipped inside. She looked up at him, and Justin wished the evening could last longer. Forever. Her expression grew serious. "I'm really proud of you, Justin. God's really gotten ahold of your life."

He shut the door and walked to the driver's side. He hadn't wanted it to happen. Wasn't even sure when it had. Maybe he started to realize it when she told them she'd gotten the job at the elementary school.

Whenever it was and however it happened, he'd fallen in love with Megan McKinney.

Chapter 18

There never was any heart truly great and generous
that was not also tender and compassionate.

ROBERT FROST

Colt didn't know when or how it happened, but he'd fallen in love with Megan McKinney. He sat perched on the edge of his favorite recliner, elbows planted on his knees, and watched as she held his crying niece in her arms. Megan was the mother Hadley needed and the woman he wanted.

"She was talking all weird." Hadley sniffed. "I mean it's not like I know what she talks like normally, but I could tell she was drunk or something."

Colt leaned back in the chair and squeezed the arms with both hands. Hadley's no-good mother had gotten their phone number and called the house. Colt never would have imagined who was on the other end of the line when Hadley jumped up and raced to the ringing phone. They both assumed it to be one of Hadley's friends. Now that school was over, the girls burned up the cell phone and the land line making plans for one visit or another.

Colt dug his fingers deeper into the chair's arms. *If I'd known it was Tina. . .if I'd known she'd gotten our number, I would have changed it. Better yet, I would have torn out the land line completely.*

Megan shushed Hadley with soft tones and traced her fingers through his niece's hair. "I know that was difficult. I'm sorry it happened to you."

Megan didn't try to defend Tina, nor did she speak ill of Hadley's biological mother. Something Colt couldn't seem to stop himself from doing. She simply acknowledged Hadley's hurt and comforted her. She knew just how to handle Hadley. The right things to say and do. With each stroke of her hand through Hadley's hair, Colt found himself more drawn to the piano teacher.

"Why did she have to call me like that? She never calls me. Never writes. And I get both in a week. And when she calls. . ." Hadley shoved her face back into Megan's chest.

Colt couldn't sit there any longer. He pushed out of the chair and paced the floor. "She won't be calling anymore—I'll tell you that much."

"But I want to talk to her." Hadley looked up at him. Her eyes were red and swollen from crying, but her expression reminded him of the one she'd given him when she was just a little tyke begging him for a new pup.

She'd won him over with that look, and Old Yeller had been a part of the family ever since. But this was different. More was at stake. It wasn't safe or healthy for her to be around Tina. He had to be firm. "Hadley, I believe I know what is best. . . ."

Megan shot him a look of warning and shook her head ever so slightly. Hadley's expression switched from sorrow to confrontation, and she started to hop up from the couch. Megan grabbed her wrist and pulled her back down beside her. "Tell me what she said."

Megan pierced him with another look of warning as Hadley settled back into the couch beside her. Only because he had no idea how to handle the shifting emotions of the twelve-year-old did he turn away, inwardly growling.

"She said she wanted to come see me, but Colt wouldn't let her."

Hadley raised her voice in accusation to him. How could he possibly be the bad guy here? The woman left Hadley. Hadn't even called or sent word of any kind to Hadley in years. She was a druggie and an alcoholic. How could this possibly be his fault? "She has no right. . . ."

Megan shot him another look, this time raising her eyebrows and cocking her head to emphasize she didn't want him to talk. He looked up at the ceiling, willing the good Lord to keep him from lighting into both the women in his living room. The very notion Tina should be able to have anything to do with Hadley was ridiculous. Out of the question.

Not that Megan had suggested he let Tina traipse into Hadley's life. She seemed to simply be trying to get the girl to calm down. Still, he didn't like being told what to do. Even if it was just in glances. And he didn't like that Hadley was acting so foolish as to want to talk with a woman who'd walked out of her life twelve years before.

"She's my mom. I want to know her." Hadley's voice lowered. "But not like she was today."

"It's hard when our parents don't behave as they should." Megan put her arm around Hadley's shoulder again. "I already told you I can't remember ever seeing my dad. And my mom and stepdad hurt me a long time ago. They didn't act like parents should have."

Colt watched Megan as she spoke. Pain etched her brows. He'd been so focused on Hadley before that he hadn't realized Megan's eyes seemed a bit swollen. She still looked adorable, her blond hair framing her face and dancing against her shoulders. But something was bothering her.

She looked down at her lap. "My stepdad died on Saturday."

"Megan, I'm sorry." Colt walked toward her and placed his hand on her shoulder.

New tears filled Hadley's eyes as she stared at Megan.

Megan nodded. "Thank you, Colt." She grabbed Hadley's hand and squeezed it. "I did get the chance to forgive him. Really forgive him. In my heart and by saying the words. Just before he died."

Colt watched Hadley stare at Megan. Was she telling Hadley to have a relationship with Tina? Colt wouldn't allow it. Whatever happened between Megan and her parents was completely different than all that happened between Hadley and his brother and Tina. Her parents weren't drug addicts. They hadn't given her up before she'd been able to chew solid food.

Hadley finally spoke. "When is the funeral?"

"Friday."

"Can I go?"

Colt cleared his throat. He wasn't sure that was the best of ideas. She was still sore at him because he hadn't taken her to his brother's funeral. She was already dealing with all these crazy emotions from her mother's contacts, which he would be sure were stopped. A funeral probably wouldn't be the best place for Hadley.

He watched as Megan looked from Hadley to him. He knew she thought the same as he did.

Hadley looked up at him. She stood and put her hand on Colt's arm. "I want to be there for Megan, Uncle Colt. She's been there for me. For us."

Colt studied his niece. She seemed more grown up than he'd ever seen her. She needed to do this. To support her piano teacher. The woman she'd grown to love.

He looked at Megan. She was the woman he'd grown to love as well. He wanted to be there for her. To give her someone she could lean on, could glean strength from.

He lowered himself onto the couch beside Megan. It was probably the closest he'd ever been to her. She smelled good, like flowers. She looked wounded, like a hurt pup. He wanted—no, needed—to be there for her. "If you don't mind, I think Hadley and I would like to go with you."

Megan looked away from him. He knew he was acting more intense than he'd ever been before. But his feelings were suddenly so evident. So real. He needed to protect and care for her.

After several moments, she nodded, and he knew he would do anything to make Megan happy.

Maybe going to the funeral wasn't such a good idea. He and Hadley walked into the small foyer of the funeral home. He felt uncomfortable at funerals for people he knew, but to go to one where he didn't know the person who'd passed was a little more than uncomfortable. More like torture.

Around ten people sat in folding chairs waiting for the memorial to begin. Only two stood in front of the casket offering condolences to the family. He watched as Megan welcomed a hug from an elderly woman. Despite the discomfort, he had to be there for her.

Hadley's teacher, Marianna, stood beside Megan. Along with a tall, thin, dark-haired man, whom he assumed to be Marianna's fiancé. At least he thought Megan had mentioned her sister was engaged. Next to them was a very fair woman with short, curly red hair. She must be Megan's mother.

She and Megan didn't stand by each other. Marianna kept her hand around her mother's arm, but Megan stood away from the two of them, on the other side of the man. What had happened between Megan and her parents? She'd mentioned making a bad choice as a teenager. But didn't lots of teenagers make bad choices? And Megan was so upright and wonderful. Whatever she'd done must not have been that bad. Nothing like his brother and girlfriend anyway. It was pretty obvious Megan wasn't doping it up.

He studied her mother more closely. She seemed sad beyond the death with a deep to the core pain. He remembered Megan also mentioned her parents weren't Christians. He'd pray for this woman—for her salvation, and also that she would be able to open her eyes and see how remarkable Megan was.

Hadley pressed her hand against his arm. "Let's go see Megan."

Colt nodded and followed his niece to the front of the room. His cheeks warmed and his collar seemed tighter with each step they took. Funeral homes made him nervous.

He exhaled a long breath. The last one he'd been in had his brother all neatly groomed and inside a brown box. He blinked hard trying not to remember the look of his only sibling in that coffin. His whole family, everyone but Hadley, had been taken off the face of the earth. His church family had always been closer to him than his brother. Still, burying Connor had been like stripping off a piece of his body and shoving it into the ground. Hadley was all he had left, which was why Tina had to stay away from her.

Megan looked up and saw Hadley. A slow smile spread across her lips, and Colt knew they'd done the right thing by coming. She wrapped her arms around his niece. "It's good to see you."

Hadley, who once again seemed more grown up than he'd ever seen her, folded her arms around Megan. "I'm sorry."

Colt didn't know when Hadley had started growing up. Only yesterday he was teaching her how to mount a horse. Now she was comforting the woman he loved in her time of need. A fleeting thought that Hadley was strong enough to deal with tough issues passed through his mind. He pushed it away. Strong enough or not, it was still his job to protect her.

Megan released a quick sniffle then let go of Hadley. She looked up at Colt, and he didn't wait for her offer. He grabbed Megan up in a deep hug. He wanted her to feel from every ounce of his strength she could count on him to care for and protect her, no matter what the situation.

He felt her quick intake of breath and knew Megan's resolve was crumbling against him. He pressed her tighter against him. She needed to know he could handle her hurts. She was safe with him.

After several moments, she released her hold, and though he didn't want to, he let her slip away. He grabbed Hadley's hand, and they moved to the front row and sat down. A few more visitors offered condolences, then Megan and her family walked toward him and Hadley.

Megan motioned to her mother. "Colt, Hadley, this is my mother, Barbara."

He shook the woman's hand. It was cold, and she never made eye contact. Colt's heart went out to the woman. How hard would it be to lose the person you loved? It was the one blessing he was thankful his parents hadn't had to endure. They passed away together. One didn't have to hurt without the other.

While Hadley shook her mother's hand, Megan motioned to her sister and the man. "You already know my sister. This is her fiancé, Kirk."

The funeral director announced the ceremony would start, and Colt nodded and quickly shook Kirk's hand. The family sat beside them. Megan beside him.

Megan sucked in a deep breath when the man shut the casket. Colt reached over and grabbed her hand. She squeezed his and didn't let go. He tried to focus on the minister's words. The man said Megan's stepfather had accepted Christ on his deathbed with his daughters present. Colt wanted to ask Megan about it. She'd said she had forgiven him. He wondered what had happened. He wished he and Connor had the same type of good-bye. Instead, he'd arrived at the morgue with his brother already dead. Overdosed.

He glanced at Hadley. Her eyes filled with tears, but they didn't spill over her lids. He should have told her about her dad. Deep down, he knew it was pride that kept his lips sealed. He didn't want Hadley to hurt. He wanted to protect her. But he hadn't wanted her to see the man who was her father and his brother. The Baker name was above such ugliness. Such sinfulness.

He studied his niece. She sat beside him, her shoulders back and her chin up. He knew she thought of her dad, of the fact she hadn't been able to say good-bye to him. He'd taken that from her. Couldn't give it back to her now. Or ever.

She was stronger than he'd given her credit for. And he was sorry. On the way home, he'd tell her.

The message finished, and Megan stood up and walked to her family. Feeling a few too many waves of emotion, Colt looked down at Hadley. "You be okay if I step out to the restroom?"

She nodded, and Colt noted once again the strong disposition of his niece. He should keep his eyes open when it came to that girl. The slight lift of her chin was proof she was more like him than her daddy. She was made of strong stuff. And the fact she had an obvious attachment to God made her even stronger.

He swallowed back the knot in his throat. He needed to get out of this room. The stench of death and the reality of his wrong to his niece turned his stomach. He walked out into the foyer and found his way to the restroom.

After splashing cold water on his face and sending up a quick prayer for forgiveness and strength, Colt made his way out of the restroom.

"Colt is the kind of guy I want to see Megan with."

Colt stopped. The hushed voice came from Megan's sister.

"Who's to say she isn't with him? He's here at the funeral, isn't he?"

Colt stepped back closer to the restroom door. It was a man's voice. Probably her fiancé's.

"I'm worried about her liking your friend. That Justin guy she works for. He's wrong for her."

Colt narrowed his eyes. He'd meant to look into that man. Justin Frasure. Megan's boss. He'd had a bad feeling when Megan mentioned him that day at the pond. Her sister evidently didn't approve of the guy.

"Justin has never said one word about liking Megan." It was the man's voice again. "And she hasn't said anything to you either."

"She doesn't have to."

Colt couldn't listen anymore. He stepped back into the restroom and peered at his reflection. He loved Megan McKinney. Justin Frasure would have to move out of the way.

Chapter 19

In three words I can sum up everything
I've learned about life: it goes on.
ROBERT FROST

It was going to be another bad day. The month of June passed in a haze. Megan worked, taught piano lessons, and helped Marianna prepare for the wedding.

She managed through the motions of life. She avoided Justin. He was just entirely too cute, and she simply needed to be away from him. She tried to avoid Colt, though he made it a bit more difficult. After every piano lesson, he had ice cream sundaes ready or the horses groomed to be ridden or a board game spread out on the dining room table. She knew he was trying to help her feel better. Colt had the best of intentions, just like when he kept her father's death from Hadley. But he had a hard time taking the hint when a girl just needed some space. He couldn't fix her, and she'd gotten to the point she wanted to avoid going to his house because she didn't want to *do* anything.

Her mother visited a lot. Preparations for the wedding, she

said. But Megan knew it was more than that. She was grieving her husband's death, and she wouldn't allow herself to show it. Or admit it. She'd grown colder with Megan, but Megan didn't have the strength to care. She grieved in ways she hadn't expected. Her father's last plea for her to forgive him played like a broken DVD in her mind. How she wished for the time to start anew with him.

"Get your shoes on. You and I are going out."

Megan shifted on the couch and looked up at her sister. She nodded. It was Saturday. She didn't have anything better to do. Except continue to sulk. "What do we need to pick up for the wedding?"

"Nothing!"

Megan frowned at her sister. "Then what are we. . ."

The front door opened, and their friends Julie and Amber walked inside. Marianna pointed to the girls. "And I've recruited support."

Amber grabbed Megan's hand and pulled her off the couch. "You've been brooding for a month."

Megan stuck out her bottom lip. "I have not."

"Oh yes you have," said Julie, "and you've had reason to be sad."

"Bill was the only dad we'd ever known," said Marianna, "and I'm thankful he received Jesus as his Lord."

Amber pointed at Megan. "But you need a reason to stop moping."

Megan crossed her arms in front of her chest. "I am not moping."

"You need a haircut." Julie lifted several strands of Megan's hair off her shoulder.

Marianna wrinkled her nose. "Yeah. I don't want you looking like 'The Shaggy D.A.' for my wedding."

Megan giggled at the memory of the old movie she and her sister used to watch when they were little. "My hair is fine." She cocked her eyebrow and pointed at her sister. "I'm taking that as an insult."

"It was an insult," stammered Marianna.

"Actually it's quite thick," said Amber. "You know I've always been jealous."

"But the dead ends kinda stink." Julie waved her hand in front of her nose. "And when was the last time you washed it?"

Megan's mouth fell open. She placed her hands on her hips. "My hair does not smell bad. I'll have you know I just washed it yesterday."

Megan stopped her tirade when she realized Amber, Julie, and Marianna were all trying to hide back chuckles. She felt a smile lift her lips. "You got me."

Marianna wrapped her hand around Megan's elbow. "That's the first smile I've seen in weeks."

Julie opened the front door. "Our appointments are in fifteen minutes. We've got to get out of here."

"We're all going to get our hair cut? Really?" asked Megan.

"We've gotta look good for the wedding," said Julie.

Megan let out a deep sigh and smiled at her friends and sister. "Let me get my shoes."

She went into her bedroom and grabbed a pair of flip-flops off her shoe rack. Dropping them to the floor, she noticed how bad the nail polish looked on her toes. She walked back into the living area. "Maybe we could stop and get our toes done, too?"

Marianna placed her hand over her heart. "My sister is rejoining the land of the living. She's asking for a pedicure."

Julie scratched the top of her head. "Megan loves a pedicure like a dog loves its bone."

"Like a horse adores its carrots," said Amber.

"Like a pig loves its slop," said Julie.

Megan lifted her hand. "Okay. Now, you're just getting gross."

Amber placed the back of her hand against the side of her mouth in a fake whisper to Julie. "But seriously, check out those neglected toenails."

"Hey! They don't look that bad." Megan swatted Amber with the back of her hand.

Julie shook her head. "Honestly, Megan. I've never seen so much peeling paint on your little piggies."

Marianna raised her pointer finger in the air. "Then it's settled. Haircuts then pedis. Maybe a little pizza afterward."

Amber groaned. "No fair. You know I'm trying to lose five pounds so I can fit in my bridesmaid dress."

"I don't have to lose anything." Julie pumped her fist. "Pizza sounds great to me."

Megan laughed as they continued to argue on their way out to the car. She still felt a deep loss in the center of her heart. Part of it probably had to do with her continued near-estranged relationship with her mom. Still it would be good to go out with her sister and friends. She needed this. She hadn't realized how much so until they pointed out her toes.

She looked down at her feet. It was true. She'd never let her nails get so chipped. Even one of the rhinestones on the flower design on her big toe had come off. It had been too long since she'd had a pedicure.

Julie and Amber started to banter over who would sit in the front with Marianna. Megan inwardly chuckled as she slipped into the backseat behind her sister. It was going to be a good day after all.

Megan lifted her shoulders when Justin approached her desk. She had no reason to still feel so anxious around the man. She saw him each day at work, each weekend at church, and on Thursdays at Bible study. It was obvious he'd changed since accepting Christ. Women didn't flock to his office, except those who brought along husbands and sought out adoption help. She had to admit Justin was not the man he'd once been. And she liked the man he'd become. More than liked. Admired.

And that is why her stomach rumbled like a volcano about to erupt each time he did approach her.

He stopped in front of her desk and shoved his fists in his pants pockets—dark charcoal pants that fit him to perfection. The deep-green button-down shirt he wore simply did not do what it should—cover and disguise the muscles bulging from his chest and arms.

Seriously, what was God doing when He formed this man in his mother's womb? Was He experimenting with different physical features to see what combination formed the most beautiful of the entire race? *Gotta give You credit, God. If that's what You were doing, You did good.*

She bit her bottom lip. She would not salivate over her boss. She would not. And quite frankly, she was getting tired of always having to remind herself not to slobber in his presence.

She looked up at him. His dark brown eyes studied her. And she realized he was nervous. Justin Frasure—nervous? To talk to her?

She almost snorted aloud, but the scared puppy dog expression he wore stopped her short. "Can I help you, Justin?"

He swallowed and averted his gaze. Looking back at her, he pulled his fists out of his pockets and wrung his hands together.

What in the world was he doing? He acted as if they didn't see each other practically every day of their lives. He reminded her of a high school boy about to ask a girl on a. . . Uh-oh. Her heart sped up. Surely he wasn't about to. . . She inwardly shook her head. No, it wasn't possible. She was nothing like Justin's type. She wasn't ugly, but she most certainly wasn't flashy or drop-dead gorgeous.

"I was wondering"—his gaze bore into her with an intensity she'd never seen—"if you'd go to a charity ball with me."

Megan lifted her eyebrows and placed her hand against her chest. "Me?"

His expression switched from intensity to amusement. "Yes, you, Megan. I enjoy being around you more than any other woman I've ever known."

Heat washed over Megan's cheeks and neck. He hadn't exactly proclaimed his undying love, and she most certainly didn't want him to do so. She didn't know what to say. She needed to stay away from Justin Frasure. He was her tempting fruit. When she was around him, she thought and felt things she didn't want to think and feel. It was safer to stay away, to say no.

"It's a charity ball to raise funds for overseas adoption. It's formal attire." He reached into his pocket and pulled out several bills. "I wouldn't want it to be a hardship, so. . ."

Megan looked at him with uncertainty. He was giving her money for a dress. It was a nice gesture. Maybe it meant he didn't intend it as a date, simply as a professional outing. She could handle that. She owed it to the company. She'd be training her replacement in the next few weeks. It wouldn't hurt to go with Justin to an event.

"A business date? That would be fine." She took the money from his hand. "Of course I'll go with you."

A glimmer of something passed across his features. Was it regret? Or sadness? She didn't know and didn't want to think about it.

He jutted out his chin. "A business date. Sure. It's short notice. The dinner's this weekend. Is that okay?"

Warmth spread over her cheeks again, as she realized she'd grabbed the money out of his hand without finding out if she could even attend the function. She nodded quickly. "Sure. That's fine. I've got time to look around for a dress tonight."

He opened his mouth then clamped it shut before he turned on his heels and walked back to his office. If she didn't know better, she might have believed he was about to offer to go with her to pick out the dress. She didn't want him to tag along. It would be hard enough to attend a formal dinner without swooning all over the man. And if she could, she'd leave her lips home for the evening. If only that were possible.

She looked at the clock on her computer. Thankfully it was time to leave. She needed out of the office. Needed to clear her head. Going to the mall to shop for a formal gown to go on a "business" date with the most beautiful man God had ever created would be just the thing to help get her mind off Justin. She rolled her eyes as she grabbed her purse out of the cabinet and headed out the door.

Once at the mall, she made her way to one of the nicer department stores. It was one her wallet had never allowed her to venture inside. She hadn't counted the cash Justin gave her until she'd reached the mall. He'd given her more than she made in a week. All for a dress and pair of shoes. Which meant they needed to be nice. Which meant Megan's stomach rolled because she'd never bought anything that nice.

"May I help you, miss?"

Megan turned and saw an adorable, petite brunette. Her hair was cut like Tinker Bell's, her makeup dark, and she wore a diamond in the side of her nose, but her clothes and shoes made her edginess appear even more professional and gorgeous. Maybe this woman would help her think outside of her usual wardrobe choice—though hopefully not too far out. Megan swallowed. "I'm looking for a formal gown, and I need it this weekend."

The woman clapped. "Then we need to get to work. No time for alterations." She extended her hand. "By the way, I'm Avery."

Megan shook her hand then told the saleswoman her dress size. Avery placed her finger on her cheek and studied Megan's shape. Megan squirmed under the intense scrutiny until Avery grabbed her arm. "Girl, you have a knockout shape. I want to be sure we enhance all the right places."

A thrill raced down her spine. She'd never shopped like this. Never had anyone study her to bring out her best physical qualities. She wanted to be around people who cared about who the person was not what she looked like. Still, it was fun to think of purchasing something special.

Megan gaped at the mounds of dresses Avery pulled off the racks. "I'm going to try on all of those?"

"Maybe." Avery shrugged. "Unless the perfect dress pops out at us before you're through the stack."

Megan went into the dressing room and slipped into the first dress—an aqua strapless gown with sequence beading at the top. The color was beautiful, but it made her hips look bigger than they were. She stepped outside of the room to show Avery. The saleswoman shook her head and sent her back inside. "Next."

She took off the dress then tried on a deep red that was too dark against her skin, then a black that was too low-cut, then a pink that was too light. It was practically the same color as her skin.

She grew weary of trying on gowns and realized she was happy she wasn't some ritzy guy's wife who had to worry about perfect appearance all the time. Dress shopping was the most exhausting thing she'd done all week.

Avery handed her another dress. It was a smoky blue color, almost the same shade as Megan's eyes. Her heart sped up, and she hoped this dress looked good on her.

Avery winked. "This may be the one."

She bit her bottom lip and smiled. After shutting the door behind her, she slipped on the gown. It had a Grecian look with cutaway shoulders and deep slits in the front and the back. The jersey style gathering made the slits modest yet sensual. A thick band of sequins the same color of blue fit perfectly around her waist. From there the gown flowed like a waterfall all the way to her toes. It was perfect.

She stepped out of the dressing room, and Avery placed her hand on her chest. "Girl, we found it." She looked at Megan. "Don't you think?"

Megan nodded.

Avery snapped her fingers. "And I know just the perfect shoes."

Megan shared her size, and then Avery raced out of the fitting area. She admired the dress. Lifted her hair off her shoulders. She'd wear her hair up. A deep sigh sounded from the back of her throat. She felt like a princess.

Avery arrived with the shoes, and just as she'd said, the silver sequined heels added just the right amount of pop to her feet. Avery shooed her back into the dressing room. "Let's get you out of it before anything happens. You're going to knock your man off his feet."

Megan didn't respond. She could've told Avery it was a business date, that her boss didn't care for her in *that* way. That she didn't want him to. But she felt so beautiful. Though she'd fought against it for years, in this dress, she wanted to impress the man she loved. To see his expression swell with pride that she belonged to him.

She had to get out of the dress and fast. Fanciful, romantic notions were not in her future. As soon as she finished her last weeks at the firm, she would start school in the fall as a music teacher, and she'd be away from Justin. Well, except for church functions and Bible study. But she could try to keep her distance in those settings.

Once dressed in her own clothes, Megan followed Avery to the counter to check out. Avery motioned to a woman in the back then looked back at Megan. "It was a lot of fun dressing you up. I hope you enjoy your date."

"Thank you so much, Avery. You were a huge help."

Megan looked back at the counter and sucked in her breath. The stunning redhead stood behind the register. Justin's old client. What was her name? Sophia. While she rang up the purchase, Megan fumbled through her purse to find the money Justin had given her.

Maybe she won't recognize me. Won't remember me.

"I know who you are." Sophia pointed at her. "You're Justin Frasure's secretary, right?"

Megan shifted her weight from one foot to the other. Shouldn't the woman just ring her up and let her get out of there? Knowing she couldn't be rude, Megan nodded.

Sophia placed the gown in a garment bag and zipped it up. "Awfully fancy dress. It's beautiful. One of our nicest."

Megan nodded again and handed her the cash.

"Going somewhere with Justin?"

Megan bit her bottom lip. Okay, the woman was way out of line. That was none of her business. If her manager walked up on this transaction, Sophia would be reprimanded. She looked at the redhead's name badge, which listed her as a manager. Megan inwardly groaned. *That's just great.*

Lifting her chin, she looked into Sophia's eyes. "As a matter of fact, we are going to a charity ball. It's a business engagement."

Sophia studied her. Megan reached for her purchase. Sophia handed her the garment bag and shoes. A look of regret washed across her face. "I hope he doesn't have to apologize to you later."

The words punched her in the gut. Without a response, Megan walked out of the store. The look of pity on Sophia's face riled her, but it also lifted the guard around her heart that Megan had worked so hard to build. Justin might be the most delicious-looking man ever, but he was only a business date. That was all.

Chapter 20

J ustin wiped the sweat from his forehead with a rag then threw it to the floor beside his water bottle. He shifted on the weight bench to face Kirk. "What are you talking about?"

Kirk opened his palms. "Megan. I'm talking about Megan. For some ridiculous reason, Marianna thinks Megan has a secret crush on you or something. She's determined to set her up with this other guy. Colt somebody or other."

Justin tossed the information around in his mind. He'd given into his feelings for Megan. God had given him the strength to be patient. He hadn't asked Megan on an official date, even though he thought that's what he was doing for the charity ball, and she'd taken his offer a different way. But if Marianna thought Megan had a crush, then maybe he had a chance.

He didn't deserve someone like Megan. He knew that. But she never left his mind. And though he wanted to know her in every way, he had changed. He respected her. He wanted to know her as a person, wanted her to know he cared for every facet of her.

But this Colt guy? Justin looked at his friend. "Who's this Colt person?"

"Megan's giving his niece piano lessons. At the funeral, it was pretty obvious the guy had feelings for Megan. He held her hand while she cried, and. . ."

Justin swallowed back the fury that welled inside him. The man held Megan's hand. *His* Megan's hand. He'd gone to the funeral? Megan never mentioned this guy to him. Was Colt the reason she didn't want him to go with her? Not that they spent time discussing the details of each other's personal lives, but still, if this Colt guy was special to her, wouldn't he have some inkling of a clue? He did see her every day at work and a lot of days at church.

Kirk continued, "I'm really not so sure Megan's interested in the guy. She's always been kinda antiboyfriend."

Justin exhaled a slow breath. Kirk didn't think she liked him. That gave Justin hope. It also meant he was going to have to step up his game if there was another guy vying for the woman he planned to marry.

Kirk took a swig from a water bottle then put it back on the floor. "I told Marianna to just leave Megan alone, that there was no way there was any kind of thing going on between the two of you."

Justin nodded. He looked up at the clock on the wall above the floor-length mirrors. "I've gotta get out of here. That charity ball's tonight." He pulled at the front of his drenched shirt. "And I might just need a shower."

"I forgot about that. Who're you taking?"

Justin cleared his throat and averted his gaze. "Megan."

"What?" Kirk smacked his hand against his thigh. "What do

you mean you're taking Megan?"

He studied the gym floor as he shrugged. "Just a business date."

"I know you better than that. I can tell. . ."

Brandy walked up to the weight bench. "Hey, guys." She waved her hand then traced her fingers through her long, dark ponytail. "How's it going, Justin?"

"Fine." Justin grabbed his water bottle and towel and glanced at his friend. "I've got to go, Kirk."

After grabbing his wallet and keys out of a cubby, he pushed his way out the front door and popped the button on his keychain to unlock the car. Kirk barreled through the door and stood beside him. "I won't let you hurt Marianna's sister."

Pain shot through his heart. His friend had led him to the Lord and watched him grow in his faith, but he still feared he'd hurt Megan. He peered at his friend, his hands itching to form into fists to defend himself as he'd been known to do when they were teens. "I'm not the same man."

"I hope not."

Justin jumped into his car and turned the ignition. "I suppose this means you don't really believe all you've told me about how a man can change once he's found God. If I can't change, then why have I been trying?" He pointed to his chest. "Have you not watched my life these last several months?" He clenched his jaw and spit through gritted teeth. "You of all people should know God's changed me."

A look of regret flashed across Kirk's expression, but Justin jerked the car into reverse and skidded out of the parking lot before his friend had a chance to apologize. He thought Kirk, of all people, would accept him as a new creation.

He didn't deserve Megan. He knew that. His fist pounded the top of the steering wheel. It was selfish of him to even ask her to love him. "God, I just won't do it. I'll keep my feelings for her to myself. No one but You and I know about them."

He pulled into his driveway then headed into the house. "This will be a business date tonight. Nothing more."

Trying not to think about Megan or Kirk or some guy named Colt, he raced through his shower and shave. He put on his tuxedo then headed toward the front door. Out of the corner of his eye, he spied the flowers he'd bought for her. Maybe he shouldn't give them to her. He didn't want her to think he meant them to be a personal gesture. Even though he did.

With a huff, he grabbed the flowers off the table. She had every right to a bouquet of beautiful roses. She had agreed to go with him this evening. He would treat her as a date. A business date.

He made his way to the car then turned up the contemporary Christian music on his radio. He didn't want to think. He needed God's Word through music to penetrate his mind. Anything to keep his mind off Megan.

He pulled into her driveway and sent up a quick prayer of help to feel nothing when he saw her. Maybe she'd have a piece of food stuck in her teeth. Something to keep him from finding her the most adorable woman he'd ever known.

Shaking his head to clear his mind, he walked to the front door and pushed the doorbell. Marianna opened it. Her scowl was evidence enough of her opinion of the dinner date. She didn't speak to him but twisted her head and yelled, "He's here. Remember Mom's coming in the morning to work on the wedding."

She turned back to him, her eyes squinted in disapproval. Her actions were so blatant Justin found them funny. He smiled at her with a grin that usually sent women to swooning. "How are you doing, Marianna? I spent the afternoon with your fiancé."

She barely lifted her head in acknowledgment. He heard footsteps down the hall and looked to see Megan standing several feet behind her. His jaw dropped. His sweet, cute secretary had transformed into a princess.

Her eyes shone to nearly match the color of the long blue dress. Her hair was swept up with rhinestones dotting the sides and top. Wisps fell and kissed her cheeks and neck. Like he wanted to do.

Justin swallowed and willed himself to think pure thoughts. He needed to keep his mind away from his feelings for her. He feared if she took one step closer, he would grab her in his arms and kiss her with the intensity he'd spent many a day wishing he could exhibit.

She smiled, and Justin forced himself to close his mouth. Remembering his manners, he extended the flowers toward her. "Megan, these are for you."

Megan bit her bottom lip, and her face and neck brightened. That was the Megan he was used to, the one he'd fallen in love with. *God, it's just not right that she looks like this all dolled up. How am I supposed to keep my feelings to myself?*

Her hand brushed his when she took the flowers from him. He winced. *God, help me keep my hands to myself, too.*

"They're beautiful, Justin. Thank you." She handed them to her sister. "Will you put them in a vase for me?"

Marianna curled her lip, but she took the roses and headed into the kitchen.

Megan looked back at him and smiled. "Are you ready?"

No food in her teeth as he'd hoped. No lipstick on her pearly whites either. He nodded and extended his arm. She touched the inside of his elbow, and Justin felt his insides shake. He'd never experienced this. He wanted Megan, but in every way. He wanted to be near her, to talk with her, laugh with her. And right now, he couldn't deny he wanted to wrap her in his arms and kiss her with every ounce of energy he could muster.

He didn't know how he was going to make it through this dinner. Pray. He'd have to have constant contact with God to make it through. *You hear that, Lord? You're on double time tonight.*

They walked to the car, and he opened the door. Once she slid inside, he closed it and walked to the other side and got in. Megan arranged her dress to avoid as many creases as possible. "So, do you like it?"

Justin gripped the steering wheel. He hadn't even told her how gorgeous she looked. He'd been so dumbfounded he'd forgotten the most important thing a woman wanted to hear. "It's amazing. You are beautiful, Megan."

She didn't look at him. She focused her attention out the windshield. "Sophia sold it to me."

Justin cringed. He knew exactly who she meant. He hoped the woman didn't ask about him. More importantly, he hoped she hadn't said too many entirely true but ugly things about him either. Judging by the way Megan stared at the windshield, he assumed Sophia said plenty. "Well, she has terrific taste. You're gorgeous."

Megan didn't respond, and Justin realized Sophia may have been a blessing in disguise. If Megan spent the evening cold and collected, he wouldn't fall all over himself trying not to reveal his feelings for her. He couldn't run from the past anyway. There would always be a Sophia somewhere. And Megan shouldn't have to deal with that.

He drove into the garage and parked his car. Megan stepped out before he had time to walk to her side to open the door. He started to grab her hand to escort her inside when she stepped in front of him.

She looked up at him. She'd put some kind of smoky gray color on her eyelids that made the blue in her eyes the most striking color he'd ever seen. Like the darkening of the sky just before a storm.

She took a step toward him and touched his biceps with both hands. His heart pounded in his chest, and his stomach churned. Her gaze moved to his lips, and he thought he might pass out right there in the parking lot. If she kissed him again. . .right there in the parking lot. . .wearing that amazing dress. . .strands of blond hair kissing her shoulders.

He couldn't take it. He wrapped his arms around her waist and pulled her closer. Blocking the protests from his mind, he lowered his lips to hers. She answered his kiss with one of her own, and Justin sucked in his breath, begging God for restraint.

Releasing her mouth, he grabbed her arms and moved her away from him. "Megan, I. . ."

She studied him, waiting for what he would say, what he would do. She wasn't ready for a proclamation of love. He could tell by her expression she needed confirmation his intentions were good.

And they were good. And bad. But they were mostly good. And completely in right standing with God. He had to prove it to her. He didn't deserve her, but he couldn't let her go. He'd move to Africa, if he needed, to get away from his past. But he couldn't give her up. He loved her.

But first he'd have to prove it.

He grabbed her hand in his. "Megan, I'm so glad you came with me."

She seemed confused, but she allowed him to lead her. They walked into the dining hall. As usual, he had the most beautiful date in the room. But this girl was different. She wasn't for the night. She was for life.

Chapter 21

I have held many things in my hands, and I have lost them all;
but whatever I have placed in God's hands, that I still possess.

MARTIN LUTHER

Megan adjusted the fuzzy, pink bride-to-be crown on top of Marianna's head. Megan, Marianna, Amber, and Julie walked into the restaurant. She grinned as several people looked their way. She knew they were a sight with their hot pink T-shirts sporting their positions in the wedding in metallic silver lettering. Megan had designed them herself. They were more ostentatious than anything she'd ever want, but she knew her sister would flip over them.

Amber lifted four fingers to the hostess. "Table for four."

The gray-haired woman winked at Marianna as she grabbed four menus from behind the table. "Looks like someone's getting married."

"That would be me." Marianna touched the silver sash at her chest and laughed.

"When's the big day?" asked the waitress.

"Week from tomorrow," Marianna answered.

Megan shook her head. She still couldn't believe her sister would become a married woman in only eight days. They'd already moved several of her belongings from the apartment, which had sent Megan into a tailspin of emotions. She was happy for her sister, but they'd never lived apart. The thought of it left an ache in her spirit. It would leave a hole in her bank account as well—even if she would make more as a teacher than she had as a secretary at the law firm.

They followed the hostess to the booth, and Megan slid in beside Marianna. The waitress arrived, offering a round of free drinks on the house. They grinned at each other, and Amber asked for four virgin strawberry daiquiris.

Julie tapped the tabletop as she looked at Marianna. "Everything ready for next Saturday?"

Marianna glanced at Megan and inhaled a deep breath. "I think so. Mom's coming in to stay with us this week to help with final preparations."

Megan's stomach tightened. She wasn't looking forward to spending the whole week with their mother. They hadn't quarreled, but the tension was still present between them.

"What about you"—Amber nodded at Megan—"you ready for your sister to move out?"

Marianna looked at her, and Megan knew this was a concern weighing down her sister's heart. The separation would be hard on her twin as well, even though Marianna would have Kirk to keep her company. Megan would have—well, nothing. Maybe she should look into getting a pet. She inwardly shook her head. Nah. Wouldn't have time for one.

"Well, yeah!" Megan wrapped her arm around his sister's shoulder. "I'll get a warm shower for the first time in my life."

Marianna giggled as she shrugged. "If you'd wake up earlier, then maybe. . ."

Megan rolled her eyes, and the group laughed. They all knew Marianna was the last to rise on any overnight outing they'd ever attended.

"Here you go, ladies." The waitress arrived with their beverages, and they ordered nearly every appetizer on the menu.

Marianna peered at them. "You do know we have to fit in our dresses?"

"Tonight is celebration night." Julie swatted the air. "We just won't eat this week."

Megan looked at her sister. Marianna had been fit to be tied for weeks. She probably wouldn't hold down a bite of food after tonight. Kirk had proven his worth in Megan's eyes though. He'd been patient and understanding, even when Marianna melted into a mess of tears over the napkins being a shade lighter than she'd expected. Though it would be hard, Megan knew she could release her sister to Kirk's able and loving care.

"So, when does school start, Megan?" asked Julie.

"Three weeks. I begin new teacher orientation the Tuesday after Marianna's wedding."

She could hardly believe how fast the summer had gone. Only one more week at Frasure, Frasure, and Combs. The training of the new secretary was going well, and she was secretly thrilled that the new hire was an older, married woman with grown kids and grandchildren.

Her mind ventured to the charity ball two weeks earlier. She'd had the most amazing time with Justin. Dancing. Eating. Socializing. He'd kept her in the crook of his arm the entire night. She'd felt more like his girlfriend than his employee.

And the kiss in the parking lot—their second kiss. This one had been his doing. Her cheeks warmed as she thought of how she'd done nothing to stop the advance. She'd wanted to kiss him more, but he'd stopped it. He'd been the one to grab her hand, lead her into the charity ball, and then treat her like a cherished lady the rest of the evening.

That was how she felt with him. Cherished. It seemed impossible given his past. But the Justin Frasure she knew loved the Lord and lived his life trying to follow Him. She'd promised to spend her life alone, and in her mind she knew it was the safest route. But the man who'd spent much of his life chasing women occupied her thoughts at every moment of the day.

"Are you excited?"

Megan blinked at Amber's question. What had they been talking about? Oh yeah, school.

Megan nodded. "Very excited. I've already picked out several pieces I hope to sing with the different age groups."

Marianna touched Megan's arm. "My sister will be the best music teacher Fayette County has ever seen."

The appetizers arrived, and they each scooped a variety onto their plates.

"I can't wait to see the movie," said Amber.

"Then fro-yo?" piped in Julie.

Marianna groaned at the mention of frozen yogurt as she shoved her third buffalo wing into her mouth. "We're never gonna fit into our dresses."

Megan laughed. "Sure we will."

The waitress returned, and they ordered the steak dinner the restaurant was known for. Megan already felt busted, but she was enjoying her sister's bachelorette party. Dinner, movie, and dessert were probably a bit tame for today's standards, but it fit them perfectly. And she'd been waiting all week to see the romantic comedy Marianna picked.

"What are you guys doing here?"

Megan turned toward the direction Marianna was speaking. A knot formed in her throat when she saw Kirk, Justin, and Kirk's two groomsmen walking toward them inside the movie theater.

Megan took in their royal blue shirts with black lettering that named Kirk as GROOM-TO-BE, Justin as BEST MAN, and each of the others as GROOMSMAN. She couldn't stop the smile when she noted Justin's look of utter repulsion as he looked down at his shirt then around the room to see if anyone was looking at them. Everyone was.

"Raiding your bachelorette party."

Kirk grabbed Marianna in a big hug and kissed her lips. Megan bit her bottom lip as she sneaked a quick look at Justin. What she wouldn't give to feel his lips against hers like that. Again.

She brushed the thought away and tried to remind herself of her determination to stay single for the rest of her life. Kirk grabbed Marianna's hand in his then lifted it to his lips for a quick kiss. Ugh. The man made her sick. He also made her want that. What a ridiculous combination.

"Man, this ain't cool. The groom and his cronies are not supposed to hang out with us. How are we supposed to flirt with other guys?" Amber nudged one of the groomsmen in the arm. Adam and Amber flirted quite a bit, and Megan wondered if a love match would develop after the wedding.

Adam locked his arm around hers. "Flirt with other guys all you want. You gotta get me out of this lobby. This shirt is ridiculous. I'm losing cool points."

"No kidding," Wayne responded. He fell into step beside Julie.

Megan looked up at Justin. They were the only ones left in the lobby. Taking in the shirt once again, she cupped her hand over her mouth and chuckled.

He spread his arms and grinned. "What?"

"I can't believe you're wearing that."

He turned his body left and then right. "You don't think it compliments my physique?"

Oh, that was so not a fair question. What didn't compliment Justin's physique? The man was a boulder with bumps in all the right places. She knew that for a fact after touching his biceps and feeling their flex the night of the charity ball.

She averted her gaze. "It compliments you just fine."

He cupped her chin, forcing her to look back up at him. His eyes smoldered with a combination of mirth and something else. The frustrating thing was she recognized the something else from the night at the charity ball. He wanted to kiss her. And though that sounded every bit as delicious as a supersized soft drink and a bag of buttered movie popcorn, it was not going to happen. Now was not the time or place.

He grinned, and his eyes gleamed with a tease. The man was insufferable. She knew he could read her thoughts. He sobered and shook his head. "I can't believe they talked me into doing this."

"Gotta admit. I'm a little surprised to see you here."

"It was Kirk's idea." He pointed to her pink top. "I believe you showed those to him, and that's where he got the idea."

Megan twirled from side to side. "You have to admit ours are much cuter."

"Definitely couldn't argue with that."

The gleam returned to his eyes, and Megan found herself shifting her feet. She pointed toward the theaters. "We'd better get in there. Hopefully they saved us a couple of seats."

Justin nodded. Her heart raced when he touched the small of her back to guide her forward. They reached the ticket taker, and she fumbled through her purse trying to find the movie ticket. Her heart pounded against her chest, and her cheeks warmed. She hated that Justin had such an impact on her. He was just a man, for heaven's sake. True, he was gorgeous and a good kisser and a newly committed Christian. Still, the guy didn't have *everything* going for him. Of course, in her addled state, she couldn't think of anything he lacked.

Justin tapped her shoulder, and she halted her rummage through the bag. He pointed to her backside. "The ticket's sticking out of your back pocket."

Heat rushed to her face as she pulled the ticket from the back of her pants. Thankfully she was wearing her favorite jeans, the ones that looked the best on her backside. *Megan McKinney, stop thinking like that.* The thought of Justin noticing her—she shook her head. She needed to get control of her mind.

The teenage guy handed her the stub, and she moved a few steps in front of Justin. Taking several deep breaths, she regained control of herself. Justin moved beside her, and she looked up at him and flashed a mischievous grin.

"Looking forward to the movie?"

He groaned as they walked toward the theater. "About as much as I'd look forward to a root canal."

Megan laughed. She figured the romantic comedy would not be one of Justin's top movie picks. He grabbed her arm and pointed to one of the theaters showing an action film. "We could sneak into this one. No one would ever have to know."

Megan shook her head. "No way. I've been looking forward to this movie all week."

Justin wrinkled his nose, but she could still see the laughter and teasing in his eyes. "Guess I'll have to suffer through."

They walked into the theater, and Megan sat beside Marianna. Her sister scowled at Justin and then at her. Megan didn't understand Marianna. Her sister needed to be encouraging to Justin. He was a new Christian. She knew Marianna didn't want them to date, but she and Justin weren't dating. Nothing close to it.

Marianna placed her hand on Megan's arm. "I forgot to tell you Colt called and asked me to remind you not to forget the sheet music for Hadley on Tuesday."

Megan's forehead wrinkled in question. "What?"

Colt would have no reason to call and say such a thing. Megan had never forgotten sheet music for Hadley's piano lessons.

Megan watched as Kirk grabbed Marianna and pulled her closer to him. He whispered something in her ear. Something like "Stop it, that's not nice." Megan scrunched her nose. What was that about?

She turned toward Justin and realized he'd stiffened beside her. He stared straight ahead at the commercials on the movie screen. His lips were pursed into a straight, angry line.

"You can't control who she likes. He has good intentions, and he's a good man now."

Megan raised her eyebrows in surprise. Kirk's whisper must have been louder than he'd intended. She knew Marianna didn't like Justin, that she feared Justin would try to hit on her like he had the other women in his past. But she didn't know Marianna thought Justin liked her.

Sure, he was attracted to her, and they'd shared a couple kisses. One was just a moment of crazy insanity, that she still didn't know what had come over her. The other was simply about the moment getting the best of him. They were all dressed up and headed to the charity ball. He'd had a moment of weakness. He'd been a perfect gentleman the rest of the evening. Never once did he make her feel uncomfortable. He'd actually made her feel special being on his arm. But that didn't mean he had feelings for her.

She sneaked another peek at Justin. He sat stiff and rigid. Was that the expression of a man who was jealous? Was he jealous of Colt?

A thread of pleasure weaved through her at the idea that Justin wouldn't want another man to be interested in her. Which Colt definitely wasn't. He was a friend. Nothing more. But Justin? Could she honestly say he was just a friend?

Something in her liked that he might be a bit jealous. The lights dimmed, and the movie started as Megan continued to war within herself about the possibility of Justin having real affection for her. Did she want him to have feelings for her?

She settled back in the chair, determined not to think about it, and enjoy the movie she'd been looking forward to watching. A strong hand reached over and grabbed hers. She sucked in her breath as Justin opened her hand and weeded his fingers through hers.

She looked at him and realized he studied her. His gaze seemed to ask if his touch was wanted. She ignored the warning signals flashing in her mind and gave in to her racing heart. With a blink of affirmation, she squeezed his hand and turned her attention back to the screen.

She felt like a middle schooler on her first date to the movies with her boyfriend. Just because he held her hand in the movie theater didn't mean he really liked her. Take Colt for example. When he held her hand at the funeral, she didn't feel anything. He was just her friend. It was the same with Justin. Even if it didn't feel like it.

Chapter 22

All truths are easy to understand once they
are discovered; the point is to discover them.

GALILEO GALILEI

The problem is she thinks I'm just a friend. Colt grabbed the tea bags out of the pantry and smacked them down on the countertop. He didn't have to search far into Justin's life to learn the man was a womanizer. He'd played more women than Colt had competed in rodeos. Megan deserved better. She needed someone who was constant and faithful, someone she could trust and who would love her every day of his life. *Someone like me.*

The phone rang, and Colt picked up the receiver. "Hello."

"Hi, Colt."

Colt exhaled a long breath at the sound of Tina's voice on the line. He looked at the clock. Time had gotten away from him, but she was right on with the time they'd arranged. Part of him still worried he'd agreed to let Hadley talk on the phone with her birth mother twice a week. And he'd only agreed to the phone visits after she'd promised to start and stay in rehab. Tina had been true to her promise. He'd checked up on her to make sure.

"How are you doing, Tina?"

"I'm doing pretty good." Her voice sounded happier than he'd ever heard it. Tina had been nice enough, if not overtly shy, when she first started dating his brother, but Colt had never gotten the chance to really get to know her. "I'm enjoying beauty school, and I've gotten two new houses to clean."

Colt smiled into the phone. He really was glad Tina was cleaning up her life. Though he didn't tell Hadley, he'd agreed to pay for Tina to go to beautician school on the condition she kept her grades up and stayed sober. It was her responsibility to find part-time employment. She'd surprised him when she'd started cleaning houses, but she must do a fairly good job, because she was cleaning four houses a week. He'd been checking up with the owners as well.

"That's terrific, Tina. How many days?"

"Thirty-one. I'm still taking one day at a time."

He was proud of Hadley's mother. Everything in him wished it hadn't taken his brother's death for her to realize her need to straighten out her life. And to get to know her daughter. He still worried if he'd made the right decision, but seeing Hadley's expression each time she talked with her mother was proof enough the girl needed to know the woman, if only a little bit.

"I've been watching the clock. Tuesdays and Sundays are the best days of the week."

"Hadley enjoys talking to you also." Colt started to pull the phone away.

"I've started going to church, Colt."

He pulled the receiver back to his ear. "Tina, that is wonderful. That's the best news I've heard."

"Please pray for me." He heard her voice catch, and Colt's heart tightened. The little time he'd spent with Tina on the phone, he'd come to realize he liked her as a person, and he wanted her to come to know Christ.

"I already do."

"Is that Mom?" Hadley raced into the kitchen and swiped the phone from his hand before he had a chance to respond. "Hey Mom."

It surprised Colt that Hadley had been so quick to call Tina "Mom" after having no relationship with her the first twelve years of her life. He listened as Hadley talked about Megan coming over in a bit for piano lessons.

Colt filled a pan full of water and placed it on the burner. He was looking forward to Megan's visit. But he didn't have a clue about how to get her to see he wanted more than friendship from her. Each time he tried to hint at a date, she mentioned some kind of wedding obligation she had with Marianna or the charity ball with Justin.

His cheeks burned at the memory. He'd wanted to insist she tell her boss to take a hike, but he'd bit his tongue. *If I could get her to see how much I like her, then it would be my place.*

He growled to himself. He had no experience with women. Every time he considered simply coming out and being honest with Megan, his hands would clam up, his mouth would go dry, and he'd find himself hiding out in the living room away from her and Hadley.

Tonight he'd talk to her. He and Hadley had made homemade blueberry ice cream. After Hadley's lessons, he planned to ask Megan to go for a walk with him around the property. Her sister's wedding was in a week. After that, she'd be available to go on dates. He hoped she'd agree to go to the upcoming rodeo with him and Hadley. And not just as a friend.

"Uncle Colt! Mom wants to talk with you."

Hadley's voice sounded from the living room. He walked to her and took the phone. "Hi again, Tina."

No one responded, and he looked at the screen to see if Hadley had accidentally hung up. It appeared to still be connected. "Hello?"

"Colt." Tina sounded nervous. "I have something I'd like to ask you."

"Okay."

"Please don't answer today. Just say you'll pray about it. Please."

Colt's gut twisted. He didn't like the sound of her voice. He had a feeling he knew what she was going to ask, and if he was right, the answer was no.

She continued, "I'd like to see Hadley. Maybe next Saturday?"

"We're busy. Going to a friend's wedding."

"What about before or after? Please, Colt."

"No. She's not ready."

"She's not, or you're not?"

Her response pierced him in the heart. Of course he wasn't ready. He didn't want to see the woman who'd run off with his brother, watched him die, and now wanted to slide her way back into his and Hadley's lives. "The answer is no."

"Please just agree to pray about it."

"Fine. I'll pray about it." The water boiled, and Colt turned off the burner. "Gotta go."

Before she could respond, he hung up. There was no way he or Hadley would be seeing her mother on Saturday.

Colt listened as Hadley played a song he didn't recognize on the piano. Megan said it was some popular song played on one of the children's networks on television. He didn't know the tune, but he could tell Hadley did a good job playing it.

The kid was a natural with the piano. It didn't surprise Colt. His brother had been a whiz on the guitar. Apparently Tina had a good voice. It was how she and his brother met. Connor had been in a high school band, and the drummer invited Tina to sing for them. All too soon, the band became a thing of the past, and Tina and Connor got hooked on drugs.

"That was amazing. I can't believe how well you're doing." Megan's voice floated through the air. "You'll be teaching me before long."

Colt took the break as his cue. He grabbed two glasses of sweet tea off the counter and walked into the music room. "Who needs a drink?"

Megan smiled as she took a glass. Her blue eyes glistened in perfect contrast to the light brown shirt she wore. He could tell she'd been trying to get a little bit of sun before the wedding. Her skin was still fair, but just a hint of a tan touched her nose and cheeks. She shouldn't worry about darker skin. Her ivory color was gorgeous.

"Thanks, Colt. You make the best sweet tea."

Colt opened his mouth to ask if she'd take a walk with him once the lessons were over, but Hadley stopped him. "Megan said she'd help me pick out a dress for the wedding when we're done." She lifted the back of her hair. "And maybe figure out what to do with my mop."

Megan touched Hadley's hair. "You have one of the most beautiful mops of hair I've ever seen."

Colt agreed. Hadley's long brown hair was beautiful. It seemed to have grown thicker over the last few months. He remembered Tina's hair had been like that when she and Connor first started dating. The last time he'd seen her, it was short and thin. Abuse had taken its toll.

Colt wasn't ready to admit defeat. He wanted the opportunity to spend time with Megan. "Remember, Hadley. We made some blueberry ice cream to share with Megan."

Megan raised her eyebrows. "Seriously? That sounds absolutely delicious." She patted Hadley's leg. "Get to practicing, young lady. I want some of that ice cream."

Hadley giggled as she placed her fingers on the keys and started on a new tune. Her practice would be done in less than ten minutes, so Colt walked back into the kitchen and took down three bowls. He filled them with ice cream. "Girls, it's ready when you are."

Hadley stopped playing, and she and Megan filtered into the kitchen. He handed them each a bowl, and they walked to the back porch to eat on the deck.

Colt watched as Megan drank in the expanse of his backyard. He loved that his land rolled out for acres. God's creation rejuvenated him, and he knew Megan felt the same way. She was a perfect match for him. Even in her choice of where to live.

With her spoon, Megan pointed to the bowl. "This is really good."

"You want some more?"

She shook her head. "Oh no. Marianna, the girls, and I had such a big bash for her bachelorette party. We ate just about everything we could get our hands on." She laughed, and Colt smiled at the sound of it. "Marianna is scared to death we all won't fit in our dresses."

"You'll look terrific in your dress."

Megan snorted. "Wait till you see it." She opened her arms. "It's yellow! Yellow!" She pointed to her skin. "This is not a skin tone that goes well with yellow." She smacked her leg. "Pale yellow at that."

Colt laughed at her dramatics. Megan was easy to be around. She made him smile, and Hadley loved her. She was already a good friend, but he wanted more.

Hadley dropped her spoon in the bowl with a clang and looked at Megan. "You ready to pick out my dress?"

Colt wasn't ready to lose her to his niece once again. "Why don't you go ride Fairybelle for a while? You know our rodeo is a couple weeks away."

Megan perked up. "Can I take a ride on Daisy?"

Colt's heart sunk. This day was not going at all as he expected. He'd wanted to have some alone time with Megan.

"Well of course." Hadley responded in her don't-be-silly tone.

Megan looked at Colt for affirmation, her eyebrows raised, and she lowered her lip in a pout. Colt grinned. How could he resist?

He motioned toward the barn, and Hadley grabbed Megan's hand and guided her away from the house. Colt watched them go. Part of him wanted to follow after them. The other part of him didn't feel like he'd been invited.

He pushed that thought away. They wouldn't care if he tagged along. They were his horses and his barn after all.

He got up and headed toward the barn, shaking off his grumpy feelings. Neither Hadley nor Megan knew of his plans to spend time alone with Megan. He was glad the two of them enjoyed spending time together. It was exactly what he wanted in his wife. Someone who would love Hadley as much as he did.

He'd just get on his horse and take a ride alongside them. He reached the barn and opened the door. To his surprise, Hadley and Megan were already mounted.

"Betcha I'll beat you to the old oak tree," Hadley hollered.

Megan yelled after her. "Of course you'll beat me. I'm riding Daisy." Daisy whinnied, and Megan patted her neck. "I didn't mean that as an insult, girl."

Colt started toward her. Maybe he'd just ride along beside Megan a little ways behind Hadley. They'd get the chance to talk on horseback. Before Colt could say anything, Megan waved as she kicked Daisy's haunches. "See ya later, Colt."

His easygoing filly took off like she was racing for the world's most luscious apple. It seemed every female on the farm didn't want him to have any alone time with Megan. If he didn't know better, he'd think Megan was avoiding him altogether.

Chapter 23

Anger is an acid that can do more harm to the vessel
in which it is stored than to anything on which it is poured.
MARK TWAIN

Megan tied the 137th thick red bow on the back of the white satin-covered fold up chair. Only sixty-three left to go. Not only was her back stiff, but she felt as if her fingers would fall off. Putting fancy silver napkin rings around two hundred napkins earlier that morning hadn't helped.

Marianna tapped her shoulder. "Megan, the bows look great, but be sure you tie them the same size." She pointed to a table in the back. "Those look a little smaller than the rest."

Megan bit the inside of her lip. It took every ounce of strength not to let her sister have it. She'd stayed up until the wee hours of the night tying extra ribbons to the table centerpieces, had gotten up before the rooster to rush over to the reception venue to start decorating, and had been working ever since. She looked at her watch. It was after three, and she still hadn't eaten lunch.

Marianna continued, "You'll be able to finish these in an hour, right? We have a nail appointment to get to."

Megan exhaled a slow breath. It wasn't possible. She'd worked all morning and hadn't uttered a single complaint, but it simply wasn't possible to wrap all those chairs in only an hour. She didn't want her sister to go Bridezilla on her, but she had to be honest. "Marianna, I just don't think—"

"I'll help you finish." Her mom grabbed several lengths of red ribbon. "Don't worry, Marianna. The chairs will be ready in time to head over to the nail appointment."

Marianna's features pinched into a stressed-to-the-max expression. "But what about the candy bar? Do you have the dishes ready to be filled tomorrow? And the punch bowls? And what about the silverware?"

Megan's mother placed both hands on Marianna's shoulders. She pressed a kiss to her cheek. "It's all ready. Stop stressing."

Megan watched as her sister closed her eyes and blew out a long breath. She opened them again. "I'm trying to stay calm."

Their mom's voice was tender. "You're doing great."

Marianna nodded and headed off to make sure the kitchen area was stocked with the menu items for tomorrow.

Megan smiled at her mother. "Thanks."

"No problem."

Her mother didn't say anything else, simply got busy wrapping bows around the backs of chairs. Since her stepfather's death, Megan had many moments when she wished she and her mom could make amends. She'd even played in her mind with different scenarios of how to broach the subject. Her dad's death had proven life was too short to stay bitter and angry with one another.

But what should she say? How could Megan approach her mom

with the hurt she felt yet still be a witness to her? Christians were supposed to forgive, seven times seventy, as Jesus said. Megan wanted to be a witness, to live, breathe, and walk a life like Christ's. But she needed to be honest with her mother as well. Their relationship would always be false if she didn't express her true feelings.

Maybe she should stop rehearsing what to say in her mind and simply speak from the heart. Allow the Holy Spirit to guide her words. "Mom. . ."

Her mother placed the ribbon she held on the table. "I'll be right back, Megan. Marianna's friends have arrived with the cake."

Megan looked toward the door. Amy and Timmy walked in carrying the wedding cake. Even from a distance, Megan could see that the three-tiered, square, white cake was beautiful. Huge white sugar roses with red tips dotted the first and third tiers. Red ribbon was wrapped around the bottom of each tier.

They disappeared into the kitchen area, and Megan knew they were putting the cake in the refrigerator they'd cleared out to keep the confection fresh. She was thankful Justin had left the decorating party to run a few errands for Marianna. Now that Megan thought of it, maybe her sister sent him off on purpose to avoid any confrontation between him and Timmy.

Megan hadn't seen the couple since the first day Justin visited church. They hadn't been back. Marianna told her they'd been visiting her and Kirk's church. It bothered her they'd stopped going to church, and yet she understood how awkward the situation was. Amy had been a friend to Megan, not as close as she was to Marianna, but it still hurt that she didn't see Amy at church anymore.

Megan tied another red bow on the back of the chair. She tried not to think of Amy or Sophia or any of the other women who'd been part of Justin's past. She tried not to think of Justin, even though her mind seemed bent on conjuring him up every second of the day.

The irony was the more she thought of Justin, the more time she spent with him, the less she remembered her high school boyfriend. The night at the charity ball, when Justin kissed her then released her and guided her into the dinner, she'd seen the yearning in his eyes. He'd wanted to kiss her more but not overwhelm her. His actions were in direct opposition from Clint's all those years ago. They made her want or at least consider the desire for more than a life of singleness. Maybe she could fall in love. Maybe she could put the past behind her.

"Megan."

She jumped and placed her hand on her chest as she turned to the male voice behind her. "Timmy, you scared the life out of me."

"Sorry 'bout that."

Megan could tell his body was tense, as if he were ready to pummel anyone who went against him. Megan looked at Amy. She'd aged since Megan last saw her. Not in hair color or physical wrinkles or blemishes—she just seemed to carry the weight of something, possibly her marriage, in her eyes.

Megan forced a smile as she hugged Timmy and then Amy. "It's been awhile since I've seen you two."

"Well, we definitely can't go back to church with that man there." Fury raged in Timmy's voice.

Amy shifted her weight from one foot to the other as she stared at the ground.

Megan felt an urge to defend Justin. Timmy's anger, though Megan understood it, wasn't fair. He and Amy divorced because of his indiscretions. Justin and Amy—the very thought of their relationship made Megan's stomach turn—still, their evening together wasn't until after the divorce was final. Sure, Megan understood not wanting to be around your spouse's past mistakes, but to be so angry and ugly about it when you'd made the same choices didn't make any sense.

Timmy's words slipped through gritted teeth. "You know he forced her."

"What?"

Timmy pointed to Amy. "He forced her."

Megan looked at Amy. Her face reddened as she placed both hands against her mouth. Megan's stomach coiled, and she covered it with her hands to keep from retching. Clint's hands on her arms. His lips pressed hard against her lips. It all came rushing in at rapid speed. She closed her eyes to keep the tears from falling.

"Amy told me about your boyfriend. What he did to you in high school."

Megan opened her eyes. She looked at Amy. Tears fell down the woman's cheeks as she placed one hand against her temple.

How would Amy know? Only one possibility. Marianna must have told her. But why? That didn't sound like her sister. She knew how badly that night hurt her, how it had changed her life.

"We've heard you're his next target," Timmy continued. "You need to know the truth about him. Who he is."

Megan looked at Amy. The woman's whole body shook. Timmy was oblivious to his wife's pain, and he most certainly didn't care about hers.

And her sister told her private business to Amy, and Amy told Timmy. How could Marianna do that to her? Justin forced Amy?

He forced her? He was like Clint?

Megan's head started to spin. A chill washed over her, and her stomach churned. With her hand across her mouth, she raced for the bathroom.

"Don't let him do it to you, too!" Timmy's voice yelled across the room.

Embarrassment added itself to her agony as she pushed open the stall and hurled what little bit of breakfast she'd eaten that morning. Her body wouldn't stop trembling, couldn't seem to stop. She grabbed a wad of tissue from the toilet roll and wiped her mouth. She opened the stall door and bumped into someone.

"Excuse me." She looked up and saw her mother. Her heart plummeted.

"I saw what happened." Her mom's voice was low, and Megan knew she couldn't handle any kind of confrontation from her mom. It had been eight years. Eight years. She wanted to be over what Clint did. Wanted to be free. She wanted to love Justin. But he was the same as Clint.

The thought made her head pound, and new tears swelled in her eyes. What kind of warped person continued to fall for evil men? Men who mistreated women for their own selfish designs. She silently begged her mom not to accuse or berate her. At the same time, with what little strength she still had, she lifted her shoulders and pushed out her chin to prepare for her mother's onslaught of words.

Her mom's stoic facade melted, and Megan watched as pain etched her mother's features. She wrapped her arms around Megan and pressed her head against her shoulder. "I'm sorry."

A dam broke inside Megan's heart and spirit, and she cried

against her mother's shoulder. She released the pain until there was nothing left in her.

"It's okay, Megan," her mother cooed as she raked her fingers through Megan's hair.

Her mom's tenderness opened the old wound, and she knew God covered it with medicine, cleaning it out, allowing a place for true healing.

Megan sniffed, and her mom held her tighter. Clint had stolen her purity. Her sister betrayed her trust. Justin was not the man her heart wanted him to be. He was the man her head knew he was.

Her heart was shredded.

Megan followed her sister, Julie, Amber, and her mom into the nail salon. It took every ounce of restraint not to lay into her sister for sharing her past with Amy. She didn't want to ruin Marianna's day tomorrow. As her mom told her repeatedly in the bathroom, Marianna loved her and would have shared that information only if she felt it absolutely necessary.

She still didn't understand how telling Amy was absolutely necessary. And Justin. She knew he had been a scoundrel, but what Timmy said made him criminal. She just couldn't imagine Justin doing such a horrible thing. She thought of her parents' disbelief in Clint's actions. They hadn't wanted her to date Clint, but they never expected him to hurt her. She hadn't expected it either. But he had, and her life had never been the same.

"You sit here."

The Cambodian woman's directions to sit in the massage chair snapped her from her thoughts. Megan forced herself to smile and nod at the woman as she settled into the chair. She dipped her feet in the almost-too-hot water and pressed her head against the chair.

Marianna released a loud exhale. "I think everything is ready for tomorrow."

"It looks great. We've done a good job, if I do say so myself," added Julie.

"I don't care if I never see another roll of red ribbon and tiny bottles of bubbles in my life," said Amber.

Megan couldn't help but grin. Amber had spent the entire day tying small red bows around the neck of the bubbles that would be passed out to the attendees to use for sending off Kirk and Marianna.

The group continued to talk, and Megan tried to focus on allowing the chair to loosen her tense muscles. She prayed God would help her understand the afternoon's events and why she felt attracted to Justin, of all people. Now she felt repulsion for Justin. She didn't want to walk down the aisle with him. Didn't want to see him later that evening at the rehearsal dinner.

God, how am I going to make it through the dinner? God didn't respond, and she felt more frustrated.

"Megan, did I tell you Colt called today?"

Megan opened her eyes and looked at her sister. She hoped her aggravation with her wasn't as obvious on the outside as she felt on the inside. She shook her head. "No. You didn't tell me."

"He wanted to make sure it was all right with me if he brought Hadley's mother to the wedding."

Megan lifted her eyebrows. That was a surprise. She was glad he was allowing Hadley and Tina to get to know one another. Hadley loved talking with her mom, but he was going to let her come for a visit? God must really be working on his heart. *Is that why You're being quiet with me, God? Colt's taking up all Your time?*

Marianna continued, "I think it's terrific he's such a good dad to Hadley. He's so faithful and devoted."

"Definitely the kind of guy a gal would want to end up with," added Amber.

"I wonder if he's interested in anyone," said Julie.

Megan pressed her head against the chair once more. She closed her eyes. Their matchmaking was obvious. But she had news for the lot of them. She and Colt were friends, and that was all. She'd spent years not wanting a man in her life, and after this afternoon, she planned to continue to stay that way. Megan mumbled, "Maybe you should go for him, Julie."

Megan heard her sister's huff, but she didn't respond. If she said much more, Marianna would be hearing an earful for telling Amy about Clint.

"God will bring the right man into Megan's life."

Megan opened her eyes and studied her mother who sat three chairs away from her. Had those words actually come from the woman who gave her birth, who raised her, then accused her of being a foolish liar? The woman who'd never picked up a Bible to Megan's knowledge until she and Marianna bought her one when they were teenagers?

Megan noted Marianna's expression revealed she was just as surprised by their mother's words. Her sister nodded. "You're right, Mom."

The small Asian woman sat in the chair in front of Megan. She tapped Megan's leg, and Megan lifted it out of the water for her to start the pedicure.

Did her mother believe her now? The memory of that night

washed through her mind. Clint had died in the car accident. Megan had grown more physically ill with each passing day until Marianna talked her into telling their parents the truth.

"You never should have dated him. If you'd listened to us, this never would have happened," yelled her dad.

"She's lying."

The words had slipped through her mother's lips like a snake slithering through a pasture. They'd contained such vehemence, such vileness. Megan didn't understand it. She'd never gotten over it.

She sneaked a peek in her mother's direction. Her mom watched her. Megan couldn't decipher her expression. She knew a discussion between them was coming. Though she felt disconnected from God, she prayed He'd see her through it.

Chapter 24

There's nothing like a good cheating song
to make me want to run home to be with my wife.
STEVEN CURTIS CHAPMAN

Justin straightened the red tie around his neck. He looked past his reflection in the mirror and realized Kirk's face rivaled the primary accent color of the wedding. Justin put his hand on his friend's shoulder and pointed to the couch. "Why don't you have a seat for a second?"

Kirk nodded and pulled at his solid white tie. "Is it hot in here?"

Justin grinned as he reached for the pitcher of water on the table. He poured a glass and handed it to his friend. "No. The temperature is fine. Feeling nervous?"

Kirk took a quick swallow then waved his hand. "Not in the slightest. Why would I be nervous? I love Marianna. I want to marry her. I want to promise to take care of her for the rest of my life, to provide for her, to be responsible for her well-being." He bent forward, placing his elbows on his knees and lowering his head between his legs. "I think I'm gonna be sick."

Justin bit back a laugh. If his friend weren't so serious, he'd rib him for his dramatics. He patted Kirk's shoulder. "Take a deep breath, man. It'll be all right."

Kirk looked up at him. "What if I lose my job? What if I lose my insurance? You know she gets kidney stones. Can you imagine the hospital bill without insurance?"

Justin shuddered. He didn't know she struggled with kidney stones. He'd passed one three years ago. Worst pain he'd ever experienced. Poor woman. He hated that for her. He focused back on his friend. "Marianna is a teacher. I'm sure she can get insurance."

Kirk placed his hand on his chest. "But I'm the man. I'm supposed to provide for her."

Justin grinned. "Sounding a little chauvinistic, aren't we?"

Kirk peered at him. "Justin, I'm serious."

"Man, I know. I'm just kidding with you." He sat on the chair across from Kirk. "I know you want to be sure you can take care of her. But isn't that God's job? And isn't that part of marriage? Taking care of each other in the good and bad times. You've got a job. You're good at it. You can't worry about the future."

Justin thought of Megan. He should be listening to his own advice. He wanted her to be his future. He worried about his past rearing its ugly head. He didn't want her to experience any pain or discomfort by running into women he'd once known. But he had to trust God with all of that. He couldn't let the past dictate the life God had for him now and later.

Kirk sucked in a deep breath and took another drink of water. "You're right, man."

Justin stood and offered his hand. "Come on. We've got a wedding to go to."

Kirk nodded as he took Justin's hand and stood up. He looked in the mirror and adjusted his tie. "Do you think she'll think I look okay?"

Justin shook his head. "I am not discussing your appearance with you. You're fine."

Kirk grinned as he headed to the door. "I bet she'll look beautiful."

"She looks like Megan. Of course she'll look beautiful," Justin mumbled.

Kirk stopped and turned toward Justin. "Look. We never talked after that night at the gym. I was wrong. You are different. I know you won't hurt Megan. I. . ."

Justin grabbed his shoulder. "I know. But now's not the time to talk about me and Megan. You're about to get hitched."

Kirk blew out a long breath. "Don't say it like that. I think I feel sick again."

Justin nudged him forward. "Get out there. You'll be fine once you see her."

Justin followed Kirk into the sanctuary. They made their way to the front of the church. Marianna, Megan, their mom, and the other girls had done a good job fixing the place up. He liked the red flowers and the little splashes of yellow.

Looking out at the congregation, his legs started to twitch. He enjoyed being the center of attention. Nothing better than walking into a crowded room with a beautiful woman draped on your arm. But weddings were not generally his thing. He couldn't remember the last one he'd attended. Grooms didn't tend to be big chums of his.

Still, he was anxious to see Megan. She'd mentioned the

bridesmaid dress not being a color that suited her skin tone, but the comment had been made in passing. He knew she wanted Marianna to have all that her heart desired for her wedding. Megan's selflessness was one of the qualities he loved about her.

He shifted his weight from one foot to the other. He wanted to see her. Wanted her to walk down the aisle for him. Not to be a part of her sister's wedding. He scratched his neck, wondering if the wedding would ever start.

Sneaking a peek at his friend, he saw the sweat beading on Kirk's brow. If the ceremony didn't start soon, he'd be picking his friend up off the ground. Justin reached into his pocket, pulled out a handkerchief, and handed it to Kirk. Kirk nodded his thanks and wiped his brow.

The music started. The group silenced as one of their friends made her way down the aisle. Another friend followed. Then came Megan.

Justin drank in the pale yellow, strapless dress with the thick red sash around the waist. He took in the length of her neck. The ivory color of her skin. Her hair was pulled up, much the same way as it had been for the charity ball. Though he tried to shake the thought, he wondered how the small of her neck would feel beneath his lips.

She looked at him, and their gazes locked. At first she seemed glad to see him, pleased with his appearance, possibly as eager to be near him as he was her. Then the wall lifted in front of her eyes. She masked her expression then looked away from him.

He had to convince her of his affection. He'd tried to hide his feelings, to spare her of his past long enough. God didn't want him to live in the past. He was going to tell her.

Megan moved to her place across from him. The music changed, and Marianna appeared in the doorway. Justin looked at his friend. Kirk's eyes welled with tears, and his nerves seemed to fade away. Though he never would have believed it possible, jealousy welled inside Justin.

He wanted what Kirk had. He sneaked a peek at Megan. She beamed in her sister's direction. He knew the two of them were close, and he wondered what life would be like for Megan now that her sister would be married. He knew she had to be a bit sad at their soon-to-be separation.

He would be happy to fill Megan's time if she'd let him. Marianna made it to the front of the sanctuary, and out of the corner of Justin's eye, he caught a young girl waving toward them. The girl sat beside an older version of herself and a large, blond cowboy of a man.

Megan partially lifted her hand and grinned then focused back on the ceremony. Justin looked back at the attendees. The preacher spoke of love never failing and always remaining honest and true, and a bunch of other good, wholesome things, but Justin couldn't take his eyes off that family.

Was that the guy Kirk mentioned at the gym? Colt somebody or other? Kirk had said Megan was giving the niece piano lessons, and that the Colt fellow was her uncle whom she lived with. If that was them, then who was the look-alike sitting beside the girl?

Justin looked back at the oversized cowboy. The man scowled at him with a vehemence Justin hadn't seen since the last time he was in the same room with Timmy. He wasn't a betting man, too busy with the girls to worry about games, but Justin felt confident the man was the Colt guy who had his eyes set on Megan.

Well Justin had news for him. He wasn't going to get her. There had never been a woman Justin felt willing to go the distance with, to fight to keep in his life. Megan was different. He wanted her until death did them part. The thought sent a shudder through his body. He never thought he'd feel this way.

One of the tech guys handed Megan a microphone. She glanced his way. Her chest rose and fell as she bit her bottom lip. The music started, and Justin wished he could hold her hand, assure her she'd do a great job.

Megan's gaze shifted to her sister and Kirk as she started to sing of love and commitment. Surely her voice rivaled the angels. Her soft pitch wrapped itself around him. Tears glistened in her eyes as she gazed back at him. His feet itched to go to her, to take her in his arms and promise all the song said.

The song ended, and he turned his attention to Kirk and Marianna as they exchanged their vows. Love and adoration reflected from Marianna's eyes. Though he couldn't see Kirk, he knew his friend felt the same. This was what he wanted. The next wedding he attended would be his own. With Megan.

Justin took Megan's hand in his and guided her to the dance floor. Marianna and Kirk had shared their first dance as man and wife. As planned, the wedding party would join them at the beginning of the next song.

He wrapped his arms around her tiny waist. She averted her gaze, but he stayed focused on her face. He loved the slight smattering of freckles on her cheeks, nose, and forehead. From a distance, her skin was so clear, so smooth, but up close, the freckles showed. He wanted to trace his lips along the line of those freckles, to kiss each one in turn.

She lifted her gaze to his for the briefest moment, and he noted pain behind her eyes. What had upset her? Maybe it was the wedding. He knew Marianna was moving out, that the two of them had never lived apart. He needed to be a comfort to Megan, to let her know she could count on him, spend time with him whenever she felt lonely or missed her sister.

"Did you bring anyone with you to the wedding?"

Her voice was hesitant, and Justin frowned. "Who? Like my dad?"

"No. I mean a date."

A fist seemed to tighten around Justin's heart and squeeze. Why would she think he'd bring a date to the wedding? "Megan, I haven't gone on a date since I became a Christian. Unless you call the charity ball a date."

And he did. He'd had such a wonderful time with Megan. They'd laughed through dinner. She'd acted comfortable, even witty around his colleagues and other so-called prestigious members of Lexington's society. And the kiss. He couldn't look at her lips without replaying their kiss. The one touch wasn't enough. It only whet his appetite for more.

"I don't call the charity ball a date."

Megan sounded angry, but her expression was sad. He didn't know what was going on. They'd had a terrific time yesterday morning putting up chairs at the reception and wrapping ribbons around napkins. He hadn't even seen her since then, so he couldn't fathom what he'd done to upset her.

He tightened his hold around her back. She stiffened, but he didn't care. He loved her, and whatever he'd done to upset her, he needed to make it right. "Megan, you of all people know I'm not the man I was four months ago. I don't want a new woman on my arm every evening. I want—"

"May I cut in?"

Justin turned at the sound of a man standing behind him. The overgrown, blond cowboy looked at Megan with the stupidest smile across his lips. A blush rose on Megan's cheeks, and Justin couldn't tell if it was because she liked the guy or she was surprised he'd ask to interrupt their dance.

Justin inhaled a deep breath. He was a new creation, and part of that was to be civil, even when he didn't feel like it. He couldn't force Megan to love him. She had to do that on her own. The wedding party song had ended. He should let her dance with this guy and then ask her for the next.

Justin forced a smile toward the man and then to Megan. He dipped his head. "Sure."

The man released a throaty sigh when he took Megan's hands. Justin wondered if the guy would drool all over her. He headed toward the punch table and grabbed a filled, dainty glass off it.

He let out a breath. He was behaving as a good Christian man would. He wasn't a Neanderthal. He didn't own Megan. He couldn't force her to stay at his side the entire night.

"The wedding was beautiful, wasn't it?"

Justin turned and nodded to Megan's mom. "It was."

"I'm so proud of Marianna. She picked such a fine gentleman of a husband."

Justin looked at Marianna and his friend. Kirk twirled her around on the dance floor. She laughed as she wrapped her arms around his neck and pulled him close to kiss his lips.

Justin's gut tightened. He wanted that to be him and Megan. He shifted his gaze to Megan and the cowboy.

"Their stepfather was a good man. So kind. Gentle. Wouldn't hurt a fly."

Justin tried to focus on Megan's mother's words, but then Colt lifted his hand to Megan's cheek. Justin's blood burned hot. No one would touch his Megan. He handed the cup to Megan's mother and nodded. "Excuse me."

He bolted onto the dance floor, grabbed Colt's shoulder, turned the man toward him, and said, "Don't even think of touching Megan like that."

The man frowned, and Justin drew back his fist.

"What are you doing?" Megan screamed.

He didn't care what she said as his fist connected with the man's cheek. The guy stumbled a few steps back then lunged toward Justin, knocking him off his feet.

Megan squealed, but he ignored her as he hammered the guy with a right punch. The man returned the favor with one of his own. He was stronger than Justin thought, but it didn't matter. He'd take whatever the man dished out. By the time this was over, the blond cowboy would know he'd better keep his hands off Justin's girl.

Chapter 25

It's no wonder that truth is stranger than fiction.
Fiction has to make sense.
MARK TWAIN

"Please, Megan. It's your last day in the office. Let me take you to lunch."

Megan looked up at Justin, taking in the deep purple and blue coloring around his left eye, as well as the slit on his bottom lip. She still could not believe he'd hit Colt. For as long as she lived, she'd never be able to fully wipe the vision of the two burly men rolling around on her sister's wedding dance floor. Over her.

She thought Marianna was going to go into cardiac arrest. Even Kirk was punched in the arm trying to break the two of them up.

Eighth grade, Mike Clark and Stan Bowling—that was the last time she'd seen such a ridiculous display of fists.

She didn't want to talk to Justin. She couldn't remember another time she'd felt so humiliated. Hadley cried her eyes out—her mom trying to comfort her. Megan had been glad to see the woman attend the ceremony.

Colt had been just as bad as Justin. He didn't try to stop her boss's insanity but joined in on it. He looked every bit as beaten as Justin with a busted nose and split lip.

She exhaled a long breath and shook her head at her boss. "Justin, I have a lot to do. Tomorrow is my first day of new teacher training."

Justin's dad walked up behind him and patted his son's shoulder. "Come on now, Megan. Go to lunch with the man." He winked, and Justin tensed. "He obviously wants to talk with you."

She found it infuriating the man who had been a lawyer for three decades found his son's skirmish at the wedding humorous. He'd actually congratulated his son for getting in a few good punches. Justin had squirmed under his father's praise. She knew he didn't want that kind of honor, but it served him right. What was he thinking attacking Colt like that? To her knowledge, the two men had never spoken a word to each other.

Justin looked at her with the most ridiculously pitiful puppy dog eyes she'd ever seen. She wanted to stay angry with him. He'd flattered more women than she could probably imagine. He'd forced himself on Amy. He started fights with perfectly innocent men. And yet he still sent butterflies to dancing a rumba in her belly.

She needed her head examined. There was obviously something very wrong with her. Maybe common sense was only delivered to one infant in a mother's womb, and she had missed out.

"Please, Megan. Just lunch."

She snarled her lip. Despite her better judgment, she nodded. "Fine."

The senior Frasure laughed as he walked back to his office. "Have fun, you two."

Megan pinched her lips together as she reached into the drawer and pulled out her purse. The new secretary had already left for lunch. Megan had planned to skip it all together and make sure she had everything ready for her last day.

She glanced up at Justin. He fidgeted with his office keys. He seemed nervous. He had no reason to act that way. Unless he assumed she might pummel him herself for his behavior at the wedding.

He opened the door, and she walked outside into the warm July air. Normally Kentucky was sweltering this time of the year, but a cold front had cooled the area, and it actually felt nice stepping out into the sun.

Justin cleared his throat. "I thought we'd head over to the café. Eat outside so we can talk."

She nodded, and they walked the two blocks in silence. For someone who wanted to talk with her, he certainly had very little to say. They went into the café, and she ordered a turkey and swiss sandwich on rye bread. He asked for the same, which she found weird, because she'd never known him to eat turkey.

She inwardly shrugged. But what did she really know of the man? They sat together at church, shared scriptures and thoughts at Bible study, worked side-by-side. She thought she'd gotten to know him well. But she never would have guessed him to force himself on a woman or to use his fists instead of his words. He was a lawyer, for heaven's sake—a professional at using words.

There was probably plenty she didn't know about him. Stuff she wouldn't want to know.

He pulled out a chair for her at a table that sat at the far end of the café's grounds. The place was bustling with people enjoying the warm weather, and Megan determined to watch those around her instead of the man she was with. She noted a baby who sat across from his mother. She grinned when the child pulled out or spit out each bite the mom tried to place in his mouth.

"Megan, I've got to be honest with you."

Justin placed his hand on top of hers, and a flash of electricity bolted through her. She hated how her body responded to him. Traitor!

"Okay. What is it?"

She tried to keep her expression blank, her mind on guard, as he looked at her with a sincerity that threatened to make her melt into a pool of foolishness.

"I love you."

"What?" She jerked her hand away from his and frowned. Did her ears need cleaning? Possibly she should make an appointment with her doctor when they went back to the office. Teachers need good hearing. His gaze was so sincere and sappy that she shook her head. "What are you talking about?"

Justin raked his hand through his hair and tapped the tabletop with his other hand. His leg shook beneath the table. She'd never seen him so uncomfortable. She was beginning to feel a bit unnerved herself.

"I don't know what to say. I've never done this before. Never felt like this before. I want to be with you all the time. To talk with you. To dance with you. To kiss you." He peered into her eyes, and Megan swallowed the knot in her throat. "And when that man tried to touch your face, I just—"

Megan lifted her hand to stop him. "Wait a minute. You hit Colt because he was dancing with me?"

He grabbed her hand again. "You're not listening to me. I love you, Megan. I. . ."

She pulled away again. Her heart pounded in her chest. Her head thumped. "I don't love you."

He leaned closer to her. "But you haven't even given me a chance. Let me win your heart. Let me—"

She raised her hand again to stop him. The words that slipped from her lips had been a lie, and her mouth burned from having said them. Her chest tightened with the urge to take them back, but she wouldn't be a fool a second time. Determined to stay strong, she peered at him. "Do you know why I don't date?"

He clamped his lips shut.

She leaned forward. "Do you?"

He shook his head. She must have looked half crazed, because his brow etched with concern. He needn't be worried. She'd let him know the truth. The ugliness of what Clint had done, and what he, Justin, did to Amy. Maybe he'd never considered Amy's side.

"I went on a date with my boyfriend." The words hissed through her lips, and suddenly she felt ready to say them. To tell him everything. No matter how he reacted or what he thought. He'd hear every disgusting thing she needed to say. "And he took me to our favorite spot to park."

Her mind shifted, and she was there. Up that mountain. Looking over the cliff.

The moon was high. The stars shining. The air clean. Clear. Warm. Clint pulled the blanket from the backseat and laid it out in front of the car. She joined him on the blanket, cuddled up beside him, invited his kisses.

He touched her cheeks with both hands, and she wrapped her hands around his neck. How she loved to kiss Clint. She could kiss him for hours.

Then he pushed her back against the blanket. With all her strength, she tried to push him back to a sitting position. He wouldn't have it. He wanted her to lie back. She'd thought if he only continued to kiss her, it would be all right.

But it wasn't. His hands moved away from her cheeks. She tried to push them away. The look in his eyes shifted, and she knew something had changed. She tried to sit up. Told him no, but he wouldn't listen.

She snapped from the memory and looked at Justin. She wondered how long it had been since she'd spoken. His expression was etched with concern and fury.

"What happened?" His eyes smoldered with a dare for her to speak the truth. He didn't want to hear it, but he would.

"He forced himself on me." She squared her shoulders. It was the first time she'd admitted the truth since the night her parents blasted her for sharing it. She'd been unprepared for their cruel words and disbelief. But she was older now. Wiser. She dared Justin to contradict what had happened.

She bored her gaze into Justin's, ordering him to silence while she finished her confession. "Despite my objections. I told him no. I pushed him away. He continued. The bruises on my body healed, but the marks he left in my heart remained. I don't want a man. I don't want to love. I refuse to."

Justin lifted his hand as he shifted his gaze to the ground. She sat back, startled by the vehemence of her words. So, he thought her tainted. Found the act disgusting. Good. Maybe he would feel remorse for what he had done to Amy.

He looked up at her, and Megan sucked in her breath at the pain that laced his features. He grabbed her hand in his and rubbed his thumb against her palm. "Megan, I'm sorry."

She jerked her hand away. "Are you sorry for Amy, too?"

He frowned. "You know I wish I could take back my past." He shook his head as he leaned closer to her. His gaze implored her to believe him. "You don't think I forced myself on Amy?"

Her stomach churned. "But Timmy said—"

"Timmy is mad about what happened with me and Amy, but I never forced myself." He moved his chair around the table and closer to her. "I would never do that. Megan, you have to believe me."

Megan looked at the uneaten sandwich on her plate. She hated what Clint had done to her. She hated that she thought of it all too often, especially lately with her heart determined to open up again. She hated Justin's past, what Timmy said, the way she felt for Justin but didn't want to. Her thoughts swirled until she felt she would get sick. She placed her napkin on the table, prepared to run away. Away from her past and present. Away from Justin.

"My past is disgusting," Justin's words interrupted her thoughts. "I wish I could take it back. Say I didn't see women for my own personal wants. I can't. But I never forced a woman. Never."

His firm voice strained against the last word, as if he couldn't comprehend a person behaving in such a vile manner. She wished she couldn't. The memories streamed like a movie in her mind.

His hand cupped her chin, and he tilted her face toward him until she looked at him, their faces mere inches apart. His eyes spoke of earnest sincerity and care. "I'm so sorry that happened to you, Megan. I love you. No matter what happened that night. . .it wasn't your fault."

Megan pushed away from him. Her chest weighed heavy, and she struggled to catch her breath. Standing to her feet, she opened her mouth to speak. Her thoughts escaped her, and she raced away from the café. She didn't want him to be sorry or for him to love her.

She didn't want him.

Megan pushed open the front door to her apartment. She couldn't go back to the office. Facing Justin again would be more torture than she could bear. "What are they going to do? Fire me?"

She shut the door and leaned against it. That wasn't the right attitude to have, and she knew it. But it didn't matter. She couldn't talk to Justin. She didn't know if she'd ever be able to look at him again.

She pushed off the door, dropped her purse on the couch, slipped off her shoes, and walked out to the back patio. She could get past him if she never saw him again.

Thursday night Bible studies rushed through her mind, as well as the fact he sat with her at church. She'd just be like Timmy and Amy and switch churches. She had a legitimate excuse. She could say she wanted to spend more time with her sister. That since Marianna and Kirk were married, she didn't get to spend much time with her. It would be the truth.

She thought of her friends at Bible study, and how they'd seen her through some of her darkest moments, even if they didn't know the reason behind those times. And the kids in children's church. How could she give them up? She'd been Meggie to precious six-year-old Hannah since the child's first Sunday in church, at a mere six weeks old.

She leaned against the patio fence. A young mother and her two little boys played some kind of game in the park area behind the apartment. The little boy moved a piece then jumped to his feet and squealed in excitement. Megan couldn't help but smile when the mother offered him a high five.

She'd seen the small family playing in the park area before. Since spring, a year ago. The first time she'd seen them, they passed a bouncy ball to each other. So much had changed since that day.

Megan had been worried and fretted over a good grade in a college class. Now her sister was gone. Her boss had gone over the deep end. And she was embarrassed to go to the piano lesson scheduled for the following evening.

Her cell phone rang. She looked at the screen. Justin. There was no way she was answering the call. She placed the phone on the patio table and looked back at the young family. The phone beeped, and she knew he'd left her a message.

She couldn't talk to him. How could she talk to him? How could he love her? It was ludicrous. First off, she was nothing like the women Justin was attracted to. She knew she wasn't ugly, but she didn't look like she'd just walked off a supermodel's runway. Those were the kind of women Justin liked. She was simply a small-town girl who liked simple things in life. The fact she lived in a city now was just a matter of logistics. It wasn't who she was in her core.

Besides, she didn't want to care about him. She wanted to be single. Too much risk was involved in loving a man. She'd been hurt before. She didn't want to go that route again.

He hadn't forced Amy. She could tell it in his expression. She thought of Amy's reaction to Timmy's words. The woman hadn't known what to do to calm her husband. Megan felt sorry for her.

She looked up at the clear blue sky. It was a perfect day for horseback riding. She longed to take Daisy on a ride, tie the animal to a tree, and lie on a flat rock, basking in the warmth of the day. She wanted to think about when times were simple.

"God, it was supposed to be just You and me. I was always happy with it that way. Why did Justin have to ruin it?"

God was quiet. It frustrated her He always seemed silent. She still completed her Bible studies, still said her prayers, but it was as if she simply walked through the motions. No two-way communication she once felt with God.

But why was He avoiding her? She hadn't changed. Sure, she had feelings for Justin, but she'd done her best to keep them at bay. Aside from the one moment of weakness or whatever it was, when she kissed him at the restaurant, she'd been a rock. Hadn't led him on at all.

Okay, so maybe she did kiss him back at the charity ball, but he'd caught her off guard. And she was all dressed up. It was an easy mistake to get wrapped up in the moment. That's all it was. A mistake.

Her cell phone rang again. She looked at Justin's name once more. She pushed out of her chair, left the phone on the table, and walked back into the apartment. She didn't care about him the way he cared for her. She didn't.

"God, it's me and You against the world."

Peace didn't fill her spirit. No nudging of comfort wrapped her heart. She grabbed a soft drink out of the refrigerator, popped it open, and took a long swig. "God, I start new teacher training tomorrow. I'm going to be a music teacher. It's what I've prayed about. It's what You wanted for me. You've blessed me with the job."

Megan picked up the newspaper she'd left on the kitchen table and threw it away. She placed her morning glass in the sink then moved to the living room and fluffed the throw pillows. She flopped onto the couch and petitioned God again. "Can't we just focus on tomorrow? Get excited about my first day of training?"

Frustrated with the silence, she grabbed the remote off the arm of the chair and turned on the television. It wasn't as if God spoke audibly to her anyway. She shouldn't expect Him to nudge her heart or fill her spirit.

Besides, God was silent with a lot of people a lot of times. She'd just keep reading her Bible and saying her prayers. It wasn't as if she'd done anything wrong. She hadn't forced herself on Clint, hadn't asked her parents to respond as they did, hadn't encouraged Justin to love her. She'd done nothing to warrant God's silence.

In the depth of her heart, she knew that was the problem. She'd done nothing. God was calling her to do something, and it terrified her. She shook her head and turned the television up louder. She didn't want to hear Him.

Chapter 26

'Tis better to have loved and lost than never to have loved at all.
ALFRED, LORD TENNYSON

Colt flipped the thick T-bone steak on the grill.

"Almost ready?" hollered Hadley.

"Won't be much longer." With a pair of tongs, he turned the foil-wrapped corn on the cob. He took two spatulas to flip the foil-wrapped potatoes, onions, peppers, squash, and zucchini. His mouth watered just thinking of filling his belly with the delicious grilled food.

He wiped his mouth with the back of his hand and winced. It had been a week since the wedding, so his nose had healed up pretty much all the way. But he kept hitting the split in his lip, opening it back up, and causing it to take longer to heal.

His blood boiled when he thought of Justin Frasure. He could've pressed charges on the no-good scoundrel. Set him up for a world of chaos as he had to work through all the legalities and still keep his lawyer reputation intact. To Colt he was nothing but a hoity-toity womanizer dressing up in an overpriced monkey suit for a living.

JENNIFER JOHNSON

The man deserved the inconvenience of a going-nowhere law suit.

Colt watched as Hadley tossed a beanbag at the wooden corn-hole board. He'd decided not to put his niece through all that. Especially now that her mom was calling her twice a week and visiting whenever he let her.

Besides, he smiled as he turned the steaks again. He'd gotten in a few good punches on Justin Frasure. The lawyer wouldn't soon forget he'd tried to take on Colt Baker.

He grinned at Megan, Tina, Hadley, and her new friend, Valerie. Megan ran to Tina, and they high-fived when Tina threw the last beanbag and it swished straight into the hole. Hadley placed her hand on her hip and stuck out her bottom lip. "I thought adults were supposed to take it easy on kids."

Megan tousled Hadley's hair. "Now what would that teach you?"

Colt chuckled as he took the vegetables off the grill. Supper was finished, but he knew the game was almost over, so he decided to wait to call them.

It was Hadley's and Megan's turns to toss the beanbags toward the board Tina and Valerie stood beside. Hadley tossed first and missed the board completely. She stomped her foot and huffed. Megan tossed and missed as well.

If his count was right, Megan and Tina only needed three points to win. Hadley tossed again, and the bag landed on the board. Valerie whooped, and Hadley grinned. Megan would need four points to beat them.

Megan tossed and hit the board as well. Back to only needing three. Hadley tossed her third bag and hit the board, but Megan tossed and knocked it off. The last throw and Hadley missed. Megan threw and landed it in the hole. Tina squealed and ran to

Megan, and they twirled around in a hug.

"You beat a couple kids. Don't be so happy." Hadley's tone was unkind. She'd always struggled with accepting a loss. Colt started to reprimand her when Megan wrapped her arm around his niece.

"You know, you've gotta be willing to lose sometimes. It was just a game, so lose the 'tude."

Hadley smiled up at Megan, but Colt noted the set in her jaw. She was still angry at the loss, but she wasn't going to say anything disrespectful to Megan.

Colt sucked in a long breath. Only one of the many reasons he'd fallen in the love with the woman. She knew how to handle Hadley. She didn't get all upset about Hadley's outbursts. Didn't make things a bigger deal than they were. However, she still acknowledged and addressed it. Hadley needed a mother like that.

Tina hadn't been sure how to respond. Colt had seen it in her eyes. She was about to apologize for winning or something like that. She wasn't ready for motherhood. He was happy she was trying. He was proud of all she'd done to clean herself up and try to be part of Hadley's life again. But only for visits. She wasn't ready for the real deal. And he couldn't imagine if and when he would ever be ready for Tina to be a real-life mom to Hadley. Probably never.

Colt motioned them to the patio table. "It's ready. Come eat."

Hadley perked up, grabbed Valerie's hand, and raced to the table. "Mom, you want a soft drink?"

Tina nodded and leaned toward Megan. "I love it when she calls me that."

"You're her mom. What else would she call you?"

Colt bit back a response. Well, Tina, for one thing. If he had his say. It seemed weird Hadley had taken to calling the woman who hadn't been in her life for twelve years by a name she hadn't earned.

They sat at the table and passed the food around. Once everyone had their plates filled, they held hands to say grace. He'd hoped to sit beside Megan, but somehow he'd ended up beside Tina and Valerie. Once the amen was uttered, he looked up at Megan sitting across from him. He didn't mind she was his focal point for the meal.

"Can we go riding after we eat, Uncle Colt? Maybe go to the pond and toss rocks and swing?" Hadley's question came with a mouthful of food.

"Don't talk with your mouth full," Megan reminded her, and Colt couldn't hold back the grin at how easy parenthood was for her.

He swallowed his own mouthful and nodded. Wiping his mouth with a napkin, he added, "I think that would be a lot of fun."

Valerie clapped her hands. She was still a bit bashful in front of him. Didn't say much. But it was obvious the idea set well with her.

Tina's shoulder dropped, and she looked down at her plate.

Megan touched her hand. "What's wrong, Tina?"

She shook her head. "I've never ridden a horse." She lifted her gaze and smiled, but Colt could tell she wanted to go with them. "You go without me."

Colt sat back in his chair. That suited him just fine. While Hadley and Valerie played around, he may get a chance to talk with Megan alone. He itched to spend time with her, but no matter what he planned, something always got in the way.

Megan frowned and looked across the table at Colt. "That's nonsense. Tell her."

Colt lifted his eyebrows. "Well, I. . ."

Megan looked back at Tina. "You can ride out there with Colt. He's got the biggest horse I've ever seen. Thunderbolt won't have a bit of trouble packing the both of you." She glanced back at Colt. "Right?"

"Right." Colt blew out his breath as he put down his fork. All of the sudden, he wasn't hungry.

Colt scooted into the booth beside Megan at the frozen yogurt place. It was the closest he'd been to her all day. Hadley and Valerie had left them alone at the pond, just as he expected. Instead of being able to spend time with Megan, he'd been a third wheel while she and Tina talked about everything from cooking to hair products.

Tina finally left, and he'd offered to take Megan and the girls for a treat.

"I've never been here before," said Valerie. It was the first time she'd spoken to them without using Hadley as a go-between.

Megan pulled her spoon out of her mouth. "It's my favorite. I love getting to pick between the different flavors."

"And all the toppings!" Hadley added. She looked into Valerie's cup. "What did you get?"

"Cotton candy and birthday cake yogurt topped with M&M's, gummy bears, Snickers, and cherries."

Hadley lifted her eyebrows. "Can I taste it? You can taste mine. I got peanut butter and chocolate yogurt with chocolate syrup, peanuts, and cherries on top."

Colt turned his cup toward Megan. "I feel quite plain with my vanilla and chocolate syrup."

Megan laughed, and her eyes twinkled as she lifted her brows and said, "Can I try it?"

Hadley wrinkled her nose. "Are you making fun of me?"

Colt shook his head. "Absolutely not. You're entirely too cute to make fun of."

Satisfied with the comment, Hadley turned back to Valerie, and the girls took another bite from each other's cups.

Colt tried not to stare at Megan as she took another bite of her frozen yogurt. Her cheeks and nose were burnt from the afternoon in the sun, which made her blue eyes sparkle lighter than the noonday sky. Her hair was messy from the day of riding and cornhole playing. She'd traced her fingers through it and pulled the mass of it back in a clip, but it was still messy, and very cute.

He'd wanted time alone with her all day. For weeks, actually. Though they weren't exactly alone, the girls were so absorbed in each other that this was his chance to talk to her. If only he knew what to say.

"I had a lot of fun today."

She spoke before he had the chance. He nodded and nudged her with his shoulder. "Me, too."

He inwardly berated himself. Why had he just nudged her? What were they? Ten years old, and she was his neighborhood buddy? It was no wonder he hadn't had girlfriends. He had no idea how to interact with women.

He wanted to tell her she was beautiful, to ask her on a date, to tell her she was the perfect woman for him. She was a country girl with a pure heart. She was good with Hadley and easy to be around. She didn't run around chasing men. He liked that most about her.

"I needed today. To just have fun." She looked at him. The seriousness in her eyes made him squirm. She lifted her hand as if she were patting the air. "You know. No heavy. Just with friends."

He inwardly growled. She thought of him as a friend. That was good. Marriages lasted when the husband and wife were friends. His mom and dad had been the best of friends. But they also looked at each other like they'd hung the moon and stars, too. He wanted that from her as well.

He settled back in the seat. It had been a long week for her. Her sister got married. She quit her job. For which he was thankful. And she started her teacher training. He'd give her a week or two. She probably needed a good friend right now. The fireworks would come later.

"How was your training this week?"

She smiled. "It was amazing. I'm going to love it. I should have gone into education from the very beginning."

"You'll do great."

"I think you're right. It already feels so natural and fulfilling. I've always loved kids. I don't know why I didn't think of it before."

"Hello, Megan."

Megan's face blanched, and Colt turned toward the male voice.

Justin spoke again. "Hanging out with Colt, I see."

Colt jumped to his feet and clenched his fists. If the guy wanted to go another round, then he'd be happy to oblige him.

Megan slid out of the booth and stood between them. He didn't look down at her. He kept his gaze focused on Justin. The man wanted to go another round. The want was plastered all over his face. The skin under his eye was still green. Colt would be sure to find his mark on that spot again.

"Stop it."

Hadley whimpered from across the booth, and for a moment, Colt started to unclench his fists. Justin grinned, as if Colt was too weak to stand his ground, and Colt straightened his shoulders. This time the guy wouldn't get in a single punch.

Megan's hand shoved his gut. "What are you two? Middle schoolers? Stop it, right now. This is ridiculous."

Justin opened his mouth, and Megan turned toward him. Colt winced when she placed her hands on Justin's chest. "I won't have it. I mean it."

Justin looked down at Megan. His expression shifted, and he looked as if she were the dessert he hadn't had the chance to eat. He started to lean toward her, and Colt's muscles flexed.

Before Colt could react, Megan pushed Justin away. "No." She lifted her finger to Justin. "No. I'm here with Colt."

Pain washed across the guy's features, and Colt had never felt such pleasure. Justin didn't look back up at him but turned on his heels and bolted out the door.

Triumph. He was the victor. Megan had said the words herself. She was with him. Not the no-good, womanizing jerk of an ex-boss.

He wanted to wrap his arms around her. Twirl her through the air proclaiming Megan McKinney had chosen him. She'd said it with her own mouth.

He looked at Megan. Tears welled in her eyes as her gaze studied the door. His heart sunk. If she was his, then why was she watching the door that Justin bolted out of?

Chapter 27

Lead us not into temptation.
Just tell us where it is; we'll find it.
SAM LEVENSON

Justin's head thumped as he shifted his sports car into gear and raced down the street. "God, I've lost my mind. I was going to get into another fight with that man. I haven't acted like this since high school."

He parked in his driveway and jumped out of the car. He raced into the house and grabbed some gym clothes out of the dryer. He wanted Megan. He wanted her with a passion he had never felt. She was the first woman who'd ever told him no. His mind retraced his life trying to remember a time he'd been rejected. Even in elementary school, he landed the girlfriends he selected. He played the positions he wanted in sports. Went to the schools he wanted. Got the grades he wanted. Clothes, toys, electronics, cars, and anything else his heart desired, he got. No one and nothing rejected him.

Now he wanted Megan. And she wouldn't have him.

He punched the back of the couch as he made his way out the

front door. Kirk warned him the Christian life wouldn't be easy. He'd said things about Justin having to surrender his will to God's purposes.

He jumped back into the car, threw his gym bag in the backseat, then pounded the top of the steering wheel. The Christian life hadn't been easy for him. He'd sought out a list of fifteen women to apologize to. Half a year ago, he'd been proud of his little black book. He'd gotten rid of it when he accepted Christ, and truthfully it had hurt.

The wheels of his car squealed when he took a sharp right without braking. "Let's just be honest." He spoke to the windshield. "Some really fun times had been had with the girls in that book."

Things had been simpler for him back then. He got what he wanted when he wanted with no promises of commitment.

He made more money, too. Divorce was a booming business. Lots of people were doing it, and he made a pretty shiny dime off the decimation of marriages. Adoption had proven not quite as popular. He made money but nothing like before. Even cut his bill for a few clients who were slipping into debt trying to finalize their adoptions.

Kirk's words the night of the men's retreat slipped through his mind. "It's going to be harder than you think, Justin. You've belonged to the world all your life, and God isn't of this world. Satan is doing a lot of reigning on earth."

Justin had been in such a euphoric state, excited about his new faith, eager to serve God. He knew the apologies wouldn't be fun, and he expected the dip in his finances when he changed what he represented.

After parking in the gym's lot, he yanked out the keys and

grabbed the bag from the back seat. "I've done everything You said," he growled to the Spirit. "Why can't I have Megan? You know I love her. You know she's different."

Ignoring the Spirit's assurance that God was in control, Justin stormed into the gym. He changed in the men's locker room then made his way to the treadmill. He turned his iPod to one of his old favorites, a song he hadn't listened to in months. Skipping the warm-up, he pressed the treadmill's buttons to a fast pace and ran.

He closed his eyes, trying to rid his mind of Megan's words that she was with Colt. He focused on the rhythm. His blood pumped, and a pinch formed in his side. He ignored it. The pain felt good. Kept his mind off Megan. Off God.

Someone poked his arm. He opened his eyes. Brandy. He pulled out his earphones.

She smiled at him. "Trying to break the machine?"

Justin slowed the treadmill and smiled at her. Brandy was the kind of woman he used to like to take out. Long hair, amazing eyes. Legs that seemed to go on forever. The skimpy blue jean shorts she wore were proof of that. Her strapless top did more than hint at what lay beneath it.

He wiped his forehead with the back of his hand. "Just letting off a little steam."

She shifted her weight to one foot and placed her hand on her hip. "I'm just now getting off. You could shower up, and we could go get a drink." She shrugged. "Maybe let off a little steam without trying to kill yourself."

In the back of Justin's mind, he knew he needed to say no. He'd spent months running away from temptation. Where was Kirk when he needed him?

On a honeymoon with his wife, that's where. He had what Justin wanted. And Justin was tired of waiting. Tired of trying to fix his life to always have his past thrown back in his face.

Amy had told Timmy he forced himself on her? He knew Timmy had conjured up that story. Still, he'd been hated, accused, and misunderstood more since becoming a Christian than he ever had before. And he was tired of it.

It was time to have a little fun. He looked at Brandy. He could tell she'd be happy to supply it.

He jumped off the machine. "Give me ten minutes to shower and change, and we'll get out of here."

Justin took another gulp of the soft drink. He tried to listen as Brandy talked about the unfairness of her university professor for her summer class. He'd forgotten many nights in his past life had gone this way. He'd sit across the booth from a drop-dead gorgeous gal while she whined about one topic or another. He'd feign interest until dinner was over; then his date would hint at dessert. Never one to turn down a bit of fun, he'd comply.

He frowned. *I really was a jerk.*

"So, did you have Dr. Honeycutt for English 101 when you were at UK?"

Justin blinked. He hadn't caught the last few things she said, but he shook his head. "I don't think so."

"Oh, you'd remember him." She raised her hand level with her neck. "Really short. Comes up to my neck. Bald head. Wire-framed glasses."

He shook his head again. He hadn't had freshmen-level English in ten years. In truth, he hadn't realized Brandy was quite that young. He knew she was a college student, but. . . He grimaced. Wait a minute, she was taking English 101. Surely she hadn't graduated high school just a couple of months ago. "How old did you say you are?"

"Nineteen." She leaned across the table. "Last year was my first year at UK, but I kinda enjoyed myself a bit much." She reached over and touched the top of his hand. "I'm taking a few classes over so my dad doesn't take away my college money."

His stomach turned. The girl was a baby. Legal. But it was obvious she was not looking for the things Justin now wanted.

Maybe that was a good thing. He'd been playing the Christian card for several months now, and where had it gotten him? A guy lying about him. Several women mad at him. His dad thinking he'd lost all his senses. A dip in his bank account. And it most surely had not gotten him Megan.

He sat up in the booth, determined to pay better attention to Brandy. He'd let the evening play out. Enjoy eating dinner with a woman who wanted to be with him.

"So, where was your gym buddy tonight?"

Justin clenched the napkin in his hand. He didn't want to talk about Kirk. He didn't want to think about his friend while he sat across from Brandy. "On his honeymoon."

Brandy lifted her eyebrows. "The dude got married?"

Justin chuckled. "Yep. Last Saturday. I was his best man."

Brandy smiled as she twirled her fork through her pasta. "I bet you looked mighty fine in a tux."

She winked, and Justin warmed at the flirtation. He'd missed

269

this—having his ego stroked a bit. The verbal sparring that was sure to set the mood for romance.

He thought of Megan walking down the aisle in her yellow dress. The one she looked beautiful in, even though she'd been concerned about the color. He remembered her voice, clear and perfect, as she sang to her sister and brother-in-law. The love she felt for them reflected in her eyes. He blinked and shook his head. He would not think about her.

He smiled at Brandy. "I suppose I didn't look too shabby."

Brandy placed her elbows on the table then rested her chin in her hands. "Bet it was hard to cage up all those muscles."

He flinched. He was a good-looking guy. Didn't deny it. And he'd always loved being flattered by beautiful women, but Brandy's comment felt wrong. Insincere. Shallow.

He pushed the uneasiness away and grinned at her. "I managed."

He was determined to have a good time tonight. No thinking about Megan. Or God.

"I'm glad your buddy's gone. We've finally got the chance to get to know each other."

He felt her foot rub against his leg. He was pretty sure it wasn't an accident.

"No offense, but your friend kinda gives me the creeps."

Justin frowned. "How so?"

"Just the way he acts and talks." She leaned against the booth and flipped her hair behind her back. "Did you know he gave me a business card inviting me to his church?" She huffed. "A business card, for crying out loud. I mean, who does that?"

Justin bit the inside of his lips. When he'd joined his church, he'd included an invitation to the services on the back of his business cards. He'd received several perplexed looks when passing them out, but he'd been eager to let clients and the world know of his newfound faith.

He pushed his plate away, trying to fight the sickness that warred in his belly. "I'm done eating if you are."

She placed her napkin in her plate. "Absolutely. Let's get out of here."

Justin motioned for the waitress then paid their bill. His heart pounded in his chest as he guided Brandy back to his car. Determining to ignore it, he opened her door then raced over to his side and slipped in.

Brandy placed her hand on his leg. He looked at her, and her grin would have battled the Cheshire cat's for mischief. "Back to your place?"

Justin nodded. "Sure."

He turned on the radio, and contemporary Christian music spilled through the speakers. He growled as he pulled one of his old CDs out of the glove compartment. The last thing he needed to hear was Third Day belting out about God's love.

He started the engine. Brandy hummed along with the tune of one of his past favorite songs. The foul language in the lyrics surprised him. Had those words always been there?

Of course they had always been there. It wasn't like someone sneaked into his car and changed the words of the CD he had put away in his glove compartment.

He glanced at Brandy. Took in the long, tanned legs. Brown hair spilled down the front of her strapless shirt. She winked as she started to sing the lyrics.

His stomach actually hurt now. Acid welled in his chest.

Something he'd eaten had disagreed with him. He pushed back the thought that he knew it was more than that. Stopping at the red light, he realized if he turned left he'd go toward his house. If he turned right, he'd head back to the gym. And Brandy's car.

His spirit warred within him as he stared at the red light. He didn't want Brandy. He wanted Megan.

But Brandy would be a nice diversion from the rejection he felt from Megan.

He wasn't that man anymore. He'd been changed when he accepted Christ.

Didn't he deserve a little fun? He'd lived his faith for months, yet Megan's sister still looked at him as if he were the devil himself. Kirk believed Justin would take advantage of Megan.

Okay, so he apologized for that, but his initial response was not to trust Justin. Was living a life of faith really working for him?

The light changed, and Justin continued to stare at it. His mind and body warred about which turn to make.

Brandy pointed toward the windshield. "It's green."

He sighed and turned. Within moments, he pulled into the gym's parking lot. Confusion covered Brandy's face. "What are you doing? I thought we were going to your place."

Justin pulled his wallet out of his back pocket then handed her a business card. She shook her head. "I don't understand."

"Turn it over."

She rolled her eyes. "You're kidding me, right?"

"I wish my faith had been obvious to you earlier. I'm sorry it wasn't. But I would love for you to join us at worship some time."

Brandy released a disgusted breath as she opened the car door. "Gimme a break."

She slammed it shut, and Justin waited until she'd gotten in her car and driven off before he left. He made his way back to his house then flopped down on his knees, resting his head against the couch's cushion.

"God, You kept me from sin. I was so close. I wanted it, but You kept me strong. Thank You."

He got off his knees, grabbed his Bible from the end table, and settled into his chair. He opened to Philippians. Even though he had memorized chapter 4 in its entirety, he wanted to read it again.

From the world's perspective, Paul had everything going for him before Jesus halted him on that Damascus road. Justin smiled at his Bible, "God, when You stop a guy, You really stop him. You change his whole world."

In the midst of that change, when pain, suffering, trials, and persecutions came along, Paul learned to be content. Justin would do the same.

He looked up at the ceiling. "I still love her, God. I still see her as my future wife."

Peace swallowed him up, and Justin knew God was in control of all of it. He didn't want Justin going around acting like a teenager, punching men who were smart enough to realize Megan was the most wonderful woman on the planet. He didn't want Justin seeking out other women to fill a void that belonged to his future wife.

God wanted Justin to trust Him, so he would.

Chapter 28

I can forgive, but I cannot forget, is only another way of saying,
I will not forgive. Forgiveness ought to be like a canceled note—
torn in two and burned up, so that it can never be shown against one.
HENRY WARD BEECHER

Having washed down the last chair, Megan sat back and looked around the classroom. Her music room. Kirk and Marianna worked together to put up posters. Her mother set a pile of music workbooks on the table then sat down beside her.

"It's really coming together nicely."

Megan grinned. "Yeah, it is. Two weeks and I'll be teaching twenty to thirty kids at a time in here."

"You ready for it?" her mother asked.

Excitement jumpstarted the butterflies in her belly. "I'm so excited I could just burst."

"You'll do a good job. You and Marianna were both always so good with kids."

Megan turned and studied her mother. Her red curls lay a little longer on her shoulders than they used to. Her makeup wasn't fixed to perfection as she used to wear it. Even though she'd done remarkably well, Megan knew her mom still grieved their dad's death.

They still hadn't officially hashed out the past, but her mother had softened toward her. Megan didn't know if it was because of her mother's kindness or because of God's constant hammering, but her heart had become tender toward her mother as well. In time they would deal with the pain from the past. For now she would enjoy the relationship they were building.

The gesture seemed crazy and uncomfortable, but Megan reached her arm around her mother's shoulder. The tension faded, and she warmed as her mom responded to the sideways hug. "I'm really glad you came to help."

"Me, too."

Megan let go, and then her mom tapped her leg. "So, have you heard from either of those boys? Justin or Colt?"

Marianna scoffed. "At least she's done with her job at Frasure, Frasure, and Combs. She'll only have to see Justin at church." She winked. "Unless you start attending with us."

"Justin's a Christian now, Marianna. You need to give him a chance," Kirk reprimanded.

"Are we talking about the same guy? The one who ruined my wedding reception by punching out one of my friends?"

Kirk placed a hand on his hip. "Colt is not one of your friends. You barely know him, and Justin most certainly did not ruin our reception."

"He sure tried. Chasing after my sister. She is not going to be just another one of his conquests."

Megan gritted her teeth at Marianna's words. She still hadn't confronted her sister for telling Amy about Clint.

"Don't involve yourself in my business, Marianna." The words slipped out with more anger than she'd meant to convey.

"What's that supposed to mean?" asked Marianna.

"That means you blabbed about Clint to Amy."

Marianna walked away from Kirk, grabbed Megan's arm, and guided her into the hall. "I did that for you."

"Telling others about my past is not helpful."

"Megan—"

"It embarrassed me. Infuriated me. It hurt." Megan rested her hand against her chest. "I don't want people to know about it."

"I don't want Justin to hurt you."

"*I* have to make that choice."

Megan pursed her lips and stared at her sister. Marianna had to understand she could not tell people about her past without her consent. Her sister blew out a long breath. "You're right. I'm sorry." She wrapped her arms around Megan. "Forgive me?"

"Just stop trying to keep me away from Justin. I'm a big girl. I haven't seen him for days, and when I do, it's all platonic."

Megan remembered Justin's declaration of love, and a shudder washed over her. He'd believed her about Clint. He hadn't blamed her, and she couldn't help but believe Justin that Timmy made up a lie.

"Okay. No more talk about Justin."

They walked back into the classroom, and Marianna picked up and handed the glue gun to Kirk. She sneaked a peek back at Megan and winked. "I still think Colt would make a terrific boyfriend. Surely you saw the way he looks at you."

Megan bit back a growl. Marianna was grating on her last nerve.

"Quit trying to make her like that guy. If she doesn't like him, she doesn't like him," retorted Kirk.

Marianna snarled and swatted her hand at her husband. Megan lifted her eyebrows and pointed toward her new brother-in-law. "I agree with Kirk. Colt and I are just friends."

"But the way he looks at you—"

Megan cut her off. "He does not look at me as you suggest. We are just friends. I think I would know it if he felt anything else for me."

"Then why'd he fight Justin?"

"'Cause Justin hit him first, and boys are weird." She looked at Kirk. "No offense."

Kirk nodded. "None taken. I was a bit surprised by the display myself. Haven't seen Justin physically squabble with anyone since high school. He must really care about you."

Marianna gasped. "Kirk, you take that back." She looked back at Megan. "Besides, it doesn't matter if he likes you. He's the last guy on the planet you'd like, right?"

Megan growled, "Marianna, I thought we just decided in the hall—"

Their mother interrupted, "Megan, honey, why don't you and I go get the supplies you need and maybe grab a bite to eat for all of us. I'm getting hungry."

Megan looked over and spied her mother waving her list of supplies in the air. A break would be good. She needed to clear her mind and get out of the classroom for a few minutes. Even though she appreciated her sister's and Kirk's help, she needed a reprieve from Marianna.

Megan nodded. "That sounds like a good idea."

"Yeah." Marianna walked to Kirk and took the glue gun from his hand. "We'll go, too."

Their mother jiggled the keys in her hand. "Why don't you two stay and fix the broken bookshelf? We'll bring you back something."

Megan bit back a sigh of relief. She loved her sister, but the woman would not stop hammering her about Colt and Justin.

Marianna frowned. "But—"

"That sounds like a great idea." Kirk wrapped his arms around Marianna. "I've never made out in an elementary school."

"Ew!" Marianna punched his arm. "We will do no such thing."

Megan giggled as she walked out of the room. Before opening the bathroom door, she heard Kirk respond, "I was just kidding."

She looked atrocious after spending the morning cleaning and rearranging the classroom. After washing her hands, she splashed water on her makeup-free face to clean off any remnants of dust or grime. She pulled off the University of Kentucky ball cap, ran her fingers through her matted hair, then fixed the ball cap again.

Leaving the bathroom, she took her purse from her mom, then they walked out of the school. She sat in the passenger's side of her mom's car and buckled her seat belt.

Her mom pulled out of the parking lot. "We'll go to the store first."

"Sounds like a plan."

Her mom didn't respond, and the old awkward feeling she'd known when she'd spent time alone with her mother resurfaced. Megan clasped her hands in her lap. Things hadn't changed as she'd hoped.

"You know, I'm really proud of you. Your dad was, too."

Megan looked at her mom. "I'm glad."

She cleared her throat. God had hounded her for months to talk with her mom, to be honest, to forgive, to restore their relationship. She knew feelings sometimes had to come after obedience. She shifted in the chair. "Mom, I should have listened to you and Dad about Clint. . ."

Her mom shook her head, and Megan was startled to see tears stream down her mother's cheeks. "We were wrong. Bill and I talked about it a ton of times, but we were both so stubborn. Didn't want to admit. . ."

Megan sucked in her breath and pinched her lips together as her mother pulled into the store's lot and parked. Her mom shifted toward her. "You weren't the first teenager to like a boy your parents didn't approve of." She placed her hands against her chest. "I did it myself."

Megan focused on her breathing. She'd never witnessed her mother crying so hard. Years of pain seemed to surface on her mother's body, and Megan's heart began to melt.

Her mom placed her hands on her cheeks. "What he did to you. . .and we couldn't even confront him. I never comforted you."

Her mom's words came fast and short. Megan searched her purse for a tissue and handed one to her mom. She never expected this. Thought she'd have to forgive her mom without an apology, without her belief Megan had been hurt by the boyfriend.

Megan leaned over and hugged her mom the best she could in the front seat of the car. "It's okay. I forgive you."

"It's not okay. The things we said. We hurt you. How could you possibly forgive me?"

Megan thought of the many times she'd said those words to God when she knew He wanted her to forgive her parents. But

God's working in a woman's heart was a wondrous thing, because in the depth of her spirit, she knew she did forgive her mom. She shrugged. "Because of God."

Her mom let out a long breath. "Megan, I'm sorry for what I did, but I'm not ready for all that God stuff."

Megan noted her mother's hardened spirit. She'd already backed away from Megan. Deep concern laced its way through Megan. Her mother needed the Lord, but she was still saying no.

Her mom scooped her purse into her hands. "Marianna is constantly harping on me about 'Jesus this' and 'Jesus that.' I'm not ready to believe in a God that would take my wonderful husband from me." She lowered her voice. "Or who would let a man walk out on me when I was trying to care for twin babies."

Megan grabbed her mom's hand before she could open the door and slip out. "Mom, I'm glad we're better."

Her mother's expression softened. She leaned over and kissed the top of Megan's head. "Me, too."

Megan's heart floated as they walked into the store. The two of them laughed as they made their way through the aisles picking up colored folders, hot glue sticks, markers, tape, and a mound of other items.

Her mother pointed to a poster of a kitten playing the piano. "That is absolutely adorable. It would look so cute on your door."

Megan nodded. She didn't have the heart to tell her mom the only kitten she'd want on her door would be in the form of a UK Wildcat.

She grabbed it out of the case. "I'm going to get it for you."

Megan smiled. Hanging a kitten on her door wouldn't kill her. She'd just tape a UK bumper sticker beneath it.

"Hello, Megan. Mrs. McKinney."

Megan sucked in her breath at the familiar voice. She turned, and her hand went to her ball cap. She didn't want the man to know she cared what she looked like in front of him. Didn't want him to know he sent her heart to pounding and her stomach to gurgling. "Hi, Justin."

Her mother grinned. "I see your face is healed up."

Megan grimaced, but Justin grinned as he touched his eye and then his lip. "The lip took a little longer. Every time I opened my mouth, the thing would split back open."

Her mother's eyebrows knit together, and Megan feared she'd scold him for the behavior at the wedding. Not that he hadn't earned a good scolding; it was just that Megan didn't want it to happen now. At the store. From her mother.

Justin looked at her. His eyes still spoke of the words he'd said a week ago. Words she couldn't believe were true. He said, "I haven't seen you in a week," as he shifted his weight from one foot to the other. Part of her loved that he acted nervous. "I mean. How is the training going?"

Her mother answered. "Actually we've been putting together her classroom this morning. Kirk and Marianna are helping."

He smiled at her mother. "I haven't talked to Kirk since the wedding. Did they have a good honeymoon?"

Megan forced herself to take slow even breaths as Justin and her mother chatted about palm trees and ocean views. The man's presence sent her heart into a tailspin. It wasn't just his looks. She thought of the conversations they'd had at Bible studies, the way he'd treated her as an employee, the change she'd watched God fashion in him. Though he'd acted like a complete idiot at the wedding reception, she still secretly thrilled he was willing to defend her from possible suitors. Even if Colt was nothing of the sort.

Justin and her mother stopped talking, and he focused on her again. "It's good to see you, Megan. I—I missed you at Bible study on Thursday."

She swallowed. She hadn't been able to go. She wanted to. She needed to. But she wasn't ready to spend an hour with Justin, even with five or six other people there.

She nodded. "It's good to see you, too."

She hated the truth of the statement. For the rest of the day, she'd think about how good he looked in the cream-colored polo and hunter-green shorts. She'd wonder where he was going, since he wasn't dressed for work, and berate herself for hoping it wasn't somewhere with a woman.

Justin walked away, and Megan felt his departure all the way to her toes. She looked at her mother and forced a smile. Her mom was studying her, and it was Megan's turn to shift her weight from one foot to the other in nervousness.

Her mom finally spoke. "That man is crazy about you."

It was on the edge of her tongue to deny it, but Megan blew out a slow breath and nodded. "I know."

Her mom pressed her elbows against the cart's handle. "Your sister vehemently dislikes him."

Megan giggled. "You can say she hates him."

Her mom cocked her head to the side. "No. Marianna is determined *not* to say she hates him."

Megan averted her gaze. Knowing her mother still watched her, she focused on the different designs of note cards. She leaned down to pick up a cute package.

"What do you think of him?"

Megan grimaced. She knew her mom was going to ask her. She could say she agreed with Marianna, that she didn't care for him in the slightest. She'd tried to force herself to believe that for several months, but it hadn't changed her heart. And she knew God didn't honor her not coming clean with Him on her emotions. "I don't want to, but I think about him all the time."

"Hmm." Her mom pushed the cart away from the note cards and posters aisle. She looked at the list Megan had made. "Did we get everything?"

Megan frowned. That was it? Her mom wasn't going to say anything else? Biting back a growl, Megan nodded. "I think we got it all."

They got into the checkout line, and her mother insisted on paying for the items. Megan thanked her, and they walked to the car. They placed the bags in the trunk then got back in the car.

"Marianna's told me all about him."

Megan did not want to talk about this. She'd spent so much time trying to get Justin out of her mind. She and her mother were finally getting along. The last thing they needed was a guy to talk about. Megan clicked her seat belt. "She's definitely not his number one fan."

Her mother chuckled. "No. She told me he's known for his womanizing."

Megan nodded. "He definitely was."

"Was?"

Megan swallowed. "He's changed since he's become a Christian."

"Hmm."

Her mother started the car and pulled out of the parking lot.

They drove through a fast-food drive-thru then back to the school.

Even though her mother ordered her a meal, Megan wasn't sure she could eat. Just seeing Justin sent her stomach to whirling. And the way he looked, and the sporadic questions of her mother. Megan placed her forehead against the window, hoping the coolness of the glass would ease her pounding head. She wouldn't be able to hold down a single bite.

Her mom parked the car, and Megan reached for the tray holding their soft drinks. Her mother grabbed her hand, and Megan looked at her. "Megan, I don't know about his past. I suppose we all have a past to deal with."

She looked up at the sky, and Megan couldn't decide if her mom was talking about herself or Megan. Probably a little of both.

She gazed back at Megan. "There is one thing I'm pretty certain of. That man is no Clint. After years of seeing the difference between Bill and your biological father, I can tell."

Megan watched dumbstruck as her mom got out of the car and bumped the door shut with her hip. Her mother approved of Justin? She hadn't approved of Clint, even though the only things he'd done prior to dating her was sneak out of the house and skip a few classes, but she liked Justin?

Megan knew Justin was different. He was a new creation in Christ. And probably her parents saw something in Clint her love-struck teen eyes couldn't grasp. *Well, obviously that was very true.*

She shook her head. Still, she couldn't believe her mom liked Justin. Not being able to help herself, she chuckled aloud. "That man knows how to get a gal on his side."

She opened the car door and slipped outside. She knew it was more than that. She looked to the heavens. "God, when I get home, we're going to sit down alone and have a little talk. And I plan to do most of the listening."

Peace flooded her spirit, and she knew God would be more than happy to share His will with her.

Chapter 29

We must accept finite disappointment but never lose infinite hope.
MARTIN LUTHER KING JR.

Colt hung up the phone. He'd had a good conversation with Tina. He was proud of how hard she'd been working at beauty school, and she'd kept a grocery store job and her house cleanings for two months. Proof enough she was staying sober. His brother had never lasted at a job longer than two weeks.

Hadley walked into the kitchen and picked up an onion off the counter. "Want some help?"

"Sure." He handed her a paring knife out of the drawer then turned on the stovetop. He poured a bit of olive oil in the pan then placed the marinated steak strips in the skillet. He grabbed another knife out of the drawer and sliced a bell pepper.

Hadley wiped her eyes with the back of her hand. "I love fajitas, but the onions are killer."

He picked up another pepper. "Wanna switch?"

She nodded and gave him the onion. "Did you have a good talk with Mom?"

"I did. How 'bout you?"

Hadley and Tina had been on the phone for at least an hour before his niece handed over the phone. Hadley begged for him to let Tina visit during the week. He'd been hesitant, seeing how the woman had become more involved quicker than he'd anticipated, but he gave in.

When the woman showed up with a container full of makeup, he'd been sure he'd made the wrong choice allowing her to visit. She picked at Hadley's eyebrows with tweezers and put different creams on her face. He let her slather on the makeup for about as long as he could take it. But when he decided to tell her to stop, she turned Hadley around, and he couldn't believe how good she looked. And still young.

Tina had done a great job. The look of pure excitement beaming from Hadley's face was an added bonus.

Hadley sighed. "I like it when she comes over."

"I know you do."

"But she doesn't know how to be a mom yet."

Colt rested the knife and the onion on the counter and studied his niece.

Hadley continued, "She wants to—I can tell. But right now, she really wants me to like her." She pointed to the skillet. "You'd better flip that meat."

Colt jumped. If he didn't pay better attention, he'd burn their favorite dinner. At least one of their favorites. He flipped the meat and added a bit of salt to the cooked side. "What do you mean?"

"Well, you know how you"—she giggled—"and even Megan will get onto me if I do or say something I shouldn't. I think Mom's afraid to."

She shifted toward him and sighed. "Okay, so I'll just tell you the truth."

Colt's stomach muscles tightened. What happened between her and Tina? Were they keeping secrets? Was Tina just fooling him? If she was, he'd yank away the phone calls and visits quicker than Old Yeller could gulp down a piece of beef. "What is it?"

The words came out harsh, angry. He cleared his throat to mask his worry. If she didn't think she could tell him what happened, she wouldn't. He'd learned long ago that Hadley was an open book until she felt like he was going to be upset; then she'd clam up, and it would take him days to get to the truth of any given situation.

Hadley must not have noticed, because she got her hands to moving even before she opened her mouth. The girl wouldn't be able to utter a peep if something happened to her hands. "Well, I was telling her about this boy from the rodeo." Her face reddened, and she clasped her hands.

Colt sucked in a deep breath and willed himself to stay calm. He hadn't noticed any boys talking to Hadley at the last rodeo. "Go ahead."

"Well, there was this guy, and he told me I was pretty, which I really liked, because I don't get that too much."

"Hadley, you're a beautiful girl."

She shook her head and waved for him to stop. All the same, he made a mental note to tell Hadley what a pretty young lady she was growing into whenever he got the chance. That was the kind of thing she was missing without a mother. If he had a wife, she'd remind him to say the words when he thought Hadley looked pretty. Like the day Tina fixed her makeup. He should have told her then.

She scrunched her nose. "But I didn't really like the way he told me, because he used a curse word."

Colt's mind raced as to which curse word would be used to tell a girl she was pretty, and in what context. He couldn't think of a single way, unless the kid was being downright vulgar, and if he was, the boy had better be glad Colt didn't catch him talking to his niece.

The steak sizzled, and Colt turned down the temperature and added the onions and peppers. He mixed them together then looked back at Hadley.

Her hands started moving again. "Anyway, I was telling Mom what he said, and I said the word, too. But just to tell her what he said, not 'cause I talk like that." She ducked her chin and cocked her head. "Well, you would have gotten onto me, told me not to say things like that. That I could get the message across without actually saying the word."

Colt let out a sigh of relief. It was nothing like he feared. Tina wasn't corrupting her. He bit the inside of his lip. "So, are you saying you like it when I get onto you?"

"Yes." Her brow puckered. "I mean no." She shrugged. "Look, don't like go all hog wild on me or anything, but I guess I do like that you won't let me be bad."

From the mouths of babes. Colt bit back a smile. He'd have to remember this little confession the next time he had to ground her for not doing her chores. He remembered Tina flinching when Hadley had acted ugly when she and Valerie didn't win the corn-hole game. Megan had reprimanded his niece but didn't let it ruin the day. Tina didn't know how to do that yet.

"You're probably right about Tina. Right now she's worried about wanting you to like her. My guess is she feels bad about all the years she hasn't spent with you."

Colt thought of all the things Tina had missed. Hadley's first tooth, first words, first steps, first time to school, first horse ride. There were more "firsts" than he could think of. Not to mention all the seconds and thirds. Every day-in and day-out moment he'd had with Hadley had formed their bond. Tina didn't have that.

A twinge of pain passed through his heart for the woman. She'd chosen her path when Hadley had been born, but she couldn't have realized all she was giving up for drugs and alcohol. Until now.

He wrapped one hand around his niece's shoulder. "I think you and Tina have made a pretty good start."

Hadley grinned. "You've done a good job, too."

He squeezed her shoulder. "You don't need to say curse words to translate what someone else said."

She nodded. "I know."

With his free hand, he lifted her chin. She looked at him with big, innocent eyes. She may be growing up, but she was still his little girl. "And you are beautiful, Hadley Baker."

Red tinged her cheeks, and he let her go. He grabbed a plate out of the cabinet and handed it to her. "Time to eat."

"Megan coming tonight?"

"Far as I know."

"Good. I've been practicing my songs. I can't wait to see her."

Colt smiled. He couldn't wait either. He would ask her out tonight. Even if he had to do it in front of Hadley, the horses, and the dog.

Colt wondered what was wrong with Megan. She smiled when

Hadley performed her songs. She went through the motions of guiding his niece through the new material. He could tell Hadley knew something was off as well.

When the lesson ended, Hadley excused herself to call back Valerie, who'd phoned during the lesson.

Colt offered Megan a large glass of sweet tea. She took the glass, drank a sip, then flopped back in a wingback chair. He frowned. "Everything all right?"

She crossed her legs and waved her hand in the air. "Just peachy."

He scratched the top of his head. He didn't have enough experience with women to know where to go from here. Did he ask her another question? Wait for her to talk? It was obvious something was bugging her. He looked around the room. He was pretty sure he hadn't done anything wrong, but one could never be certain.

"My mom and I made up."

He sat on a hardback chair across from her. "That's great. I know that means a lot to you."

He didn't really know the ins and outs of why Megan and her mother had such a stilted relationship. He knew it had been that way for years. From what he gathered, even before she graduated high school.

It didn't make much sense to him. Sure, his parents had been estranged from his brother, Connor, but that was because of drug abuse. Megan didn't have any vice of that sort. In fact, she was an upstanding Christian woman. He'd be thrilled if Hadley grew up to be like her.

The thought brought a smile to his face. He still hoped she would have the chance to see Megan as a daily model for womanhood. Though they hadn't dated, he knew she was the kind of woman he hoped to marry and help him raise Hadley.

She sat up and rested her elbows on her knees. "Colt, we're friends, right?"

He nodded, unsure where the conversation was going.

"Why do you suppose Justin hit you that night at the wedding reception?"

Colt clenched his jaw. He couldn't stand that guy. He knew God didn't want him to hate anyone. Knew God said to pray for one's enemies. But that man made it hard to heed the Lord's words. "Because he likes you."

Megan stood and opened her arms wide. "Wrong. Apparently he loves me."

Colt gripped the arms of the chair on both sides and ground his teeth together.

She smacked her hands against her thighs and started to pace. "Yup. Told me himself. The man went all Neanderthal at the reception because he thought you were flirting with me." Megan threw back her head and snorted. "Like that would ever happen."

Colt wrinkled his nose. Why was it that no matter when he saw Megan and no matter how many times he determined he would ask her out on a date, his plan would get thrown back in his face? Was he really so bad at showing his feelings that Megan had no idea he was attracted to her?

She stopped pacing in front of him then leaned down in front of his face. "Apparently he really"—she lifted up her hands and made quotation mark gestures—"loves me. Like for life. Like now he doesn't want anyone else. Even though he's dated half the state."

Colt stiffened. He did not like the way this was going. He cared for Megan. He was the one believing she was for life. He was better for her. Justin wasn't good enough.

She lifted up her pointer finger and thumb. "Okay, so maybe that's a wee bit of an exaggeration." She smacked her thighs again. "But not much."

He opened his mouth to speak, but she started again. "And apparently my mom approves of him. Of course, Marianna doesn't. She wants me to go after you. Which is ridiculous. I keep telling her we're just friends."

A knife of dawning seemed to twist in his heart. They really were just friends. He wanted more, but Megan didn't see him in that capacity. Maybe if he'd been more vocal earlier on, he'd have had a chance. But it was pretty obvious Justin held her heart. The truth of it sickened his stomach.

Colt leaned back in the chair. He hurt for Hadley the most. Megan would make a terrific mother. He grimaced. He thought he loved her. For himself. Even if Hadley wasn't around. He inwardly nodded. Yes. Of course he loved her. She was a good pick. Christian. Pretty. Talented. Loved the farm.

Irritation swelled within him that she would fall for Justin. He was the better man. A husband a woman could be proud of. His heart twisted. He did hurt, but he needed to cipher through the pain and the humiliation. Which one weighed heavier?

For now, he'd listen to her rant until she realized the truth. And he would start praying for Justin. He'd pray the man would one day be worthy of Megan.

She opened her arms wide. "My mom. That's the biggest joke of all. I've never told you why my mom and I had such a bad relationship. Let's just say it has something to do with the hang-up I have about men."

She raised her eyebrows and pointed to her chest. "And I earned my hang-up. I dated one guy in high school." She lifted her pointer finger in the air. "After him, I swore to never, ever fall for another guy."

She smacked both hands against her knees. "But Justin Frasure. The Justin Frasure. The most gorgeous guy on the planet who could have"—she cocked her head—"and *has* had, any woman on the planet."

She marched back over to the wingback chair and flopped back down in it. She grabbed the iced tea and took a long swig. Placing the empty glass on the table, she leaned back in the chair and looked at him, her expression the most pitiful he'd seen. "Justin Frasure?"

The words hurt, but he had to say them. "You love him."

She shook her head. "But why?"

He shrugged. "Because you do."

Megan closed her eyes, and Colt sucked in a long breath. He would hold his emotions at bay. God would see him through this.

She opened her eyes and stood to her feet. She picked up her purse and walked toward him. "Tell Hadley I said bye." She leaned over and kissed his cheek. "Thanks for being such a good friend, Colt."

Colt didn't move as she walked past him and out the door. He touched his cheek with his hand. He'd finally gotten a kiss from Megan. A kiss of good-bye.

He looked behind him and spied Hadley peeking around the corner. "You care about her, don't you, Uncle Colt?"

He bit his bottom lip. No use trying to hide the truth. She'd know he was lying anyway. What kind of example would that be? He nodded.

"She didn't know."

He shook his head. He knew she didn't.

Hadley walked into the room and knelt beside him. She nestled herself under his arm. "I love you, Uncle Colt."

He kissed the top of her head. "I love you, too."

Things hadn't gone as he planned. His heart felt weak and weary from the hammering it took the last several minutes. He'd been taught that God had a plan in all circumstances, and he'd always believed it. Knew it when his brother and Tina ran off. Knew it when his parents died. Knew it through the daily raising of Hadley. He'd have to know it again.

He looked up at the ceiling and offered a silent plea of help from God to see him through once more.

Chapter 30

Justin walked into the Bible study room. He knew Megan wouldn't be there. She'd been getting her classroom ready for school to start the following week. Plus, he assumed she was still avoiding him. He missed seeing her. Missed knowing her presence was just outside his office door. Missed hearing her voice when she answered calls or reminded him about meetings. The new secretary was doing a great job, but it wasn't the same.

He nodded at their leader, Kat, as he took a seat beside Brian. He leaned toward Justin, "Ya missing softball yet?"

Justin nodded. "A little."

He didn't want to admit the softball games and practices had been his lifeline. Especially when Kirk married, left on his honeymoon, and was now busy setting up house with a new wife. He'd needed activity to keep his mind off Megan. Unsure how Brandy would respond to him, he'd limited his gym visits. Still hadn't decided if he needed to switch memberships.

Out of the corner of his eye, Justin noticed a familiar form. He shifted and watched as Megan walked in the door. She glanced at him and offered a slight smile. Justin's heart pounded. He wished she'd sit by him like she used to, but she passed him and sat by one of the women.

Kat opened her Bible. "It's five after. I think we'll go ahead and get started."

Kat rubbed her hands together. "I hope y'all don't mind. I know we've been studying Paul's life for a while, but this week God laid something else on my heart."

Justin sneaked a peek at Megan, her attention centered on Kat.

"And I mean, God just wouldn't let it go." Kat opened her hands. "Have you ever had that happen? You have a plan, an agenda of some sort, and God is just determined you're going to change direction?"

Justin thought of his life before becoming a Christian. He'd been on the fast track to becoming one of the most prominent and wealthy divorce attorneys in Kentucky. Figured he'd settle down and get married one day, but not until he'd sowed all the wild oats a man could handle.

Then God stepped in and changed all that. He wanted to be an attorney, but not for wealth or fame, but to help others who had legal needs—like adoption. He'd started donating to a local counseling group whose sole purpose was to assist struggling couples with the hope of reconciliation. He looked at Megan. And he wanted a wife. Wild oats were a thing of the past.

Kat spoke again. "I want to focus on Jeremiah 29:11, where God tells us He has a plan for us, and that His plan is always for our good."

Megan lifted her hand, and everyone looked at her. She glanced at Justin, and he had to remind himself to keep breathing. She looked back at Kat. "I had a plan. Thought I'd spend my life doing my agenda." She made a fist and pumped it through the air. "Me and God against the world. I was going to sing contemporary Christian music." She grinned and glanced around the room. "We all know God switched that plan on me."

Kat chuckled. "And those elementary kids will be thankful. You'll be a terrific teacher."

Megan's cheeks brightened, and Justin thought how cute she looked when she was embarrassed. Though he didn't say it aloud, he agreed with Kat. Megan would be the best music teacher.

Megan cleared her throat. "I also thought I'd spend my life single." She glanced at him again and then averted her gaze.

Justin frowned. Was she talking about Colt? He wasn't the right guy for her. Justin couldn't stand the thought of it. And he most certainly wouldn't sit here and listen to her talk about it. Before Megan could say another word, he scooped up his Bible, stood, and walked out of the room.

He strode down the hall to the exit. Part of him felt bad leaving like that, but he wasn't ready to hear Megan talk about Colt. Sure, she deserved a guy like the blond cowboy. A guy who'd been a saint since birth. But that didn't stop Justin from loving her. From praying God would have mercy on his worthless personhood and allow a woman he didn't deserve to love him back.

He pushed through the door, and the hot August air smacked his face. He yanked his keys from his front shorts pocket then wiped his face with his hand. Maybe a dip in his pool would calm his nerves and cool his heart.

He'd promised God the night he saw Colt and Megan together at the frozen yogurt place that no matter what, he would allow God to lead his life. Megan choosing to fall for Colt stung worse than any yellow jacket he'd ever come into contact with, but Justin wouldn't lose his faith.

He heard the door open behind him, but he didn't look back. He didn't want to discuss his feelings with anyone right now. Waving his hand, he said, "Sorry to leave so quick. Got something I need to do."

"What do you need to do?"

Justin stopped at the sound of Megan's voice. He turned on his heels and studied the woman who'd stolen his heart. He felt sure she'd spent most of the day working on her classroom. Her blond hair was pulled up in a ponytail, but some of the shorter strands had escaped and touched the sides of her cheeks and the back of her neck. She didn't have on a drop of makeup, and she sported an old Wildcats T-shirt, navy blue shorts, and flip-flops.

He crossed his arms in front of his chest. He loved this woman. He'd told her as much, but she'd said straight to his face she didn't feel the same. "I need to do stuff."

Great comeback, Frasure. That's telling her.

She squinted at him. "Stuff? You come to Bible study. I start talking about God's plan for my life, and you walk out to do"—she lifted up both hands and made quotation marks—"stuff."

Her sassiness drew him like a magnet, and he took a step toward her. It was none of her business what stuff he needed or didn't need to do. He had every right to walk out of that room. "Yes. That's right."

She thrust out her chin and took a step toward him. "Well, that answer isn't good enough."

"Who isn't it good enough for?"

She pointed at her chest. "For me."

He stepped toward her again. If he reached out his hands, he could take her in his arms. The desire warred within him. He raised his eyebrow. "It's going to have to be good enough."

She pinched her lips. "Justin."

He couldn't take anymore. She was just too close, and she smelled too good. Like some kind of fruity lotion. He grabbed her arms and pulled her to him. Pushing away the knowledge that this may be his last kiss, he pressed his lips to hers.

He took both her cheeks in his hands. He didn't want to let her go. She wrapped her arms around his waist and deepened the kiss. Knowing he had to let her go, he pulled away and searched her eyes for the truth. "I couldn't sit in there and listen to you talk about Colt."

Megan's jaw dropped, and she pushed away from him. "Colt?" She lifted her hands and shook her head. "What is it with everyone thinking there is something going on between me and Colt? We're just friends."

She obviously hasn't taken in the way the guy looks at her.

She punched his arm. "I was talking about you."

"Me?"

"Yes, you." She rolled her eyes and shifted her weight. "Didn't you just tell me last week you loved me?"

He raised his brows. "Yes I did. And you said you didn't love me."

She bit her bottom lip and scrunched up her nose. "Well, maybe that wasn't the complete truth."

"You love me?"

"I do." Her cheeks darkened, and Justin thought his heart would float out of his chest.

He grabbed her arms then wrapped his arms around her, pressing her as close to him as he could get. He looked up at the heavens. "Thank You, God."

She pushed away. "I'm not going to love you if you're going to smother me to death."

He laughed, scooped her into his arms, and twirled her around. "I knew it. I knew you would have to love me back."

She patted his chest. "Seriously, Justin. I'm going to barf on you."

He placed her back on her feet, and his mind traveled to the night he'd taken Brandy to dinner. He had to tell Megan. Had to start off with complete honesty. Especially given his past.

He sobered, fearing she wouldn't believe him. "I've got to tell you something."

Worry etched Megan's face, and he wished he hadn't had that moment of almost weakness. If he told her and she walked away believing he was who he used to be. . . He shook the thought away. He couldn't hide the truth. "Remember the night I saw you and Colt at the frozen yogurt shop?"

Megan frowned, and Justin saw her take in a long breath. "Yeah. Why?"

"I was really upset when I left there. I went to the gym. There was this girl who'd been hitting on me since I started working out there."

Megan took a step away from him. "What happened?"

"Wait a minute." He touched her arm. "Give me a chance to finish."

She crossed her arms in front of her chest. She looked ready to bolt but hadn't done so yet.

"I took her to dinner, and she offered to go back to my place."

Megan lifted her hands and spun on her heels. "Bye, Justin. I won't go there. I have too much in my past. I have to be able to trust you."

Justin reached for her arm and spun her back toward him. "Nothing happened. I took her to her car. I'm not that guy anymore. And I love you."

He watched as Megan stared at him, taking long breaths in and out. He knew her mind churned with what decision to make. It would hurt if she walked away, but he'd been honest. Their relationship had to be based on truth.

Her expression softened. "I believe you."

He took her hand in his. "It's going to be truth all the way for you and me."

"I'd like that."

He grinned and nudged her arm with his elbow. "Unless you're wearing a really ugly outfit and you ask my opinion, and I know if I tell the truth I'm going to get in trouble."

Her jaw dropped, and she punched his arm. "You'd better tell me if an outfit looks ugly."

"Don't worry, I do promise to tell you if you have something in your teeth."

"Justin Frasure!"

He twirled her in front of him and placed a quick kiss on her lips. "Would you like to go get some frozen yogurt with me?"

She pointed back to the church. "What about Bible study? They'll wonder where we are."

"They'll know we're off making out somewhere."

She punched him again. "We are not."

He rubbed his arm. "You know if you don't stop, you're going to give me a bruise."

Megan grinned. "My purse and Bible are in the room."

"Don't worry. We'll be back before the study is over."

Megan cocked her head. "Well, it is my favorite place."

Justin raised his eyebrows. "Oh honey. We're not going to that one. We're going to the chain store on the other side of town. I'll never go to that one again."

Megan lifted her fist to punch him once more. He stuck out his bottom lip and pointed toward the spot. "Bruise?"

Megan laughed and wrapped her hand around his arm. "Okay. Take me to the chain. I'm sure it's just as good."

"It's even better." He pointed to his chest. "Because you're going with me."

She shook her head. "No. It's because you're going with me."

He sobered as he placed a kiss on the top of her head. "You are right. It's better because of you."

He opened the car door, and she slipped inside. As he walked around to the other side of the car, he offered up a silent prayer of thanksgiving.

Epilogue

I dreamed of a wedding of elaborate elegance,
A church filled with family and friends.
I asked him what kind of a wedding he wished for,
He said one that would make me his wife.

UNKNOWN

Megan's hands grew clammy, and her heart beat with a staccato pattern against her chest. She loved her job as a music teacher and felt the first five months had gone well. There was no reason to be so scared about being asked to see the principal. And yet she felt like one of her fifth-grade students who'd gotten caught doing some punishable activity.

She knocked on Mrs. Carey's office door. The sandy-haired woman motioned her inside. Megan entered then clasped her hands as she stood in front of the massive mahogany desk. "You wanted to see me?"

Mrs. Carey motioned for her to take a seat. Megan sat on the edge, holding her back straight and shoulders up. A smile lit up her boss's face, and Megan let out a breath. "I just wanted to check with you to see how your first semester of school has gone. Christmas break is just around the corner, and you've done such a great job, I haven't had much of a chance to talk to you."

"I love it. It's even more rewarding than I'd hoped." Megan's mind raced with all she'd experienced. The career choice was challenging. She spent more hours in the building than she'd ever anticipated. But the students! How she loved the eagerness and excitement on the faces of the first and second graders whenever she pulled out the instruments to practice playing and singing at the same time. The older students had been eager to learn the historical Kentucky music pieces and were quick to come up with motions to the songs they'd perform for their parents at their concert in a week's time.

She shrugged. "I suppose there have been a few challenges, things I needed to learn."

She thought of the third grader who'd slammed the piano keys cover on his fingers after she'd warned him not to mess with it.

She continued, "But I can honestly say I love this job. Each day I feel more confident that this is where I need to be."

Mrs. Carey looked at her watch then stood up and motioned for Megan to do the same. Megan frowned. She knew her boss was busy, but she'd called her in to talk. Now she acted as if she needed to get her out of the office.

"That's lovely, Megan." She opened the door and guided her out. "I knew when we hired you that you'd be perfect for the students." She motioned for Megan to follow her. "Come on. I'd like to visit your room."

Megan's stomach turned. Her room? She hoped the students in her last class had placed their songbooks back in the cubbies. She normally checked, but she'd been in such a rush about the meeting, she'd let the last class leave without double-checking.

Mrs. Carey smiled. "I haven't been in there for a few weeks. You'll have to show me some of the things the students are doing."

Megan's mind raced. She did have her daily learning targets on the board, right? They were supposed to be posted and current each day so the students knew exactly what they were to be learning that day. Megan's lessons were always planned bell to bell, but for some reason she was always forgetting those targets.

Megan fretted over her desk. She wasn't sure her papers were as neat as she'd like them to be for her principal to visit. They weren't bad, but she wished she'd had time to be sure everything looked as she'd want it. Sucking in a deep breath, she opened the door to the music room.

"Surprise!"

Megan gasped and placed her hand against her chest when she spied all of her fourth- and fifth-grade classes squeezed into the room. Soft music played from her computer. She recognized the song— "Will You Marry Me?" The title swam through her mind, and she sucked in her breath.

She watched as the children lifted up a banner that had been hidden around the bottom of their legs. She looked around the room. Her hands trembled and her legs grew weak. Where was he?

The words "Will you marry me?" spieled from the song and were painted in bright red letters across the banner.

Megan lifted her hand to her mouth as tears formed in her eyes. She saw movement from the back corner. She bit her bottom lip when Justin appeared wearing a tuxedo and carrying a dozen red roses. She drank in his love-filled yet smug expression. He knew he'd surprised her, and he was proud of himself.

The kids giggled, and she realized several of her colleagues and her principal stood in the door. She could tell by their oohs and aahs that they were as teary-eyed as she.

Justin reached her, and she bit her lip as he bent down and kissed the top of her head. He handed her the flowers then lowered himself to one knee.

Megan wiped her tears with the back of her hand. Her boyfriend was proposing, and she'd be a black-eyed raccoon before she'd have the chance to say yes.

Her heartbeat raced as Justin pulled a black box from the inside of his coat pocket then opened it. She gasped at the large square solitaire on the white gold band. The thing would practically cover her finger.

He took her hand in his and looked up at her. The love in his eyes made her want to melt into his arms. "Megan, I love you. Will you marry me?"

Her body filled with wonder. A year ago she never would have imagined this possible. She wouldn't have wanted to, especially with her then-boss. So much had changed. And she couldn't believe how much she loved him.

"Yes." He pushed the ring on her finger, and she said it again, "Yes."

He stood, and she wrapped her arms around his neck and planted a quick kiss on his lips. The students yelped and whistled, and she let him go. A more fitting kiss would be had later that night.

She laughed as she looked up into his eyes. "You got me good. I had no idea."

Thrill traced his features, and he wiggled his eyebrows. "I know."

She laughed as she looked at the enormous ring on her finger. Then she pressed the roses to her chest. "I don't know how I'm going to make it through the rest of the day."

Mrs. Carey stepped forward. "You don't have to. We got you a sub." She touched Megan's arm. "You don't mind that you took a half day off, do you?"

Megan giggled as she wiped her cheeks with the back of her hand. "I don't mind."

Justin handed her a tissue then offered his arm, and Megan wrapped her hand around it. They headed toward the door, and then she looked back at her students. "Be good for the sub."

Promises of good behavior filled the room, and Megan let her fiancé lead her to his car. She looked at her ring then back up at Justin. "So, where are we going?"

"To our engagement party."

Megan's jaw dropped. "What?"

Justin kissed the tip of her nose. "Don't worry. I've got your dress in the car. We'll stop at your house so you can change. Your mom and sister and Kirk. My dad. Everyone is already there. Lunch will be served when we arrive."

Megan shook her head. "I can't believe you did all this."

"I'm good, aren't I?"

She wrapped her arms around his shoulders and pressed her lips to his. She released him and gazed into his eyes. How she loved this man. "You're very good."

"Which is why I will stay right here in my car when you go in the house to get ready?"

"What?" she asked.

He winked. "I'll need the distance to stay that way."

Megan laughed as she lowered herself into the passenger seat. She inhaled a deep breath as she looked at the engagement ring, the promise she would belong to Justin legally at a future date. Hopefully soon.

He grabbed her hand in his and kissed the top of her knuckles. He gazed into her eyes, and she thought she would melt into their deep brown depths. "You know being good doesn't come easy to me."

"I know."

He lifted one eyebrow. "Short engagement?"

"Absolutely."

Discussion Questions

1. Even though Justin became a Christian, he dealt with the temptations that plagued him before he knew Christ. Do you have a temptation that you still battle against? What measures do you take to fight it?

2. Megan was raped as a teenager by someone she knew and trusted. Then her parents didn't believe her. Have you ever been betrayed? Maybe your betrayal is not as life-changing as Megan's, but it still hurts. What can you do to overcome that betrayal?

3. Colt is a great guy. Like the elder son in the parable of the prodigal son, Colt is a steady, faithful person. However, his pride sometimes gets in the way. Is there an area of your life where pride sometimes takes over? What steps do you take to ensure you live a life of humility?

4. Both Tina and Barbara (Megan and Marianna's mom) needed forgiveness. They needed the opportunity to be given a second chance. Is there someone in your life to whom you need to extend grace? Pray that God will show you what He desires for you and that person.

5. Justin says several times in the story that he connects with Paul from Scripture. Is there a person in the Bible with whom you relate? Who is that person, and why do you connect with him or her?

6. God was silent with Megan in several places in the book because she wasn't willing to trust Him with her future. Is that true for

you? Are you hesitant to trust God with an area of your life? What is keeping you from yielding to His will?

7. The story doesn't end as Colt would have hoped. How do you react when God says no? Do you trust Him? What practical steps can you take to strengthen your faith when you don't get what you thought was best?

Jennifer Johnson and the world's most supportive redhead have been happily married for over two decades. They have three of the most beautiful daughters on the planet and an amazing soon-to-be son-in-law. Jennifer is a seventh-grade language arts teacher in Lawrenceburg, Kentucky. She is also a member of American Christian Fiction Writers. When she isn't teaching or writing, she enjoys shopping with her daughters and playing on Facebook. She's addicted to Words with Friends. Blessed beyond measure by her heavenly Father, Jennifer hopes to always think like a child—bigger than she can imagine and with complete faith.

*Other great destination romances
available from Barbour Publishing*

A Bride's Flight from
Virginia City, Montana

A Wedding to Remember in
Charleston, South Carolina

A Bride's Sweet Surprise in
Sauers, Indiana

A Wedding Transpires on
Mackinac Island

A Bride's Dilemma in
Friendship, Tennessee

Available wherever books are sold.